Everybody Liked Harry

Margo, the hundred-dollar girl for whom Harry was more than a trick, but who got her treat with a girl named Dusty...Jan, who thought she understood the man she married, but never suspected his desperate needs...Myra, voluptuous child of the love generation turned to lust, for whom an older man was a deliciously new kick...Eddie, the big money man who depended on Harry for the shame-filled pleasures that only Harry could arrange...Phil, the accountant, the worrier, the friend, who knew too much and could do too little....

Everybody liked Harry—but nobody could save him....

Save the Tiger

Steve Shagan

GOLDEN APPLE PUBLISHERS

for Betty and Robert

SAVE THE TIGER

A Golden Apple Publication / published by arrangement with
the Author

Golden Apple edition/December 1984

Golden Apple is a trademark of Golden Apple Publishers

For information address: Golden Apple Publishers,
666 Fifth Avenue, New York, N.Y. 10103.

ISBN 0-553-19830-0

PRINTED IN CANADA

COVER PRINTED IN U.S.A.

U   0 9 8 7 6 5 4 3 2 1

Everything that grows has the right to perish
—*Goethe*

Chapter 1

The icy air mass blew the cold winds down from Canada. Its spearheads split south-southwest covering Utah. But over Nevada, it slammed into columns of hot wind whirling up off the desert floor. There it halted, inverted, heated. On the news reports that night, it was called a "Santa Ana condition."

Like a vast, invisible army collecting itself for a final assault on some distant enemy, it massed and swirled in the neon-edged night over Vegas.

Then, as if by pre-arranged signal, it moved. Slowly, ponderously, it slouched west, covering the San Gabriels, pouring down through the passes, a silent, nocturnal force advancing on a broad front toward the city that lay beyond the mountains.

Sensually, it oozed through Coldwater Canyon, spreading out, hanging low and tight over Beverly Hills.

In the tall royal palms lining Bedford Drive the rats crawled over themselves fighting for space to breathe. Their angry squeals could be heard from among the lifeless fronds. But no one was listening. People do not walk the streets of Beverly Hills at night. They remain locked securely behind triple-bolted doors and intricate alarm systems.

The rats had the night to themselves. The street lamps blinking on triggered their descent from the high palms. They scurried quickly into the alleys behind the mansions, swarming over the expensive remnants of half-finished dinners.

The alley was two hundred feet behind the Stoner house; a huge swimming pool served as a moat keeping the rats at a safe distance. Harry Stoner, clad in white boxer shorts, stretched out on his king-sized bed in the master bedroom; he could not hear the rats tearing at his garbage.

1

At times like this, alone, Harry imagined he was in the bowels of some great ship listening to the throbs of giant screws. The power plant that kept it all running: the mortgage, the cars, the insurance, the Swiss school, the maid, the pool man, the tree surgeon, the gardener, the twenty-year-old Scotch, the specially cured beef, the dinners, the constant guests. He was the ball bearing. And he was wearing out . . . And no one was listening.

The air conditioner chilled the dead air, sending a sharp pain tripping through the "88" fragments. The German shrapnel had remained embedded in the tissue near his spine for almost three decades and lately those steel remnants of Krupp's genius had increased their complaints. Without warning, at random moments, their knife-like stabs pulled him back to a distant, stained Italian beach. He shuddered slightly as the last bite of pain curled through the maze of sciatic nerve ends.

Harry watched the tiny figures in the chromatic Zenith light. It was a late inning back in Baltimore. It was mid-September and the pennant race had long since been decided; but this pitcher was worth watching. His fast ball had a nine-inch hop, and the sidearm curve broke down sharply. He was hitting spots and mixing speeds. Harry no longer recognized the teams or players. He thought their uniforms were ludicrous; yellow and greens were wrong on ballplayers. Still, it was good to watch a pitcher with fine stuff.

Soon he would have to shut the game off. He would have to shower. Get dressed. Jan was having one of her dinner parties. But he couldn't concentrate on tonight. Tomorrow burned its way through the cyan flush of the Zenith. Tomorrow the buyers would be in town. The fall show. Everything on the come line. A mélange of designs and dreams draped on the slim shoulders of high-strung models; pretty shills on the runway of survival. Harry shook his head at the madness of trying to outguess the desires of millions of women six months ahead of time. And even if the line were well received, where would the money come from to finance its manufacture?

Harry knew the answer before the question flashed away. He would have to convince Phil. They would have to risk it. Everything. It was dirty, below the belt; but there were no more rules. Only referees.

* * *

Not far from the Stoner residence the Century City Hotel glowed in the soupy night. It was a towering glass erection; a neon tombstone built on the graveyard of the old Fox back lot.

Margo stood on a small balcony fourteen stories up. She wore a peignoir over her shoulders and nothing else. The lights of the city below were in soft focus, diffused by the smog and Santa Ana.

Margo could coax milk out of a crowbar. But knowing it wasn't enough. You had to perform. You had to concentrate, to blot everything out, to fuse all the talent. The "Johns" had to remember your work. That's how you built a clientele. Tricks... tricks. She had unleashed them all on Ricky.

A superlative performance: touching, squeezing, probing. Tricks. Sliding down all the way, then back up, swiveling her hips; prolonging, judging. Tricks. Like a skilled surgeon who while operating, cutting, watched carefully all the life signs. She had seen Ricky's eyelids flutter, his hands start to clench. She felt the first shudder, then another; his body arched. She had figured ten seconds. He went fifteen.

He had fallen back, gasping, mumbling, groaning... "Jesus... Jesus," and she had thought, "Yes, baby, they've hustled him pretty good, too."

Ricky was in the shower now, cooling off. At a board meeting two months from now he would remember this night. High up in some glass abattoir in New York he would listen to commercial facts and figures and his thoughts would drift back to this night. And he would remember her action.

By sheer accident of birth Ricky, a thirty-eight-year-old child, sat atop a two-hundred-million-dollar pyramid. A coast-to-coast chain of restaurants, firmly based on canned clam chowder. Margo could not fathom a society that produced such great wealth from so small a mind.

She drew hard on the Algerian tobacco. Tomorrow the buyers would be in town; and she was fully booked. In three short years, coming out of the line in Vegas, she had made it. One hundred dollars a trick. They liked her soft Colgate looks. Her curves. Her style. Her artistry. And she was off the hard-hustle. She had a platform of steady clientele. There was a cash flow whether she worked or not. There were old retainers, like Harry Stoner.

Harry had put her on the payroll that first year when she was getting started. Margo shook her head in sympathy. Tomorrow Harry would be uptight, tense; the fall show, the buyers, his whole hustle was on the line. She wished him well but hoped that tomorrow he would not have the usual emergencies; some buyer in heat at the last moment. It would be hard to say no to Harry. She hoped he wouldn't call.

Suddenly the boyish voice rang out from the suite, "Ready, baby!"

She exhaled. Now, the hardest part. Ricky would go down on her, and she would have to invent her own ecstasy. This was pure performance. Her reactions would get him off. But then the profession demanded good acting; that was the key. Acting. She smiled at a line from an old song: "Oh, Lord, why won't you make me a star . . . a star like Hedy Lamarr."

Margo took a final drag, coughed, crushed the Gauloise out, fluffed her dark hair, and went back to work.

The Southern Pacific sped through the desert night, slicing its way across the Mojave toward Los Angeles. In compartment thirty-three, Eddie Mirrell stared at the *Playboy* centerfold pinned to the wall opposite his bed. The girl in the centerfold had an "I'm watching you play with yourself" look. She wore an open shirt, exposing her large milk-white breasts with their cherry-colored nipples. She leaned over at a forty-five degree angle, hands holding onto a table. Her firm protruding ass looked like a split peach.

Eddie thought about doing it for a minute, then decided he'd save it. Tomorrow Harry Stoner was showing the fall line. He'd put the muscle on Harry to provide Margo. As he stared at the girl in the centerfold, he thought about Margo. Her mouth. Her moves. The Playmate's smiling face became Margo's face. Eddie suddenly lunged at the magazine, grabbed the centerfold and tore it to pieces. Panting, he caught his breath and sank back down on the bed. He reached up and snapped off the compartment lights.

The exertion frightened him. He knew better. The heart

attack had been a nightmare of fear and pain. Then, remembering the specialist's advice, Eddie calmed down. The doctor's words were reassuring: "It's all right, Ed. Exercise, have sex, but stay off planes."

The logic of the formula escaped him, but he accepted the conditions gratefully. Speeding through the night toward Los Angeles, a moment of joy, of expectation took hold of him. There was a very special kind of excitement waiting in the city of the Angels. Margo; and maybe she'd bring that girl along, that Asian girl, Dusty.

But Eddie's euphoria was brief. Guilt... guilt like an old infection spread slowly through his consciousness. Alice... goddammit... Alice. He owed his life to her. That sweet lady with the scarred belly. Alice.

They had met years ago, when Eddie was on the road selling a line of cheap shoes. Her father owned a specialty store chain in Cleveland and Alice was the fashion coordinator. It was for Eddie his first meaningful relationship with a mature woman.

She gave Eddie a self-confidence he never had; and through her father's connections he secured an important job in one of Cleveland's finest department stores. Eddie possessed an innate sense of what would sell and rose rapidly through the echelons of management. The years were good to them.

The slip of a surgeon's knife during a cesarean operation ruptured their relationship. They lost the child, and Alice almost lost her life. There were post-operative complications and she suffered sporadic hemorrhaging. Eddie felt the whole torturous business was in some way his fault. He could no longer become aroused with her. He thought that if he penetrated her, her agony would be increased. Despite the passage of years and the assurances of doctors, he dreaded the thought of making love with her.

They became companions, civil and pleasant, but at its core their marriage was barren and hollow. Then the thunderbolt. The heart attack. She nursed him through that. There was no single comfort Alice neglected to provide during his long convalescence.

After he recovered, his need for sexual gratification became obsessive. He began to masturbate, to collect pornographic literature, to sneak into blue movies in the middle of the day. He managed to connect with some ten-dollar hookers. But their tough talents provided only momentary relief.

He never approached the girls in the store. Only professionals. No dialogue. No involvement. No residual problems.

Now in the dark compartment he acted as his own defense counsel. He was, after all, very careful at home. No embarrassment to Alice. So what if he scored on these trips? It was necessary. It took the pressure off. The guilt subsided. Margo drifted in, shrouding his brain in a cloud of sensuality. He would not wait for tomorrow afternoon. He would see Harry early, at the showroom. Harry would make the arrangements. Christ knows, he gave him enough business. Besides, they probably had Margo on a retainer.

The train shrieked and braked sharply. Eddie raised the window curtain and looked out. They were moving slowly through a small junction. An aged Apache woman was sitting on a bench under a station light nursing a baby wrapped in rags. Eddie found it difficult to believe that her dark, shriveled breast contained any nourishment. He dropped the curtain and checked the radial dial on last year's Christmas present from Alice. It was almost a quarter to two. Five more hours and he'd be in Los Angeles.

The green hands on the small clock glowed softly in the darkness. It was one forty-five, and Harry Stoner twisted violently in his sleep.

The surrounding jungle smelled of death and decay. The gaudy, multi-colored birds shrieked their staccato lyric into the gummy night. Harry sat between the black, painted tribesmen. They all wore loin cloths, and bones pierced their nostrils. They had formed a circle in a clearing. In the center, on a raised platform, stood Billy Graham. He wore an expensive tie and nothing else. He was building to a crescendo:

"Listen to me, my black brothers; the Panthers are fucking up the Old Republic! Those Pearly Gates; the man who has the keys to those Pearly Gates is J. Edgar! Listen to me, black brothers! The Master speaks through my lips! I have traveled a long way, brothers! From the Via Dolorosa to Broadway! I am the Superstar!"

The tribesmen shouted an attenuated "Halleluja!"

Billy paused for breath, his eyes scanning the audience.

Harry leaped to his feet and shattered the silence by screaming, "You're naked, Billy! You're hanging out, Billy!" The tribesmen watched Billy, waiting for his reaction to this outrage.

Billy's eyes found the offender and their blue beams pierced Harry for a long minute. Then he raised his hand, pointing directly at Harry's heart and, in his best Doomsday voice, shouted, "Black brothers, I tell you now. I know that man! He's *'Cuban Pete, King of the Rhumba Beat!'* Get hiiiiiiimmmm!" Billy stretched the "him" into a four bar wail, electrifying the blacks.

The tribesmen rose up. Chanting. Spears pointed at Harry. Billy shrieked encouragement and Harry took off, bolting through the black mass, tearing into the surrounding green maze. He found a path and ran full out, legs pumping, lungs gasping for air. Gradually, the clamor of the following tribesmen subsided. Harry slowed to a trot . . . then a walk. Then he saw it. And froze. Horrified.

Out of the ground it rose. A giant black cobra, its head fanned out, came slowly to a ten-foot-high erection. It moved closer to Harry, swaying back and forth, measuring him like death on a slow metronome. Harry reached down into the roots of his vocal cords, begged them, pleaded with them for sound . . . for life.

Finally, he managed a low groan . . . then a small shout . . . then, with gaining power, a scream. Then another, and another, their strength increasing all the time, piercing, shattering, one scream following the other without pause, until they became one long, harrowing scream.

Jan's hand clutched his shoulder. "For God's sake, Harry . . . for God's sake." Then she mumbled something about American Airlines and dropped off.

Harry, fully awake now, pulled the covers up to his throat. He was soaked with perspiration. The air conditioner chilled his body. He moved closer to Jan, huddling into her warmth. Slowly, the chill diminished, the shock of the dream faded. But the weaving, fanned head still lingered.

He rolled out of bed, picked up his robe and slipped it on. He looked down at Jan. Over the years her softness, her total femininity, had developed a hard edge. His fault. He brought the business home with him. He never smiled and rarely spoke. He was in a trench cowering against the shuddering impact of the daily bombardment. It rubbed off. Jan had become a soldier, another member of his patrol.

Harry went into his daughter's bedroom. The playthings of her childhood still remained: dolls, puppets, drawings, records, children's books drenched the room with innocence. As he lingered in the doorway, the lyric of the elephant's song from Babar came back to him. "Rapali... Ripato ... crumda... crumda... Ripalo..."

Chapter 2

The huge living room, with its high, hand-carved ceiling, stared back at him, almost challenging him to use it. The antique clock over the fireplace showed two fifteen. He sank down into the two-thousand-dollar sofa and faced the opaque dead-eye of the Zenith.

Harry pressed the button on the Space Commander and the chalky light stabbed into the darkened room: the primary blues, yellows and reds came briefly to life, then died, receding into black and white.

George Raft was uncovering the Japanese plans for the attack on Pearl Harbor. Raft... the man who danced his way out of the Mob. Harry smiled... The Mob.

The candy store at the corner of Saratoga and Livonia. They ran Brownsville. They ran Brooklyn from that corner. It was the late thirties and Harry was in his late teens. The streets, the Mob, the older kids provided parental guidance. His mother and father had long since wound out of the fabric of his life. He remembered them as two lost children.

His mother possessed that special Latin beauty sometimes captured by Renaissance painters: eyes like black olives, with tiny circles of light at their centers; high cheekbones that curved toward a small, evenly planed nose; and soft, full lips that formed perfectly over wide, white teeth. Her face was framed by very fine black hair that spilled down over her shoulders.

Philomena Grimaldi had always been a rebel. She was

the first member of the family to be born in America. Her father died in Palermo when she was an infant; her two older brothers were married and lived in Jersey. She rarely saw them. It was her mother, Steffanna, who raised her. The code was strict, and very Catholic. But despite that matriarch's dire admonitions, Philomena was determined to become a dancer. And she succeeded.

By the time Philomena was twenty, she was one of fifteen girls kicking high, and synchronously, in one of the vaudeville palaces on Flatbush Avenue.

Philomena met Marty Stoner by chance in an old studio building on Fifty-seventh Street in Manhattan, a labyrinth of small stages and rehearsal rooms connected by winding corridors. In those grey halls one could hear the sounds of barking seals mingling with alto saxophones and the stentorian tones of some hopeful's Shakespearean recitation.

Philomena had just finished a dance class and was halfway down the main corridor when she heard a rich tenor voice. The strong voice, reaching for one of Verdi's high C's, carried through the floor. She had to meet the owner of that voice, and waited one hour in an outer room for Marty Stoner.

By the time they reached Broadway it was dark. They walked slowly up what was then truly the Great White Way. They had sandwiches and coffee in a restaurant near the Palace, where crowds lined up waiting to see Al Jolson.

She studied Marty's face and thought he looked Irish. He had bright blue eyes and a ruddy complexion topped by sandy hair, and he was tall and well built. She couldn't really tell: Stoner... Stoner... she hadn't heard it before. She asked him. Yes, he was Jewish. And did it matter? No. It did not...

It was just that... well, her mother.

Marty smiled, squeezed her hand and said, "Listen, Phil, if you don't tell yours, I won't tell mine."

In reality he had no mother to tell anything to. At the age of five weeks, Marty Stoner had been deposited on the steps of a Jewish orphanage on Hester Street, with a note pinned to his blanket proclaiming "S-T-O-N-E-R."

He received the inoculations of the time: a proper circumcision and a low-key trip through the Talmud.

The director of the orphanage played Caruso records

endlessly on a battered gramophone. Marty's right arm ached from winding the instrument, but he was fascinated with Caruso and the powerful beauty of opera.

He went to Science High School, then took a course in pharmacy and auditioned for a voice teacher. After two years, he wanted to begin a professional singing career. But the teacher warned: he was not ready; the voice was a delicate instrument, one had to proceed slowly.

Marty was twenty-five when he met Philomena. They were both night people. Marty worked the night shift in the pharmacy at St. Luke's Hospital and studied opera by day. They did the things night people do; they used the daylight. They went to zoos, all of them: Bronx, Brooklyn, and Central Park; to museums; to ball games and Coney Island with its great amusement complex, Luna Park.

On his one night off Marty would meet Philomena after her show. They'd go out to Sheepshead Bay and have clams and lobster and California wine.

They were caught in the magic of the times, and the magic of their dreams: of music, of lights, of theatre, of make-believe. It was a good time to be in love.

There was a tide of gaiety sweeping the nation. It was a time of heroes, of Valentino; Dempsey; Ruth; Chaplin; Bow and Gish; Ty Cobb and Fairbanks. And for a few dollars you owned thousands of shares of American industry. Like everyone else, Marty dabbled in Wall Street with his spare cash.

They had been going steady for six months before Philomena summoned the courage to tell her mother. By then, she had no choice. She was pregnant. Her mother had turned skeletal in those six months. They didn't use the word "cancer" in those days; the obituaries would say "long illness." Philomena dodged the issue as long as she could, but finally she said, "He's Jewish."

The death's head on the pillow screwed up and the voice was a rasp. Philomena could not marry a Christ killer! She would not have a "Mata Christi" in her house! Philomena's sacred soul would wander forever in the flames of hell! Vengeance would come!

Her mother died soon after. Marty and Philomena were married on a freezing February night by a justice of the peace upstate in Mamaroneck. Her mother's dying threats were prophetic; vengeance did come; but not from the Vatican; it came from a different holy place.

Wall Street blew its breath out with a force that tumbled the country. Lives, fortunes and dreams disappeared, shredded like the bits and pieces of meaningless ticker-tape blowing wildly through the canyons of lower Manhattan.

Marty Stoner's cash vanished overnight. It wasn't expected and it was visceral. Suddenly there was nothing. His salary at the hospital was cut in half. The future of opera would be left to other aspiring Carusos. They were forced to move from the middle-class neighborhood of Bensonhurst to the Italian-Jewish ghetto of Brownsville. Harry was six years old the year the market crashed.

The frustration of shattered dreams and fourteen hours a day of mixing formulas for the sick were too much for Marty. He began to gamble. In the beginning, it was just a few cents on the numbers, then a few dollars. Then the horses. Then the infection. Harry could remember his father saying, "Son, you can see the entire human condition played out in just six furlongs." Marty retreated into a world that had its own language: "One if two, back-to-back; round robins with 'if' money onto the place parlay... if the chalk shows... if the long one wins." The one word that remained constant was "if."

Marty worked seven days a week to support himself, Harry, Philomena and the habit. The mobsters on the corner knew the Stoners were struggling, they helped many families on the block, and on Friday nights they would send a basket of fish up to Harry's mother—in those days the Mob was shaking down the Fulton Fish Market. Harry remembered the "shookdown" fish as the best dinners in an otherwise constant diet of pasta.

The deathbed threats of Philomena's mother took on special significance as the years wore on. Philomena had indeed been consigned to hell—and while she was still alive. What then was in store for her immortal soul? She sought absolution in jugs of cheap Dago Red. She was afraid to enter a church, but she lit candles and said her private novenas; crucifixes and holy statues were everywhere in the tiny apartment.

When Harry came home from school, she would mumble drunkenly about the Son and the Father and the Holy

Ghost, and he would put her to bed whispering, "Yes...yes, Mama..."

A commercial for strawberry-flavored Feminine Hygiene broke up a meeting of the Japanese High Command. Harry got off the sofa, walked over to the wet bar, rummaged around until he found the Fundador. He poured about three inches of the amber fluid into a brandy snifter. He took a sip and felt the Spanish brandy burn its way down his throat, slowly warming the lining of his stomach. He crossed back to the sofa as a truck driver extolled the virtues of Alka Seltzer.

Raft was on again, tailing Tojo through a tough section of Tokyo, but Harry's thoughts drifted back to a tough section of Brooklyn and a large pharmacy at the foot of Atlantic Avenue. The drugstore was in a Puerto Rican neighborhood. They were the early pioneers, the first of many to trade jungles. Marty got the job as head pharmacist because he spoke some Spanish. After school Harry would help out with deliveries.

It was early evening on a July night. When Harry returned from a delivery, his father was waiting for him in front of the store. Marty was tense, and all he said was, "Let's go, son."

They walked five blocks to a tenement on Henry Street, then up three flights of wooden stairs to a door at the end of a pitch-black hallway. Marty knocked twice, a panel slid back, an eye fastened on them for a moment, and then the door opened.

The room was large, with cane chairs set in even rows. It was like a temple. About twenty men sat in the chairs studying similar papers, as if they prayed to a common god. At the far end of the room a grey-haired man sat behind a paper-strewn desk.

Marty walked up to the man. "Paki, I'd like you to meet my son, Harry. He's a good boy."

The tired face smiled and said, "Hello, Harry." Paki then looked at Marty. "You're onto a big one, Marty. The first three win."

"Win" not "won." They had their own grammar.

Paki went on, "Let's see, you had twenty to win on Skylark. She paid eight-twenty. That's eighty-two goin' on Free Again. She win and paid ten even. That made four hundred and ten onto Guilty Party. She win and paid five-forty. Christ, Marty, you got nine hundred goin' on Larkspur."

Marty smiled nervously. "Larkspur is eight to one on the morning line."

Paki shook his head. "I must be nuts to hold a four-horse win parlay. You could clean me out, Marty. Let's see, if Larkspur win you get about eight thousand."

In that room, in 1937, Harry didn't know what eight thousand dollars meant.

Paki looked down at the racing form and said, "Larkspur's goin' in the fourth at Bay Meadows." He checked his watch. "It's three o'clock on the Coast. We can get the call."

Marty nodded. "That's why I'm here."

Paki switched the radio on, then addressed the other men in the room. "Whosoever got anything goin' in the fourth at Bay Meadows, here's the call."

A few of the men moved up to the desk. There was a commercial message in Yiddish. Then an icy voice in English came on: "They're away in the fourth at Bay Meadows and here's the stretch call!"

Instantly, a heavily amplified voice boomed into the room.

"And turning into the stretch it's Try Again by a length and a half. Moving Man is second by a head. Larkspur's third and closing on the outside."

Harry noticed his father's red complexion starting to get lighter. The voice picked up:

"With only seventy yards to go it's Try Again and Larkspur. They're head and head . . . neck and neck."

Marty Stoner's face was now the color of chalk.

"At the wire . . . it's . . ."

There was a pause. Harry held his breath.

"It's Try Again by a nose. Larkspur second . . . Moving Man third. Time for the six furlongs: 1:09 and two fifths."

Paki snapped the radio off. "Sorry, Marty. Tough one to lose."

Marty was silent for a moment, then said, "Well I lost twenty dollars. That's all I bet."

Paki nodded. "I guess you could look at it that way."

Marty smiled. "Let me have twenty bucks, Paki." Marty

signed a marker and took the four fives. "Come on, we're going to celebrate."

Harry asked, "What for?"

"Son, you always know a man when he's down on his luck. That's when you see his character. I want you to remember the night your dad lost eight thousand dollars and took you to dinner to celebrate."

They went to a small Italian restaurant on Navy Street. Marty drank two bottles of red Bardolino and sang "Sorrento" with the Sicilian waiters. They ate baked clams Casino, and lasagna.

The wine had taken its toll on Marty. He stared blankly down, watching the pink, brown and white sections of his untouched spumoni melting together.

Harry touched his father's hand. "I want to ask you something, Dad."

Marty's tired eyes left the ice cream and focused on Harry.

"The thing is, Mama keeps telling me about The Father, The Son and The Holy Ghost... is she right? Am I supposed to believe in those things?"

Marty sighed. "I don't know, son. I don't know."

Harry persisted. "But what do you think God is?"

Marty smiled sadly. "To me, God is a four-horse win parlay."

That was the last time he tried to have a serious discussion with his father. By the time Harry reached his teens, his mother and father had receded from his world. They were shadows in a tenement. They spoke. They moved. But they were glassed in, trapped by lost dreams, clinging to scratch sheets and crucifixes for a salvation that never came.

Two Judo experts had Raft cornered in a back alley off the Ginza. Raft fought valiantly, traditionally, with jabs, crosses, and hooks; but a chop with the edge of the palm sliced into his neck, flinging him down.

Harry thought Raft's left hook was slow, even with the impetus added by movie magic. Harry knew all about left hooks.

He was always fighting. The Italian kids called him "Christ killer"; and the Jewish kids called him "Wop." He took boxing lessons after school from a battered club fighter at the YMCA. Harry was a natural and developed a wicked, professional left hook. The right cross did not come as easily, but it was there. Soon the kids called him "Harry."

Once in a while he got hold of a P.A.L. ticket. Ebbetts Field was a shrine. After the game, he would wait at the runway hoping for a glimpse of Dolph Camilli. The big first baseman was Harry's "Holy Ghost," and the Mob guys were the "Father."

They used to sit in the "headquarters," the back of Mom's candy store: Abe Reles, Marty Goldstein, Happy Maione, Phil Strauss. They liked Harry. He heard Reles once say of him, "That's a good kid. He don't take no shit off nobody; and he don't give no shit to nobody." It was a high compliment, and they began to throw a little action his way. Harry picked up betting slips, ran coffee, and brought pastrami sandwiches into the back room.

He remembered a handsome, tanned man coming into the back room on a bitterly cold winter day. The man was from that never-never land where they made movies. His tan seemed out of place among all those white-faced men. The man was seeking permission to have someone killed on the Coast. Before the conversation got too specific, Marty Goldstein looked at Harry and said, "Go out front and get an egg cream, kid." Harry left quickly, but didn't go for the egg cream. He walked ten blocks in the biting cold trying to forget the calm request of the tanned man for the death of some faceless stranger three thousand miles away.

Sitting now in the empty living room, watching Raft trying to hump Gale Sondergaard, Harry thought about how close he had come to full-fledged membership. The music probably saved him.

He loved big band swing and took drum lessons from an old bar mitzvah drummer on Pitkin Avenue. The Mob got him a job playing with a band in one of their hotels up in the Catskills. There was great suspense that summer.

Someone's body was chained to a pinball machine at the bottom of Swan Lake. It had been a sloppy job and all the Mob guys held their breath waiting for the body to surface. They were certain it would pop up among the bathing Margorie Morningstars. It didn't. Not that summer.

It was a memorable time for Harry. And not just the music. He received the complete sex manual. Toes up.

The vacationing married women tore into him, like jungle cats devouring a small kill. They had that musky odor of the lion house. On the weekends they ignored him, catering to their worn-out husbands. The summer ended with a final chorus of "Hatikva." And the action was back on the corner.

One night, that fall, Moey Wineburg took him to a restaurant just off the boardwalk in Coney Island. The smell of the sea mixed with odors of steaming hot dogs and cold draft beer. Besides the food, there were free, continuous movies: Charlie Chaplin and Harold Lloyd silents.

Moey Wineburg had three distinctions: he was brutally fast with an icepick; he had the bluest eyes in Brownsville; and a perennial clap that defied all known remedy.

After a few beers, Moey leaned close to Harry and said, "Listen, kid. You gotta get off the fuckin' corner. It's gonna get rough." Moey used the future tense as if, up until now, the corner had been Tahiti. "Either we're gonna wipe out them Wop cocksuckers and get a slice of the waterfront, or they're gonna wipe us." Moey bit the end of his hot dog viciously and gulped it down, belched loudly, and continued.

"Lookit, kid, there's the army. Get into it. You got no record. They'll take you. Your chances of stayin' alive are better. They got bands. You could play the drums. They have all them fuckin' parades. You know what I mean? They need drummers. You'll never see a gun. Besides, they send money home to your old lady."

Harry nodded in agreement, ate his hot dog, sipped his beer, and watched Harold Lloyd dangle precipitously over Wall Street. In those days, very few people argued with Moey. Especially when Moey took time out from his busy practice to give fatherly advice.

Uncle Sam didn't have to point. Moey had. Besides, anything outside of Brooklyn was an adventure. Harry did get out of Brooklyn, all the way to Camp Clairborne, Louisiana.

Harry didn't play the drums. He played a Browning Automatic Rifle. They had one to a squad and he played that tender instrument for the 133rd Regiment of the 34th Division. And it was a long refrain from Louisiana to Africa to Italy... sunny Italy.

But in the winter of 1943 there was very little sun in sunny Italy. An icy Alpine wind pushed a steady rain down the peninsula turning the dirt roads into knee-deep traps of cold mud, key bridges were down, and the swollen Volturno River flooded the tiny villages between Naples and Cassino—and above them, always, on the high ground, crack German units. . . .

The German retreat was classic and brilliant. Veteran Wehrmacht infantry, well emplaced Panzers and S.S. paratroopers extracted a bloody toll for every inch of ground they ceded. It was man to man, shell for shell, a violent shuddering impact of two determined armies locked together in death, misery and mud.

The wires had been sent weeks apart, but they reached him on the same night, a freezing night on the east bank of the Volturno River.

His father had collapsed and died on Henry Street. His mother had died of cirrhosis in a Bellevue ward.

Harry read the wires over and over again, stunned by the fact that death could come in pasted letters; it was almost incomprehensible that three thousand miles away people were dying of natural causes.

About his mother Harry felt more anger than sadness— that religious fanaticism and cheap wine could machine that beauty down to a yellow corpse in a city ward. About his father he could only wonder if Marty had died sweating out that fourth horse in the win parlay.

Harry could have asked the chaplain for a leave but decided not to. There were only a handful of the original men left in his platoon, and they took care of each other. They had an unwritten law: You only went home if the Germans sent you.

Harry had never known that special camaraderie before and could not betray it.

It had been some war... some adventure. The corner guys had all been killed in the electric chair. But Harry survived. The Germans just missed killing him.

The antique clock showed three thirty. The daylight was missing, but it was tomorrow. In a few hours years of work would be on the line. Harry sighed and thought, Christ, the next time he blew out any candles, he'd be fifty. Why was it still on the line? Why was it all still in doubt?

You kick like a son of a bitch, lungs bursting, the pain searing; the light gets a little stronger. Finally, you surface. And there's the life support. You cling to it. Lean on it. Catch your breath. Then slowly, subtly, it grows heavy. It begins to sink. And you're back fighting for air. But something's gone. The years have sapped your strength. Still, you have to get back up again. You have to hold on to that small piece of the pie. That tiny slice of the American Dream. A payroll instead of a paycheck. Not a big dream. Why was it so tough? He tossed that one away. Why not? Who said it would be any different?

Only the Tube, the media promised a life of Tootsie Rolls and Lollipops. And gorgeous girls who came in six delicious flavors. Everything was exquisitely packaged. But nothing worked. Not anymore. Ten-thousand-dollar cars were faulty; and animals flourished under the lids of soup cans. They nailed you. They sucked you in. Get the things . . . get the things. And maybe they were right. How could you quarrel with it? If you made it, why not live it? It was over so fucking fast . . . Christ . . . fifty, five-oh coming up.

And where was it any better? Where do you run to? To a worn-out lyric: "An airline ticket to romantic places." Used to be. Used to be. The romantic places were gone: full of loud shirts, cheap tours, cigar butts and beer cans. Today they had you. Grab the dream and you're squeezing the neck of a cobra. You can't let go, and you can't get it into the bag.

One way or another they had you. It would always be on the come line. But it was too late to lie down. Well, okay, let them come. What could they do? Put him away? Christ, the lunatics that murdered presidents . . . what was the worst they got? Three meals a day and a toilet.

The only question was, do you have enough courage to take care of your own? Harry swallowed the last of the Spanish brandy. And if he got caught . . . well, every man owed his country some time in jail.

Raft found out about Pearl Harbor. But too late. The Imperial Fleet sailed. He changed channels. Charlie Chan was wrapping up a complicated case on the back lot at

Warner's. Harry pressed the button. Gary Cooper and Akim Tamiroff were huddled behind a snow bank in the Spanish mountains, watching a battalion of Moors cantering toward a mined bridge. Cooper's hand closed over the plunger. Harry shook his head. It would never happen that way. The Moors would have sent out sappers. They'd have gone over that bridge with a vacuum cleaner. He snapped the set off.

The sudden silence was ominous. The big room seemed to be alive, animate, ready to pounce on him, to swallow him.

He got up and started out of the living room. Something stopped him. He thought he heard a child singing. It was the Elephant's song from Babar: "Ripalo... Ripati... Crumda... Crumda... Ripalo..."

Chapter 3

The Monday morning sun flaked the night out of the sky. The hot breath of the Santa Ana mixed with the pus-colored smog, forging a thick gauze that stuck fast to the skin of the city. Above Highland Avenue, the decaying sign HOLLYWOOD was barely visible. A pack of wild dogs prowled its base, pausing occasionally to spray their yellow-green urine on its splintered legs.

A half-mile east of Union Station, on the main track, the signal changed from green to amber. The engineer throttled back, and the jerking spasms of steel gripping steel continued for three minutes. The Southern Pacific came to rest with a final jolt at precisely 6:40 A.M.

Eddie Mirrell pointed his luggage out to the elderly black porter. As they started to the exit the porter said, "We sure got a hot one goin' today." He laughed nervously. "Gonna choke us today."

Eddie smiled, nodded, but didn't answer. His mind was methodically tracing the order of the day's business.

They came out of the dark terminal into the filtered light and walked up to a waiting line of yellow cabs. The driver of the lead cab saluted and quickly came around to the rear of the car. He opened the trunk, helping the porter with the bags.

Eddie gave the driver the name of his hotel, then turned to the porter and handed him two singles.

The porter smiled. "Thank you, sir. I sure hope you have a good day. Gonna be a tough one. Yes sir, gonna be a hot one today." He chuckled and ambled away.

They rolled easily through the quiet streets. Eddie felt his jacket sticking to the imitation leather and shifted his weight. He didn't care about the heat. They had arrived an hour ahead of schedule. His timetable was working perfectly. The check-in business would be fast and efficient. No crowds at this hour. He'd unpack, shower, have breakfast, then rest for an hour or so. At ten he'd walk over to Harry's office. He figured the walk to be about fifteen blocks, but despite the heat it would be all right. He'd walk slowly, leisurely. He was supposed to walk. The doctor had prescribed "A mile a day."

They crossed Fifth and Hill and a sudden, unpleasant thought entered his mind, and he played judge and jury to his own anxieties. What if Margo was sick? Margo wouldn't be sick. Why should she be sick? Hookers seldom got sick. They couldn't afford to be sick. Margo was strong; her body was as finely tuned as an athlete's. You could see the little muscles in her stomach. No it was an absurdity. Margo was fine . . .

But suppose she was out of town? Suppose she took off for Vegas or Acapulco with some wealthy John? What was the matter with him? He had almost forgotten; it was Market Week. Margo would never leave town during Market Week. The town would be flooded with hundred-dollar clients. He was here on business. That was his leverage with Harry.

He settled back, secure in his own logic. The driver mumbled something about the weather. Eddie grunted a reply.

High up, at the crest of Doheny Road, the Sierra-Alto Towers were shrouded in the morning haze. In the bedroom of a seven-hundred-dollar-a-month suite, on the twenty-fifth floor, Margo stirred in her sleep. She was naked. Her milk-white skin poured into the pink satin sheets; her legs were wide apart and her flat belly formed a smooth valley leading up to her large, firm breasts. Their stiff red nipples reflected her subconscious thoughts. She dreamed of Dusty, of being locked together with that supple, coffee-colored girl.

It was ten to seven and Margo had been sleeping for four hours. She had left Ricky at two thirty and arrived at her apartment at three, looking forward to seven hours of sleep.

Before taking the two seconals she followed an old procedure: she pulled the pin on the alarm clock turning the small hand to ten; she set the FM radio-clock for ten ten, then called her answering service leaving a wake-up call for ten fifteen. She had a full calendar for the day and prided herself on being punctual. Margo had only missed three appointments in the last three years: once she was busted; once she woke up hemorrhaging; and once, an elderly lady in a Buick smashed into her MG.

The small smile on Margo's face widened slightly. She moaned softly. The dream had improved. She felt Dusty's warm breath playing on the inside of her thighs.

The haze was less intense over Beverly Hills as if the pollutants showed some degree of respect for the lofty real estate.

Night-weary cats purred and rubbed against the stone steps, waiting for the Mexican maids to let them in. They were easy targets for the swooping blue jays.

The red-necked pool men netted their usual morning catch of nocturnal insects: the floating dots that had lost their lives in the gentle chlorinated currents.

The small clock on the night table showed seven A.M. Harry looked over at Jan enjoying the last few grains of phenol sleep. He studied the high cheekbones, the broad pug nose, the full mouth and the long black hair splayed across the pillow. Jan was past forty now, but still handsome. Her face and figure still resisted the lines of time. She would move into her middle years without being demeaned by the clock.

He often thought she bore a strong resemblance to his mother, Philomena. He shook his head, remembering all those candles, all those crucifixes in the tiny apartment and in the end, "Philomena," the saint his mother was named for, was taken down, like an "objection" after the race.

Harry reached for the intercom speaker on the wall behind him. He depressed the red button on the mouth of the speaker. "*Carmella . . . buenos dias, si . . . un café por favor.*"

Deep and mushy with sleep, Jan said, "Tell her to put some cream in it."

Harry depressed the button once again. "*Carmella, mucha crema para la señora, si . . . gracias.*" He replaced the speaker.

Jan raised herself into a sitting position. Her large, shapely breasts jiggled slightly as she made herself comfortable.

"Messy night."

In a resigned voice, Harry replied, "Doctors."

"He had his hand on my thigh all night."

Harry nodded. "Wait till we get the bill."

He pushed a button on a remote master panel alongside the bed. A color television set into the wall opposite them sputtered into chromatic life.

A handsome, plastic announcer broadcast the morning news: "Three major fires are still out of control in Northern California . . . On the National scene a spokesman for the Defense Department stated a host of lower echelon officers have been placed under arrest as the investigation into corruption of PX facilities continues . . . Several massage parlors in Saigon have been raided and shut down." Without a pause, the man held up a box and smiled. "Any dog will lick his chops if you feed him Grenadine Beef . . . why, it will make your dog sit up and . . ."

"Shit." Harry spoke and shut off the set simultaneously.

A Mexican woman in her late forties entered the bedroom. Her face was a brown blueprint of some ancient Aztec god. She glided silently toward Jan, carrying a silver tray bearing two cups of coffee.

Jan said, "*Buenos dias,*" and took a cup.

Carmella repeated the same ritual with Harry. Then, moving silently, as if directed by John Ford, she left, an Apache disappearing behind a rock.

Jan took a sip of coffee. "He was a louse. A real Thoroughbred. They ought to declare a holiday in New York."

"When's the funeral?" Harry asked.

"Tomorrow."

Harry shrugged. "Sorry about the airport thing."

"It's all right." She sipped some more and asked, "How's the line?"

"Good. Rico's a talented kid."

Jan took a big swallow, shook her head, and said, "Hard to believe Bernie's dead. God, what a bastard!"

"Screwed everybody." He pushed another button on the remote panel, activating a tape machine. "How long will you be away?"

"Oh, a week...ten days." She paused, sipped some coffee. "I wonder if he left anything?"

"A lot of pain."

"You know, Harry, he liked me. He was always feeling me up. I mean even when I was a kid."

"He never stopped."

They fell silent, lost in their own thoughts. Benny Goodman's "Stompin' At The Savoy" filled the void. After a few bars, Jan put her coffee down. "I'll call you when I get in tonight." She paused, and repeated, "I said I'll call you tonight."

Harry looked straight ahead at the dead TV set on the opposite wall and softly said, "Benny Goodman."

With a touch of annoyance, she asked, "Where are you?"

"The bull-pen...Ebbetts Field. It's two out, bases loaded...they wave me in and my curve is coming around the corner."

"You screamed in your sleep again."

"Same dream."

"See Doctor Frankfurter. Bring your dreams to Frankfurter."

"No. I know what it is. It's Willie. The black guy that parks my car. He always gives me heat."

"But that doesn't explain Billy Graham and the cobra. You should see Doctor Frankfurter."

"What for? He'll tell me it's repressed sex struggling with religion for possession of my brain. It'll cost me fifty bucks and all the time I know it's Willie."

"You can't be sure of that."

"Of what?"

"Willie."

Harry nodded. "I'm sure. You know I saved his job. You remember. I told you, Jan."

"No, I don't remember."

"I went to Landsburgh. I told him if Willie was fired, I'd pull out of the building. I went to bat for the man."

"Why?"

"Who knows why? 'Cause he looks like Ezzard Charles."

"Ezzard Charles?"

"Yes, Ezzard Charles. The most honest fighter I ever saw. He may have been over his head, but they knew his name. That goddam Willie looks just like him."

They fell silent again.

Goodman, Krupa, Teddy Wilson, Hampton, Artie Bernstein and Charlie Christian swung into "Rose Room."

Jan broke the silence. "You insulted Levitan."

"I asked him what he does."

"You know what he does. He's a business manager."

"What the hell does that mean?"

"Harry, please don't ask him what he does."

"Okay, okay ... speaking of insults ... what about the good Doctor Vogel and his wandering hands?"

"It's insecurity."

"Insecurity? Christ, the man has everything up front except trumpets."

"Everybody's using him. He's a fine doctor."

"I liked Doc Fisher."

"He still uses leeches. He's an old man."

"I know. Old and smart. He can diagnose hemorrhoids through a suit of armor."

Harry swung his legs over the side of the bed. He removed his pajama top and sat there motionless, studying the Oriental patterns on the three-thousand-dollar rug. Jan's eyes examined his back. The three scars seemed a deeper blue than usual.

The Goodman sextet leaped into "Limehouse Blues."

Sadly, Harry said, "Kamu died. It was on the six o'clock news, last night."

She said, "He died a long time ago."

"Not him. Not the writer. The whale at Pacific World. His dorsal fin became infected, from swimming in the same direction—against the current."

"What current?"

"The current in the tank."

"So there's one less whale in the world."

"Years ago, I took Audrey to see him. He was magnificent. They shouldn't be allowed to take those animals out of the sea; they shouldn't be allowed to cage them."

On the vibes, Lionel Hampton painted lightly around the melody.

Gently, she asked, "What is it, Harry?"

"Nothing. Nothing." There was a pause, and his voice brightened. "I passed Roxbury Park. The kids were playing little league."

It was a fortuitous cue and Jan picked it up. "Harry, you used to love baseball. Why don't you go to a game once in a while?"

He got up slowly and came around in front of the bed, facing her. "They still play, but it's not the same. They don't play on dirt anymore. They play on plastic. And the pitchers don't wind up."

"Wind up?"

"Yes. Wind up. You remember Johnny Van Der Meer?"

She watched him as he swung his arm in a huge arc, double pumping, kicking his leg high, then coming down into a very professional follow-through.

"That was pitching, Jan. They spat tobacco juice on the ball; they scratched their ass. They looked up at planes, cursed the batters ... they were something." He walked to the night table and switched Goodman off, then turned to her, "Goddammit, they were something."

She studied him carefully: the light blue eyes, the even features, the black hair going to grey. His figure was still trim. He used the pool. That was one thing he still enjoyed. But it was his eyes; that very pale blue color. When they wanted to, they could put you away. But lately, there were tiny menacing lights behind them.

"I really think you ought to see Doctor Frankfurter."

"Frankfurter says I murdered myself." He came around to her side of the bed and sat down.

She touched his waist. "You're always worried."

He forced a smile. "Cuban Pete never worries. Why would I worry? It only costs me two hundred dollars a day to get out of bed."

"I don't understand."

"There's nothing to understand. That's what it costs. With everything. And downtown. That's another story.

I've got to finance the new line. That's now. That's in a few hours. And we may still be audited for last year."

A trace of fear crept into her voice. "Audited for what?"

"We did a little ballet with the books last season."

"What does Phil say?"

"He's worried."

"He'd be a lot less worried if he'd get his mind out of politics."

Harry smiled. "He's not into politics. Phil's still in the Lincoln Brigade. He's still defending Madrid."

Harry stretched out, moving close to her. He pulled the pink string on her nightgown. The silk fell away. He cupped his hands around her right breast and kissed the nipple. Her hands tilted his face up; she looked into his eyes; there were no lights on, they were cool and that very opaque blue.

Harry said, "You know, whenever we leave each other I wish we had made love."

"Me, too, but it was a late night. They didn't leave till almost one. But, still, we should have. We should make love more often."

"We will. We will, Jan."

She smiled, and he spoke quickly, hopefully. "I tell you what. When you get back from New York, let's take a plane to Zurich. I miss Audrey. I miss the kid. We can see her and have a holiday." He paused. "I really miss her."

Jan shrugged. "She's better off there. Things are too crazy here. A man came out of La Scala restaurant two nights ago and was shot six times. That's only three blocks away."

He shifted his weight to his elbow and sat up. "Maybe we can get a brigade of South Vietnamese to patrol Beverly Hills. The Mexican maids can cook their rice."

"Harry, it's no joke. They're shooting horse in the toilets at the high school."

"Cuban Pete's daughter doesn't shoot horse." Harry stood up; a thin streak of pain shot through the 88 shrapnel. He walked toward the door leading to the master bathroom, opened it, then turned back to Jan. "You taking the 747?"

"I don't know. It's the ten o'clock."

Harry nodded and wistfully said, "Jan, with my arm I could have made Brooklyn . . . well, at least Philadelphia." He paused, threw her a last look and went into the bathroom.

Jan picked up the coffee cup and studied the remains of the Guatemalan grounds as if there were some sign, some clue, some way out of the dark, twisting tunnels that had become the walkways of her life.

Harry stared at his lathered reflection. He was in the bleachers at Ebbetts Field, clutching his P.A.L. ticket. The Dodgers were behind with two out in the ninth; and Dolph Camilli was moving into the batter's box. Harry whispered with the reverence of one calling up some great diety, "Dolph Camilli . . . first base . . . Dolph Camilli . . ."

From the bedroom, Jan's voice tried to penetrate the barrier of his thoughts. "I'll call you tonight! I'll call you when I get in!"

Harry whispered again. "Dolph Camilli . . . first base."

The volume of her voice climbed, pulling him out of the bleachers.

"Harry, I said I'll call you tonight!"

Automatically, he shouted back. "Okay, Jan . . . okay." He picked up the Gillette, poised to slaughter the night's stubble. But, at the last moment, he held the stroke back and softly spoke to his reflected image. ". . . Second base . . . second base . . . Pete Coscarot."

Chapter 4

The sun cast its damaged light onto the Stoner driveway.

Carefully, Harry hung the jacket of his Italian suit on the little pin over the rear door of the Lincoln. Jan had bought the suit for him at a Saks sale. He opened the front door, leaned in and switched on the ignition, then activated the air conditioner. He straightened up and lit the first Sherman of the day and thought of the small irony of these two actions: waiting for the interior of the Lincoln to cool while sucking the hot fumes of the black Sherman into his lungs.

He heard a sudden noise in one of the sixty-foot-high palms that shaded the Spanish style house. He looked up at the nearest one. Its fronds were motionless, but the rustling and squealing was unmistakable. Standing there, waiting for Iacocca's technology to cool the Lincoln, Harry remembered the last time he saw rats.

Finally, in late fall of '42, the Allied forces broke through at Kasserine Pass. Their first victory in Tunisia, but a costly one. Half the men in his platoon had been cut down by Speer's 88s and Porsche's tanks; by virtue of survival, Harry received a field promotion. He leaped over death from corporal to top sergeant.

They had stopped to regroup in a small, nameless Arab village and the camels were being generous to the desert flies who massed on each dropping, turning the brown dung black. Even the armor roaring up the dirt street could not disturb their appetites. A burned-out Panzer tank stood at the head of the street, and a German trooper sprawled out of the hatch, as if the interior of the machine had vomited him up. His stiff, purple fingers hung down the side of the turret, almost touching the small, black cross.

Harry visited the remnants of his squad in a clay-walled bar that had been converted into a recovery ward. It was surreal: the red plasma, the colorless glucose and that special yellow that comes from infected wounds; and on the walls colorful Cinzano posters of Biarritz, Cannes, and Lugano; and, over all, the smell of Lysol.

A tiny nurse weaved her way through the cots and stretchers. She looked like Linda Darnell and had not yet acquired that protective, field-hospital veneer, that fixed smile, that happy mask flashed at men with only seconds to live. She was a full lieutenant but did not try to impress anyone with her rank.

Harry thought she liked him but was hesitant about pushing it. He was out of practice. He had not talked to, been with, or even seen a girl in almost five months. But as the days wore on this pretty nurse became a symbol. A last chance. Someone at GHQ had computed the life span of a BAR man in combat to be thirty seconds and Harry had passed that allowance long ago. The nurse haunted his nights; her cute face and tiny, perfect figure became an obsession. Still he held back. She was a quality girl and probably besieged by captains and colonels.

Harry stopped by the small ward every day, helping her, running errands for her. When, finally, he asked her to lunch, she accepted and seemed genuinely pleased. They drove to the edge of the village, to an area of high, endless dunes. Fast-moving clouds cast changing shadows over the barren landscape, and small cones of swirling sand blew off the tops of the dunes, giving the desert the appearance of a shifting sea. Only the burned-out hulks of tanks dotting the high dunes spoiled the illusion.

They got out of the jeep and spread a blanket. Their picnic consisted of C rations and two bottles of 1938 Pouilly-Fuissé that Harry had been saving since Casablanca.

He listened patiently to her chatter about her home town and her family and the good life they led on a small ranch. And how she always wanted to be a nurse. She went on and on, and he let her go, listening without interruption, waiting for his chance. After she had consumed the wine, he asked her. His words sounded more like an incantation than an invitation. He was certain she'd be offended. She would pull rank and say, "Take me back, sergeant." Instead, she wet her lips and quickly said, "The supply tent, behind the motor pool, at nine thirty sharp. That's when the MPs go to the movie."

That night the desert wind carried Helen O'Connell's voice from a distant radio: "Those cool and limpid green eyes" soaked through the canvas walls of the supply tent.

They were on the floor behind a pile of plasma cartons. He was on top of her building slowly, but going well. He had his hands under her, pulling her close. The fact that she was so small excited him. He wondered how she took it and where it went. Then, just as the come-trains and coaches started to roll, he saw them. There were two of them. Big and grey. They were sitting quietly, three feet away, their beady eyes shining, locked-in, fascinated, as if they had been invited to a special showing of a blue movie.

Harry stopped.

The nurse whispered, "What's the matter?"

He replied automatically, "Nothing, nothing." He picked up his rhythm and kept going. In those days, rats or no

rats, you kept going. She could have been the last bang for
a long time; or forever.

The sounds they made when they came scattered the
rats. They made it once more, but Harry didn't enjoy it.
He kept searching the crevices of the tent for the rats. He
was sure they would crawl up on him and, at a critical
moment, take a bite.

Now, looking up at the palms, he felt a strange kinship
to these Beverly Hills rats; that, somehow, they shared
with him the experience of that desert night.

Harry dropped the Sherman, stepped on it, and slid
into the driver's seat. It was like moving off a sundeck into
a cold pool.

He backed out of the drive and pointed the blue Lincoln north, toward Sunset Boulevard.

The false voice with the sub-rosa smile came out of the
twin speakers. A Russian seaman who leaped aboard a
U.S. Coast Guard cutter had been denied asylum. The
captain of the vessel stated that to have given the seaman
asylum would have upset delicate negotiations with the
Soviets over the take of yellow tail flounder.

The abrasive voice of a housewife interrupted the
news with critical details of how she saved three dollars
a week shopping at Al's Supermarket. Harry turned the
dial. A cheery male voice was describing a special
service of a huge cemetery: children could learn American history in a mortuary, on a pleasant hillrise overlooking
the dead.

He turned to an all-news station. The detached, cool
voice spoke rapidly: ". . . the notorious Nazi doctor responsible for the deaths of eighty thousand women at Ravensbruck
concentration camp in World War II, reported to have
been seen in a sidewalk café in downtown Asunción,
Paraguay . . . In Washington, the Atomic Energy Commission stated the five-megaton test is . . ."

Harry shut it off and slipped a cassette into the tape
deck. It was "Mack the Knife" in many versions. The one
now was in German; soft and blue. Harry translated the
German.

". . . Yes . . . yes, that shark has pearly teeth, babe . . . and
when he bites . . . scarlet billows start to spread . . ."

But, as the car moved east on Sunset Boulevard that

morning, none of the very rich in their 1920 mansions were listening.

The Lincoln stopped for a red light on Doheny and Sunset. The early morning hippies, junkies, teen-age hookers, having spent the night in hallways and parking lots, were beginning to circulate. The light went to amber, then green.

She was thumbing on the corner of La Cienega. A gorgeous girl, with pressed blond hair, wearing tight jeans and a beautifully filled blouse. She smiled at Harry as he waited for the long three-way light. His brain flashed images of the Manson kids: the monster chicks drinking the blood pumping out of Sharon Tate's swollen belly.

The girl's smile widened at the sound of the horn. He watched her young breasts dance as she ran to the car. She climbed into the passenger seat and slammed the door shut.

"Thanks a lot, mister."

"It's okay. Where are you going?"

"Nowhere . . . what I mean is, I stay on the Strip."

"All day?"

"All day."

"Nothing wrong with that."

"No."

"Where do you live?"

She shook her head and yellow light shimmered all along the blond hair. "Oh, I live in a pad at Manhattan Beach. It belongs to a pilot. Not just a pilot. A captain."

The traffic light went green. Harry gently pressed the gas pedal; they rolled slowly east.

"You mean an airline captain?"

She laughed. "Yes, of course. He's old. I ball him anyway. It's groovy. Not him. I mean the pad."

He dropped the air conditioner to Low.

She spoke in sudden bursts. "Sometimes I sell the *Free Press* and I rap with a very groovy guy. He's a veteran. Vietnam. They blew his friend's leg off. He killed six people. He was stoned. It was trippy. They wanted him to testify but he stood on his rights."

She looked at him, waiting for a response. He flicked his eyes at her but said nothing.

As if picking up a lost thread, she said, "Must be

something else . . . I mean war. It's so male. It's so full of balls." She pronounced "balls" as if a pair had just fallen out of her mouth.

Harry looked at her and asked, "How old are you?"

"Twenty. Hey, what's that music?"

"German."

"Why?" she asked.

"Why not?"

"No reason." She smiled.

She studied him carefully—the greying hair, the blue eyes, the silk suit, and the pleasant aroma of an expensive cologne.

"Say, mister, how old are you?"

He hesitated for a second, then quickly said, "Thirty-eight. As a matter of fact, my birthday is next week. I'll be thirty-eight."

She sucked her lower lip between her teeth. "That's old."

Harry smiled. "Well, that all depends on how you feel . . . right?"

"Yes, I guess that's right. You know, that's a very groovy-looking suit."

"Thanks."

They were passing Orange Grove Ave. She continued to stare at him. She put her forefinger between her lips and sucked at it briefly. She then slid the wet finger out of her mouth and said, "You want to ball me?"

He shot her a look. "Ball you?"

She nodded. "Yes, right now. You can pull into a parking lot. It's early."

Harry shook his head. "It's sweet of you to offer, but I don't have the time."

She shrugged. "Okay. You can let me off at the next corner."

He maneuvered the Lincoln out of the stream of traffic and eased into a red zone at the curb. She got out quickly, but held the door open. Leaning in, she said, "Listen. Thanks. My name is Myra. I'm here all the time."

"Good. Good, Myra. Well, have a nice day."

Myra's grey eyes clouded as if Harry had said something utterly profound, some deep mystical message that defied explanation.

She spoke with a measured cadence. "Nice day?"

He smiled. "What I mean is . . . rapping with the veteran . . . and a . . . well, you know. Just have a nice day."

Still perplexed, she said, "Uh, yes . . . well, okay."

Harry nodded. "Okay."

Myra closed the door and watched the Lincoln move off, growing smaller, getting lost in a sea of multi-colored metal.

"Groovy car."

She heard the voice and turned. A tall, bearded boy of perhaps twenty-four came up alongside her. He wore chino pants and a black satin shirt. He slipped his arm around Myra's waist.

She smiled up at him and said, "A business cat. Old. But groovy. Smelled nice. You know what he said? He said, 'Have a nice day.'"

The boy shrugged. They walked west toward Schwabs.

Chapter 5

He parked in the curve behind Ula's apartment and checked his watch; it was eight forty.

Myra's voice continued to reverberate. "War must be something else." It repeated like a stylus caught in a bad groove. "War must be something else . . . War must be something else."

It was a bright, sunny day in Naples. From the top deck, Harry looked up the Via Castellano. The red medieval fort clung to the brown hills overlooking the ancient city. Across the bay, small, white puffs of smoke oozed out of Vesuvius. It reminded him of the old Camel sign on Broadway, blowing perpetual rings of smoke. The mouth of the bay was cluttered with the sunken remnants of the Italian Navy. Their masts sticking up out of the oily, green water were like rust-colored headstones giving final testimony to their brief existence.

Harry had to remind himself that he was not standing in the middle of a dream. He had made it. He was alive. He was going home. He thought, only the dead really knew the short odds of war. They did not forget. For them, time could not erode that ultimate horror; that last second when something vital was blown away.

He had come close. He knew it would be an 88. The Germans hadn't burned all the books; they saved a few on trajectory. For almost three years he had seen and heard those shells come screaming in. Their accuracy and explosive power was a true testament to Germanic efficiency. Pound for pound there was nothing their equal in the allied arsenal. Toward the end the 88s totally dominated his thoughts. Harry could see himself in their cross-hairs: no group, no cluster, no armor; just himself. They had one shell reserved for him.

The Americans had lost the initiative and the Germans had them on the beach at Anzio. The day had been a Daliesque nightmare. Veteran German artillery and Panzers in monster Tiger tanks massed on the heights rained their iron down onto the beach. Crack units of Wehrmacht infantry crisscrossed the beach with heavy automatic fire. Hienkels dropped anti-personnel "butterfly" bombs. "Goliaths," radio-controlled armor vehicles loaded with TNT, ran madly down onto the beach, smashing into the men and exploding with devastating effect. Squads of men stumbled through gelatined minefields, blowing up like struck matches.

Miraculously, Harry remained untouched into the night. They were huddled behind a small dune. Flares lit the beach with streaks of brilliant green light; it was as if hell changed color.

He heard the shell come screaming in. It did not waver. Not this time. The force of the impact was so intense, it delayed the pain for a few seconds. Before he lost consciousness, he saw the other men. They looked like a box of crushed tomatoes.

A flock of screeching gulls brought him back to reality. He had survived. He was alive. He was on the ship.

Five thousand men lined the rails. The huge grey transport was marked AP.61. From the top deck, a large black banner was draped over the side. In the center of the banner was a giant head of a red Longhorn steer and the legend, "The 34th." On the dock, a Navy band played "Begin The Beguine."

The hookers on the Via Roma would miss their action

but the Wehrmacht would not. Algeria...Tunisia...Salerno
...the Volturno...Cassino...the Gustav line..the Gothic
line...Anzio-Nettuno. They had met the best: The Afrika
Corps, the Herman Goering Division, the S.S. Panzers in
the big, grey tanks with the small, black crosses.

"*...and down by the shore an orchestra's playing, and
even the palms seem to be swaying.*"

The kids on the pier handling the ship's lines were
German prisoners, but they were not the Supermen. The
Supermen were gone. These were children in grey, thrown
in at the end. They would live to go home and make the
mark the hardest currency in the world.

Five living heads were carried up the gangway in wire
baskets. They were part of the Japanese 442nd. Their
parents in California were penned up in a concentration
camp at Santa Anita racetrack.

"*...and there we were swearing to love forever...*"

The gangway went up. The whistle screamed. The
German kids let the lines go as the Navy tugs eased them
out of the berth. The band could still be heard as they
reprised the song. The teeth of a soldier standing alongside Harry started to chatter. Harry looked at the man. He
was a staff sergeant and tears rolled down his face. There
was a slow rhythm to their descent.

Harry gripped the man's arm and said, "It's over."

The man nodded; but, suddenly, he burst into sobs, his
teeth chattering violently. Harry put his arm around the
man, hugging him, pulling him close. "It's over, sergeant.
The fucking thing is over."

"*...and promising never...never to part...*"

Ula's warm lips dissolved the fall of '45. He was lying
face down on her bed and she was kissing the scars on his
back, her mouth lingering on each. There was a softness to
her voice that was helped by the Scandinavian accent.

"What's the matter? What is it?"

It was the same question Jan had asked.

Harry turned over and looked up at her. Her green eyes
had the raw fire of uncut emeralds. He thought her body
was like a piece of fruit that would never quite ripen, that
would always be firm. Her hair, parted in the center,
cascaded down to her soft shoulders, glittering like a
lemon shower along both sides of her face.

The first time was at the Biltmore two years ago. He had given her a chance to model a few numbers in the Summer Line. It was a very wet January, and that day had been a harrowing one for him. His brain swam in a mixture of fatigue and alcohol. After the show, they wound up in a suite, high up in the hotel.

She stood over him. Naked. Legs apart. His mind blurred. He thought of her as a Nordic goddess, transformed her into some great Valkyrian bitch from whose womb sprang—the Wehrmacht, the Stukas, the endless lines of tanks, the camps, the bunkers, the shiny black boots, the small black crosses: all streaming, flowing out of that moist tunnel.

He buried his head between her legs and pressed his mouth into that pink conjunction of all that was evil and all that was exciting; as if absolution could be had by drowning in that strange serum.

He was possessed with her. That first night, and for months afterward. He had told her of the mad illusions she created in his mind; how he used her in fantasies. She listened, said nothing. She would smile and make it work.

But time, and intimacy itself, cooled Harry's drive. Looking down at him now, knowing the excitement was gone, she still tried to keep him interested. She needed Harry. And he had needed her. The relationship balanced.

She spoke softly. "It's still early."

He patted her waist and forced a smile. "No. Forget it. I better call Phil."

"What time is the show?" she asked.

"About three."

She unwound, got up and slipped into a pink dressing gown. He stared up at the white ceiling. Her voice had a plea in it. "Harry . . . I want to . . . to . . ."

He cut her off. "You don't owe me anything."

"Yes, I do. The visas, the work. Harry, I . . ."

"Forget it. Please."

"Would you like some coffee?"

"Son of a bitch."

"What?"

"Greatest bastards that ever lived."

"Who?"

"The 34th. The Red Bull Division. They were playing

'Begin The Beguine.' A guy started to cry. After all that, he started to cry."

"Would you like a drink?"

Softly, he said, "Artie Shaw."

She sat down on the bed and touched his cheek. "A drink. Some brandy."

"No. No thanks." He paused and, like a pitcher turning his back on the plate, thinking what to throw next, he said, "I miss my daughter."

Then he moved quickly, sitting up and swinging his legs over the side of the bed. His back was to Ula. He picked up the yellow Princess and, while he dialed and waited, he spoke to himself.

"'. . . what moments divine, what raptures serene . . .'" His voice had a liturgic quality. "'. . . I'm with you once more . . .'"

His tone switched back to normal. "Hello. Yes. Good morning, Gloria. Put Mr. Greene on, please." There was a brief pause. "Hello, Phil? Yes . . . no. I'm fine. Goddam car quit on me. I'm in a garage. No. No. They're on it. Look . . . I'll be down in a half-hour. Sure, talk to him. Right. 'Bye."

He put the receiver back on its slender, yellow cradle and felt Ula's arms go around his neck. Her nipples brushed against his back. Without turning, he asked, "You ever hear Artie Shaw's 'Summit Ridge Drive'?"

She whispered, "No," in his left ear, then in his right ear, "How could I? I'm a foreigner. An alien."

Harry said, "The Gramercy Five. Caught them once at the old Blackstone in Chicago."

Chapter 6

Harry carefully steered the big Lincoln around the Disneyland curves, coming down slowly through the maze of colors and styles.

Ula's apartment was in the hills above Gower Street. Her triplex was done in early Hansel and Gretel and fought for space with red-tiled Spanish casitas and glass

A-frames, as if some giant hand had opened a box of Jujubes on a rainy night and let them tumble down, sticking into the mud where they fell. And there they clung, waiting for the next assault by mud, fire and earthquake.

A flat, tough voice came out of the twin speakers: "Alls I know there wuz this ditch, see, and it wuz filled with bleedin' kids and old mama-sans. And they were getting sprayed with automatic fire . . . that's all I know."

Then the smooth controlled voice of the announcer: "And what did you do, Corporal?"

"Me? . . . I didn't do nuthin'."

Instantly a rock group started to sing the virtues of a new detergent.

Harry switched it off, thinking, "Auschwitz, brought to you by Procter and Gamble." He slipped a cassette into the tape deck. Bunny Berrigan got into the first chorus of "I Can't Get Started."

The blue Lincoln was out of the scabby brown hills and moving toward the Hollywood Freeway. He'd be at the Los Angeles Street exit in fourteen minutes. Harry knew what was ahead of him. He felt like an old club fighter going in over his head. You couldn't win. But, if you were careful, you might last.

It had been a hell of a lot easier in the old days, back in New York. Just selling. Someone else worried about the payroll. Jan had gotten him the job. She was modeling for a medium-priced dress house. It was a good line, and from the beginning the buyers liked Harry.

The men were the merchandise managers and, when they came to New York, Harry would take them to the fights, ball games, the track, a good steak at Danny's, and, occasionally, provide a hooker or two. The buyers were women. Harry would escort them to the theatre, or the Copa, or whatever French restaurant was "in" that season. Once in a while, he would go back to their hotel rooms and put in a performance.

It was the summer of '51. He and Jan were happy and high on love. Two or three times a week, Harry would bring home champagne and caviar. They'd put on some Billie Holiday records and let it all go. That fall Jan got pregnant; Harry was made sales manager; and the Chinese swarmed all over MacArthur.

Harry met Phil Greene at a New Year's party in 1957. Phil was one of the best inside men in the business. He could look at a garment and break the costs down: labor, fabrics, design, accessories, shipping. He was honest, dedicated, and a survivor of the Lincoln Brigade. Harry especially liked Phil not for being in the Brigade, but for surviving.

Phil desperately wanted to be in business for himself and when original California fashions became increasingly important, he and Harry decided to take the plunge together. They rented a loft on San Pedro Street and more space on Los Angeles Street for a showroom, offices, and a small sample factory. When pantsuits got hot, they picked up another factory in a rundown building in Long Beach. They were always beset with problems: capital, designers, labor, and the hazards of trying to outguess the likes and dislikes of the American female.

It was like riding a perpetual roller coaster. They'd crest, then plunge wildly down around the curves of financial disaster, miraculously pulling out and climbing again. Phil lived close to the vest, but Harry was always over his head. It wasn't all his fault. He could never say no to Jan, and he felt the only noble gesture left in his life was to make her happy. She was like a little girl in a very private world.

"... you're so supreme ... lyrics I write of you ... dream ... dream day and night of you ..."

He was in the center lane; the speedometer showed sixty-eight, and Bunny repeated himself. A speeding yellow Mustang swerved in front of him. Reflexively, he swung the wheel left, cutting into the fast lane. A frightened Cadillac horned him furiously. Harry shook his head, mad at himself. He should have checked his sideview mirror. Sloppy. But what wasn't sloppy? There was a lack of excellence in everything and everywhere.

And who's playing the horn like Bunny? And who's writing like that? It isn't just me. It's not the calendar. It's not the years. Things *were* better back there. Things people made were better, the arts, theatre, movies, the ball players. All were better.

He remembered old Hugh Casey, mouth stuffed with chewing tobacco, cheeks flaming red like some fire-breathing Irish dragon, lumbering out of the bullpen.

His sinker would fall off a cliff and he would get them out. And if he ran out of stuff, he'd throw his balls up at the plate.

It grooved out of Bunny's horn and swelled that classic chorus where the whole thing fuses.

Christ, they were better. He remembered, as a kid, listening to the great fights on an old radio.

Yes, they were better. Even the horses were better. Stymie. Big, red Stymie. Flying in the stretch. He'd never get a call in the early part, but coming into that final curve, that last turn, the announcer would say: "And here comes Stymie." And you could see those salmon and pink colors passing the other colors as if they were standing still. He remembered the Gold Cup Day at Belmont Park when Stymie caught Natchez at the wire. He'd run the last six furlongs in 1:08 and change, after a mile and a half. Christ almighty. Stymie. You didn't need any forms. You could throw the charts away. You knew. You just knew he'd be there. No, it wasn't age. It wasn't the calendar. Who's running the last six in 1:08 these days?

Harry caught himself. He hadn't thought of racing fractions since that night on Henry Street when his father got nosed out of the parlay in 1:09 and two fifths...

He turned onto the Los Angeles Street off-ramp. It was ten thirty. He should have called Jan on the car phone; before Ula. But he had picked up that kid... Myra.

They had been in the air twenty-eight minutes and were climbing to thirty-five thousand feet. Captain Jameson's eyes swept the cockpit. His co-pilot, navigator and flight engineer were absorbed in their respective work; the four sets of lights, switches and gauges were all normal. The co-pilot flashed a reassuring wink, and Captain Jameson left, closing the door firmly, making certain the automatic lock had engaged. The last thing he needed today was some screaming Spic waving a gun.

The captain walked up the aisle, smiling at the passengers in First Class. He never bothered with economy. Fuck them. They could listen to him on the speaker. On the way back to the flight deck, he noticed a very attractive brunette in window seat 1A. She was alone, reading *Time* Magazine, a half-finished martini alongside.

It was obvious that she wore no bra. Her full, thrusting

breasts were straining against the white silk blouse, trying to get loose, to pierce the material and expose her large, stiff nipples. But as he put the key into the cockpit door, he erased the image. He thought the woman had to be crowding forty, used up.

Jan looked dully at the magazine. She put it down and picked up the plastic glass. Making a face, she sipped the martini as if it were laced with strychnine, but kept on sipping, believing it helped ease the tension of flying.

Outside the tinted window, she saw a sea of white clouds, most of them rimmed with black. The color reminded her of Harry's hair—traces of black but more and more silver. His blue eyes had faded a little, but the lines around them were lightly etched. He was still handsome. But out of reach. Falling off the world. Screaming in the night and into yesterday. Yesterday...

She had played everything her own way ever since her childhood. Jan's parents, wealthy and divorced, had sent her to expensive boarding schools in Vermont, leaving her to find her own way. Her relationship with her parents had always been remote, formal. Her father had been in the import-export business, and due to his extensive contacts in Europe and fluency with language he was inducted as a full colonel in the O.S.S. and stationed in London. One blacked-out night a Wren driving a Red Cross lorry jumped the curb on South Audley Street and crushed him to death. Six months later, Jan's mother married a real estate man and moved to Palm Beach.

Once out of school, she was on her own. Those first few years in New York were a blur of fumbling, groping and half-hearted love-making.

She remembered dating the CCNY students. They would talk about Kafka, Molière and Tolstoi. But when the intellectualizing was over, they'd fumble for her breasts, desperately wanting to be nursed. One winter night, on a deserted road in Westchester, in the back of an old La Salle, she let a Columbia pre-med student go all the way. It wasn't painful and she considered it a humanitarian act.

Harry was something else. They met at a Beach Club out on Long Island. That summer Perez Prado was at the top of the charts and Sinatra was at the bottom. Jackie Robinson was stealing everything except wristwatches; and soon, but not yet, people would know what "Korea" meant.

Jan was a model and a good one. She was riding a rising curve of success. Socially, she had passed the students and had plunged into the East Side bubble of designers, artists, interior decorators and money magicians. She had gotten more than her feet wet but still had not met anyone that interested her.

With three other girls, she had taken a cabana for the summer at the beach club where Harry had the bar concession with a wartime friend. She had watched him, sitting alone in the bar, seldom talking to anyone. There was an abstracted quality to his presence, as if he were walking through.

The path to the ocean passed directly in front of her cabana. She asked one of her outgoing friends to stop Harry and invite him in for a drink. Up close she noticed the blue scars on his back and the etched lines just beginning to show around the eyes. It was his subdued attitude, his aloneness, that attracted her.

When they took a walk along the beach, Harry hardly spoke. She watched him as he stared at the black Atlantic and asked him if anything was wrong. He shook his head and said, "No. Everything is fine."

That night, they had dinner at Sheepshead Bay: buckets of steamed clams and cold draft beer. They were very comfortable with each other.

Harry took her to ballgames, the racetrack, and an occasional play. He never made any overtures. He'd take her home to her tiny apartment on East Sixty-eighth Street, kiss her good night, and leave.

He made a small profit on the concession, but was out of work that fall. He was drifting. Occasionally, she would ask him what he wanted to do. He would shake his head and say, "I don't know, Jan. I don't know."

She asked him about the scars, and the war; but he would never discuss it.

Harry still received a small disability check from the government, but he was running short and they began to go dutch. Then, she started to pick up the tabs.

Even now, a lifetime later, she remembered that night

clearly. It was in early December and very cold. They had seen Sartre's *No Exit* down in the Village. He didn't ask her; they just went. They took the Seventh Avenue local up to Eighty-sixth Street. For some strange reason the summer fans were on, whipping the icy air. No one complained, no one even seemed to notice. It gave the ride an overtone of comedy, as if some obscure subway technician in revolt against the system had played a practical joke.

Harry's small apartment was on West Ninety-third Street, close to Riverside Drive. A chilling gust of wind blew into them off the Hudson. When they got to the apartment, they did not speak. Harry put on Coleman Hawkins' "Body And Soul." The record kept repeating as they made love.

She knew he still loved her, but he had slipped into some dark world that she could not fathom. Perhaps they needed to be apart for a while. Perhaps Uncle Bernie had died at the right time.

She suspected Harry had a model or two hidden away somewhere, and it bothered her even though she knew it wasn't emotional.

Their own lovemaking was spotty, but still held a high level of excitement. She still moved him that way. No, all they required was a little respite from one another. She would stay in New York a little longer, perhaps even for three weeks.

She had lots of friends; there was the theatre, and the lovely East Side boutiques; and there would be parties and French restaurants. By dying, Uncle Bernie had accomplished his first good deed. When she returned, they would go to Palm Springs for a week. Yes. That would work. Harry loved the desert. Yes, they'd go to the Springs, and maybe afterward they'd go to Switzerland and visit Audrey.

Jan was startled by the metallic, computer voice that crackled through the overhead speaker.

"Good morning, ladies and gentlemen. This is Captain Jameson speaking. We are presently cruising at thirty-five thousand feet . . ."

"Fuck you." It popped out of her mouth. Low. Fast. And automatic. She didn't know why she said it. She

would have to remember to tell Doctor Frankfurter. He
would understand. He would explain the meaning of her
action.

Chapter 7

Harry threaded the Lincoln through the heavy downtown
traffic, insulated from its sounds and heat by Bunny's horn
and Iacocca's air conditioning.

The people jammed at the corners were a spray of
colors—white, yellow, brown and black. They bore the
look of patient pain as buses washed clouds of black smoke
over them. The Mexican boys, pushing clothes-racks, hurried across the street, not wanting to be caught in the
middle of a wrong color change.

As Harry crossed Seventh and Los Angeles Streets, he
noticed a group of Krishna mystics wrapped in orange silk;
shaved heads, pigtails hanging down, chanting their Hindu
lyrics at the oblivious masses.

Midway up Seventh Street he snapped the left blinker
on and pulled into a dirt parking lot adjacent to his
building. He saw Willie, wearing khakis and a plaid
sport jacket, put the *Playboy* down and come out of the
shack. Willie was stocky and very black. A goatee,
struggling for recognition, grew out of his ebony chin.
His left eye hooked down as if somewhere a stitch had
been missed.

Willie came alongside and opened the door. A wave of
noxious fumes, heated by the Santa Ana, stung Harry's
eyes. The change in temperature from the cool Lincoln to
the clammy street was overwhelming. It was like walking
into a wall.

"Morning, Mr. Stoner."

"Good morning, Willie." Harry reached into the car and
picked up his jacket. He slipped the Italian silk jacket over
his shoulders, Fellini style.

As Willie slid in behind the wheel, Harry said, "Listen,
watch my tapes, will you?"

Willie's face screwed up. His lips drew back over his teeth. "Sheeeit. Ain't nobody stealin' nuthin'!"

"Come on, Willie," Harry soothed. "I didn't mean you."

Willie shook his head. "Everyone says the same thing: 'Willie, watch the tapes. Willie, watch the lighter. Willie, watch the hubcaps!' . . . Sheeeit!"

Harry leaned into the window and smiled. "Hey, pal. I'm on your side. N double A, Panthers, right on."

"Right on to what? Fuck them Panthers. Huey Newton livin' in a seven-hundred-dollar pad. What I got?"

Harry straightened up and tried to inject some annoyance into his voice, "Chrissake, Willie. Who went through the building? Who took up the collection for Biafra? Remember Biafra, Willie?"

"Fuck Biafra. I got Biafra right here. When you goin' out?"

"I don't know. Late, probably."

Willie moved the gearshift to D, spun the tires and shrieked off. A cloud of dust tried to settle over Harry, but he moved quickly away and out of the parking lot.

He went into the dark grey lobby and waited for the elevator. He thought about lighting another Sherman, but frightened himself out of it. The elevator doors slid open, revealing a sparkling new formica interior. The grey gloom of the lobby and the shiny walls of the elevator had all the design integrity of an Easter egg.

The new interior already carried that familiar big city odor of sweat, fear and carbon. The doors closed. Harry pushed 10, leaned against the black wall and watched the indicator lights on the panel above the door: 8-9-10.

He came out of the elevator into a wide reception room done in Danish modern. Color photos of high fashion models in a variety of poses were framed on the oak paneled walls. A sign on the far wall above the receptionist proclaimed CAPRI-CASUALS. Directly underneath the sign, a pretty girl in her middle twenties sat at a long desk. She was surrounded by a typewriter, three desk phones and an old-fashioned plug-type switchboard. To her left, there was a double door marked Showroom, and to the right, a padded set of doors marked Factory Employees Only. Behind her ran a dimly lit hallway with offices facing the street side.

The girl looked up at him and smiled. "Good morning, Mr. Stoner."

"Good morning, Gloria."

He paused for a second and looked at the pink message slips on her desk. "Anything for me?"

"Yes. Al has to talk to you." Her smile widened. "My, that's a beautiful suit."

"Thank you."

The switchboard buzzed and, like Pavlov's dog, her hands leaped for the wires. Harry walked to the factory doors and went inside.

The sound of thirty-five sewing machines assaulted his ears. It was a long, narrow room with a double door at the far end. Several EXIT signs were lit over metal doors halfway down the room. The women operating the machines were either black or Mexican. Along the left wall, multicolored garments were draped over rolling iron racks. Several models in various stages of undress were getting in and out of clothes.

There was a high-frequency pitch to the work, a feverish pumping of pedals, whirling needles and guiding fingers. The rhythm of tension and expectancy hummed through the room. Even the machines took on a dimension of life. Even they seemed to know that today, futures were on the line.

A handsome Mexican man wearing a white shirt and black pants came up to Harry. His face was chiseled like a Mayan stone head. His upper front tooth had a strange rounded curve at its end, and this gave a tinge of sarcasm to everything he said.

"*Buenos, días, patrón.*"

"Speak English, Al."

"My name is Alfonso. And Spanish is a recognized minority language."

Harry sighed. "Listen, this isn't the morning for Chicano crap."

Alfonso's eyes were smoky topaz, and the little lights inside them were on. "It's marvelous the way you boil centuries of Yankee oppression down to 'Chicano crap.'"

"Look, I haven't bought a grape in three years, okay?"

Alfonso laughed. "Okay, *patrón*. You stand shoulder to shoulder with President Juarez."

"Good. We've solved that one. Now, how are you doing?"

"I'll be ready."

Harry put his hand on Alfonso's shoulder and squeezed it gently.

Alfonso smiled his sardonic smile and mixed languages. "Meyer and Rico *otra vez*."

Harry shrugged. "What else is new?"

As Harry started away, Alfonso shouted over the noise. "That's a good-looking suit, *patrón*."

But Harry didn't hear him. He was walking toward the far door at the end of the room.

Near the racks, he passed a tall brunette in panties. She was bending over to slip some pants on. When she saw Harry, she straightened up and flashed a smile.

"Lovely line, Mr. Stoner."

He smiled back at her. "Let's hope it sells."

She flicked her pink tongue across her very white teeth. "It will. It will."

As Harry opened the far door, two angry voices hit him. The voices were in sharp contrast; one shrill, almost feminine, the other, musky and rich with an East European accent.

The shrill one belonged to Rico Santoro, a dapper, thin, Mediterranean man in his late thirties. The heavy voice was Carl Meyer. He was grey, all grey: eyes, hair, and face; but there was a dignity to the old man that the years hadn't stolen. A small magenta flush crept into Meyer's grey cheeks as he shouted, "Goddam fairy! I wuz cutting patterns before you sucked milk!"

They were facing each other across a large, wooden table strewn with paper patterns and pieces of fabrics. Rico screamed back, "I will not have my designs butchered by a no-talent Cossack!"

Harry moved between them. "Okay, that's enough."

Meyer barked. "You're right! It's enough! I'm through! This time I'm through." He caught his breath and went on, "After fifty years in the business, I don't need lessons from a Roman fairy!"

Rico went up an octave. "Goddam peasant! You can be replaced by a laser beam!"

Harry shouted. "I said that's it! Now cool it! We've got a show to do this afternoon! Rico, get back inside with the girls!"

Rico went to the door, opened it, came down a few

octaves, but got the last shot off. "Just remember, Harry. You can't get a design out of a patternmaker."

The door swung shut.

Harry walked up to the old man. The hum of the sewing machines filled the sudden silence.

"Meyer, why do you do this to me?"

The old man lit a Camel through orange fingers, inhaling deeply, then blew the grey smoke up toward the ceiling. Harry thought: the old-timers, they don't worry about health hazards.

Meyer sucked on the cigarette, blew some more smoke and said, "Who can do anything to you?" The magenta flush had receded. The normal grey color had returned to the sixty-eight-year-old cheeks. "You tell everyone what they want to hear. To me. To the fag. To Alfonso. To the black people."

"Meyer, I can't have a philosophical discussion. My balls are in the wringer. You understand? Everything's on the line."

The old man said, "I don't want to talk philosophy. I want to talk business."

"Okay . . . okay. But later. We'll talk later."

"I mean it. I want to talk to you."

Harry forced a smile. "Fine. We'll talk later." Harry paused. "Meyer, look at your fingers. They're orange."

The once powerful shoulders shrugged. "So they're orange. Fifty years I'm smoking—and if I die, you know what will happen? They'll bury me. Because if they don't, I'll stink."

The old man crushed the Camel out in a red Cinzano ashtray. He picked up the cutting machine, carefully lining up the paper patterns. He was into his craft now, and didn't hear Harry leave.

As he expertly cut along the symmetry of the penciled lines he thought about the incredible injustice of talent: the haphazard way that gift fell on certain people, that elusive commodity that put a platform under the lives of monstrous children and relegated ordinary men to the daily task of survival. He smiled at a long-ago memory: the Bolsheviks—they knew about that inequity. They used it in their doctrine. "In the eyes of the State all men are equal." He muttered an epithet in Russian that could loosely be translated as "Bullshit."

Phil Greene, at fifty-nine, had kept his figure. He was still thin and tall, but the erosion of the years had attacked his scalp and his eyes. He was almost completely bald now, and he wore yellow-tinted rimless glasses with powerful lenses.

He was on the phone, chewing nervously on the wet end of an unlit cigar. The tone in Phil's voice changed from selling to pleading. "But, Mr. Norris, we cannot forget the fact that we have been banking with you for ten years." There was a pause. Phil spat a wet leaf of tobacco onto the grey rug. He spoke again, picking up speed. "Fine. Discount the orders," then, pausing for a second, he changed gears. "But that's a minor consideration. They're all first-class stores. We have a payroll to meet. Textile mills to pay. Sales commissions."

The finality on the other end of the line stopped him, pushing the tone of surrender back into his voice. "Yes, Mr. Norris . . . Yes . . . I understand. Tomorrow. Yes . . . I'll be there. Thank you."

He hung up, removed his glasses, took out a tissue and held his glasses up against the light. Looking through the lenses, he spotted something. He took the cigar out of his mouth and placed it in an ashtray. He blew on the lenses and carefully proceeded to clean them. After checking them again against the light, he put them back on, and glanced around the small office. It was oak paneled, with one floor-to-ceiling window facing the street. The only adornment on the walls was a large, framed black-and-white photograph.

Phil studied the picture. A very young man in a World War I doughboy uniform sat under an olive tree. He was smiling and waving at the camera. A vintage rifle lay across his lap.

But the boy in the photo was not in World War I. The guns of August had been quiet for twenty years. It was Spain, 1937. And while Phil no longer recognized the boy in the photo, he knew the boy was himself.

It was almost thirty-five years ago, in the olive groves of Jarama: the front to Madrid. They had held there that spring. They had fought off the thrusts of fanatic Moors, Italian infantry and the German Condor Legion. They fought, died, suffered, but they held.

And how they had been used; and how they had been

lied to. The Commissars and politicos had pushed them into the mouths of the Falangist guns. Their only equipment was their spirit. But the silver lining of their crusade had picked up some heavy tarnish on the trip from New York to Jarama. And how many had died? And to what purpose? He remembered two truckloads of boys, just boys, who took a wrong turn on the Titulcia Road and ran into a battalion of Moors. Later, after the breakout, they found their butchered bodies.

Wearily, Phil rubbed his hand across his face. He tried to erase the image of that long-ago carnage. He shuddered slightly as he thought about all the carnage that had taken place since the olive groves of Jarama. He relit the dead cigar, puffing hard. The blue smoke hung in the small room, then shifted suddenly as the door opened.

Harry came in, walked over to the couch, and sat down. There was a moment of silence, filled by the muffled sound of phones ringing and traffic noise trying to penetrate from the street below.

With a tinge of sarcasm, Phil broke the silence. "How's the car?"

Harry knew that Phil knew, but played the game. "Just a clogged plug. How'd you make out with Norris?"

"No dice. The best they'll do is a fifty percent advance on every purchase dollar. Damn shame. Rico did a brilliant job. We really should give him a bonus—a present."

Harry snapped, "Present? What the hell for? I took him with me across the country—twenty-five stores—buyers, friends of mine, took the time to show him: midis, minis, pantsuits, fabrics, silk, cottons, jerseys, wools, all prices, all styles—you think he didn't learn something? You think everything that came out of his head is original? What present? A guy shows up for work and he's a national hero."

Phil shrugged, "Still, he designed some beautiful numbers and we can make them profitably. I've been over all the patterns with Meyer."

"Does everything figure?"

"Every number, materials, labor, fittings, accessories, sales commission, packaging, shipping. It all figures. If the country doesn't nosedive, we should have a great season."

Harry got up and walked slowly to the large window, and his eyes zeroed in on the rotating rear of a young black girl in jeans, following her well-shaped ass until it disappeared around Eighth Street.

"How much cash do we need?" he asked.

Slowly, Phil ran it down. "If we write three hundred thousand this afternoon—discounted, we get a hundred and fifty from the bank. We'll need another two hundred in less than sixty days to service the re-orders, to continue manufacturing."

"What about the factory in Long Beach?"

"We're using it for three numbers. Pantsuits."

Harry turned from the window. "Get Charlie Robbins."

Phil's face went a little pale. He whispered, "Charlie Robbins?"

"That's right. Robbins. How much is the floater worth?"

A long cigar ash spilled down the front of Phil's shirt. He spoke quickly. "Drop it, Harry. We can ask the unions, the textile mills to carry us."

"We tried that last year and the word went out that we were broke. The stores damn near canceled their orders. Our salesmen got nervous. The union and the mills turned us down anyway."

Phil shook his head. "I won't get involved with Robbins."

With rising anger, Harry snapped, "Goddam it! What's the fucking floater worth?"

Phil sighed. "A hundred and fifty thousand."

Harry took a few steps toward him. "Enough to squeeze through."

Stubbornly Phil said, "There has to be another way."

Harry looked down at him. He loved this man. He loved his morality. But he had to push him over. Softly, he said, "If we were manufacturing missiles and falling on our ass, Congress would send us a certified check. But we're making dresses."

"Harry, you can't rationalize a thing like this. It's madness."

"No. It's business."

Phil sucked the heavy smoke. "You're sure you want to do this?"

"I'm only sure about one thing. We need money."

"It's wrong, Harry."

"Well, what's right? To go under? And where do *we* go? We're obsolete. Who the hell is going to hire us?"

"There's always a place for experience," Phil replied.

Harry nodded. "I know that place. Retirement Village

and an oxygen tent. Believe me, Phil, there won't be any questions."

Phil shook his head. "A fire's a fire. There are always questions."

Harry sat on the edge of Phil's desk and in a gentle tone said, "Charlie's a pro. How do you think Beckman pulled out last year? You think his fire was spontaneous combustion? We have a real shot with this line. Besides, we can't default. We can't go bankrupt. We'd be audited."

Through the tinted lenses, Harry appeared to be jaundiced. Phil pleaded, "Harry, arson! For God's sake . . ."

Harry got up off the desk, standing now, close to Phil. "Fraud or arson, the accommodations are the same. Give me the number."

Phil studied him for a moment, then opened his top drawer, took out a small, black notebook and placed it on the desk. He looked at Harry again, then got up and walked to the window.

Phil thought of the sea as he listened to Harry dial. He tried to diffuse Harry's salutory asides to Charlie through imagined waves. But the sound of the surf receded. Harry's words broke through.

"Listen, Charlie . . . We have a plumbing problem. Yes. The one I mentioned last week. It needs fixing right away. Where? . . . The Mayan Theatre? . . . No, that time is no good. We have a show at three. Yes. Five is all right. Yes, I'll have it. See you then. Thanks, Charlie." He hung up and looked at Phil. "Have Gloria draw two thousand in cash, put it in an envelope with the key to the loft. We meet him halfway down the center aisle, at the Mayan. Five sharp."

Phil turned from the window and walked to the couch and dropped down into it as if all the strength in him had expired. He spoke to the carpet. "So we cheat a little with the government . . . okay. We have call girls on a retainer . . . okay. Occasionally we use seconds in some of the fabrics . . . but arson!!" He looked up at Harry. "I'm fifty-nine. All I want to do is get out in a boat . . . and on a big day catch a fish."

Harry lit a Sherman. He thought it was the fifth or sixth. He spoke quietly to Phil. "You understand, we haven't got the license to declare bankruptcy. We invented some new arithmetic last year. We can't be audited."

"I know about that. But we didn't hurt anyone. We kept people working. We survived. So the government buys one tank less."

Harry sighed. "The government has a different word for survival. They call it fraud. They want that extra tank."

A buzzing sound came out of the little box attached to the phone. Harry pushed a button. The amplified voice of the secretary came on. "Ed Mirrell is in the showroom."

Harry depressed another button and said, "Tell him I'll be right out."

He came around the desk and started for the door. As he opened it, Phil's voice stopped him.

"The show is at the hotel this afternoon. Eddie knows that. What is he doing here?"

"He wants to get laid."

"Here?"

"Arrangements. Arrangements."

Phil sighed, "I wonder what would happen if once, just once, we said no. Buy the line on its merits or forget it. What would happen?"

"We'd lose the account, that's what would happen. Thank God he's horny. You better get hold of Margo. We have the suite reserved, don't we?"

Phil got off the couch and started toward his desk. "Yes. We have it reserved. Our friendly neighborhood whorehouse." He sat down at the desk and thumbed through the little black book until he found the right page.

From the door Harry said, "Set it up for one thirty."

Phil looked up from the book. "What the hell is going on? Fraud, arson, hookers. What the hell has happened to us?"

"Nothing's happened. It's business."

Chapter 8

It was a softly lit, wide room with partitioned booths running down one side and on the other, a glass case with sample garments and a large wet bar near the door. The oak walls were dressed with color blow-ups of high fashion models posed against the glamorous oases of Europe, and piped Muzak drifted in.

Eddie Mirrell paced the room, stopping occasionally to study the various posters. He was particularly drawn to one shot of a gorgeous brunette. She was lying prone, amid columned ruins on a Greek beach. She was in a mini-bikini, her legs spread apart, her toes touching the edge of the Aegean. The creamy foam of the surf spread across her tanned thighs.

Eddie moved closer, staring with profound intensity. The surf began to pick up motion. The white foam surged against the girl, lingering for a moment, then running back down the caramel-colored flesh and into the green sea. Eddie imagined the swirling white surf was sucking some sensual fluid from between her thighs; some invisible serum that nourished the sea; a flow of eggs that would revitalize the Homeric gods that lie beneath the waves. Harry's voice hit Eddie like an Arctic gale, blowing him off the sunny beach.

"Hello, Ed." Eddie whirled around, smiled nervously, and shook hands. Harry put his arm around Eddie's shoulder, moving him toward a booth.

"How was the trip?"

"Too long. I got to the hotel about eight o'clock. Freshened up and came back down." Eddie moved to the inside of the booth and sat down. Harry sat on the other side of the table opposite him.

He lit the seventh Sherman and blew the hot smoke up and away from Mirrell. "You look tired, Ed. Lost a lot of weight."

54

Eddie nodded. "Haven't been too well. I had a hell of a scare, Harry. A severe heart attack."

"Jesus . . . I'm sorry to hear that. You all right now?"

A little too fast, Eddie replied, "Oh, sure. I pulled out in fine shape." He shot the foaming thighs a fleeting glance, then quickly said, "I think I'd like a Scotch on the rocks."

Harry smiled his salesman smile. "Sure, Ed." And, as he started toward the bar, "You know, I'm surprised to see you here this early."

Eddie said nothing. He watched Harry fixing the Scotch.

"We have a hell of a line."

Eddie forced his thin lips into an embryonic smile. "Well, I'm here to buy. That's what I'm here for."

Harry came around the bar carrying the drink. He handed it to Eddie and sat down. Eddie studied the golden fluid for a few seconds then said, "Luck." Harry nodded.

Eddie took a long, quick gulp. Swallowed. Gasped, and caught his breath. "Bitch of a ride. I took the train."

"From Cleveland?"

"Can't fly anymore. Too dangerous. Too tense. I need to unwind. That's what the specialist said. I'm tight. I'm very tense, Harry. Bitch of a ride: ghetto to cactus, ghetto to cactus, like the click of the wheels, ghetto to cactus."

In his absence, the seventh Sherman had gone out. Harry took another one from a black ceramic cup that had a Scorpio design baked into it. Eddie sipped the Scotch, watching Harry light the dark brown cigarette. Harry took a deep drag. Exhaled. And sighed.

"I'm nervous myself. Phil and I . . . We . . . we have to write a hell of a lot of business this afternoon."

"I'm sure the line is solid."

"It is. But until we have it on paper . . . until those orders are signed . . ." He drew hard on the Sherman. "Look, Ed, you're tired. Why not give me an open order. I'll fill it personally. You can go back to the hotel and relax. You don't have to bother coming back to the show."

Eddie swallowed some more Scotch. "I don't know. I can't think about business. I've got to unwind." He paused, laughed nervously. "Tell me, Harry, is that... is that girl still around?"

"What girl?"

"You know, Harry. From last year. That uh... Margo ...come on... you remember."

Harry chuckled. "Oh, Margo...yeah, I guess she's still at the old stand."

Eddie's palm slapped the table. "Hell, Harry, that broad is a magician. Christ, she and that other girl... that Dusty..."

Harry smiled. "They're the best."

Eddie glanced at his Patek Philippe. "It's only eleven thirty. What if we arranged something?"

Harry shook his head. "Very tough. All the buyers are in town. I'm certain she's booked."

Harry got a whiff of the Scotch as Eddie leaned forward, and spoke in a hushed, conspiratorial tone. "Harry, we go way back. I can tell you. I've been dead from the waist down for years. Thirty-six hundred nights with a sick woman. Don't misunderstand. Alice's not a bitch. It's just gone. Harry, it means a lot to me... these diversions. You know what I mean?"

"Yes. I know what you mean."

The table phone rang sharply. Harry picked it up. Eddie watched him like a defendant examining the face of a jury foreman about to read a verdict.

Harry listened for a moment, then spoke into the mouth of the phone. "I'll be right in." He hung up, and flashed the sales smile. "Small problem. Listen, why don't you wander into the factory... get a preview of the line?"

As Harry got up, Eddie asked, "Are we tuned in?"

"Sure. Sure we are, Ed. Give me a few minutes. I'll get her on the phone. Relax."

Eddie watched him go, then rose and carrying the remnants of his drink walked over to the girl on the Greek beach.

Phil inspected the scorched end of his cigar. It had gone out. He thought about the inferiority of the Florida leaf; and if we send jets to Tito, why can't we import cigars from Castro? Then, giving up that political question, he relit the cigar. Harry opened the door, breaking up the cloud of Tampa.

Phil said, "She's booked... solid."

"Booked, my ass. We have her on a retainer. And that horny son of a bitch out there is going to write us a hell of an order."

"Well, you better talk to her." Phil got up as Harry came around behind the desk.

Margo was sitting up in bed. Naked. She was carefully applying Pontocaine salve to the lips of her cunt.

Ricky had worked himself into a frenzy and had bitten her, badly. But she took it. She never complained. She fed him the moans and groans he wanted to hear. That was part of it. Pro football players got mangled; lawyers lost cases; and doctors lost patients. That was the pain of being professional.

Still, despite these painful moments, the profession had been good to her. She was in good hands, Giaccomo Maltrate's good hands.

Giaccomo Maltrate was known to his colleagues as The Welder. The peacemaker. For twenty-five years he cooled tempers, soothed raw nerves, and maintained order among the "families" in the United States.

Giaccomo was a master at the fine art of negotiation. His sense of weaknesses and strengths, of temperaments and intelligence, of what to say to whom and when were legendary. He knew how to go off the center of a problem, then loop back in, to feint, to trap, but always with a chilling calm and a gentle smile. He was respected and trusted by all the capos.

When necessary, Giaccomo flew to Milan, then motored to a small village in northern Italy to report to the seventy-three-year-old capo. These trips were made only when all attempts at negotiation had failed, when someone's death was the sole solution.

The need to commit murder troubled Giaccomo, not because of any personal regard for the intended victim, but rather as a betrayal of his own art.

It saddened him that in the ultimate scheme of human relationships a bullet could be more effective than a smile.

Giaccomo had been offered the top post by the old man but had refused. He was not interested in wielding power, only in exploring the avenues of power.

One night, in Vegas, Margo turned a trick on the aging Mafioso. He kept her with him for two weeks. He spoke of her as *mia figlia*, my daughter, and wanted to help her. He placed her under his powerful umbrella and set her up with a business management firm: she was incorporated Sugar Loaf Investments. She earned close to forty thousand last year and paid next to nothing in taxes.

Margo had been busted only once. She had been careless and accepted a call without checking. Immediately after she worked on him the cop, a vice squad square named Kruger, placed her under arrest.

She phoned Maltrate. The vice squad officer never testified. They found him at six A.M. on Mulholland Drive, slumped over the wheel. All his front teeth had been pulled. Kruger should have known better: some girls you bust; some you don't. Maltrate's timing was exquisite; that week the vice squad was busy making headlines in' massage parlors.

She finished anesthetizing her pink machine, then picked up a can of strawberry-flavored Feminique and sprayed it up her hundred-dollar chute.

Later today she would work with Dusty. She enjoyed the beautiful Eurasian girl. There were times when Dusty's tongue would trigger a distant sensual stirring in Margo. She would feel a delicious throb swelling through her body and the muscles in her flat belly would tighten. It never reached an orgasm, but it was exciting and cooled her tensions. There were even times when she could forget about the watching customer. It wasn't professional. But every game had a whistle.

Margo put the Feminique down and leaned back against the padded yellow headboard. She had hung up on Phil Greene; if they needed her that badly, let Harry call. She didn't know Phil. She knew Harry. She had made her deal with Harry. The last minute . . . always the last minute.

The Princess rang. Margo picked it up. It was Harry. "His balls were in the wringer, honey. A very important buyer. I know it's the last minute but it's an emergency." Harry was going now. She could see his handsome face, the blue eyes smiling, pouring it on. Selling.

Finally she said, "Who is it, Harry?"

There was a pause as he gave her the name. The name rang a bell. A nasty one. She said, "Christ, not him! Not Mirrell! He wants the act: hot olive oil, camphor ice, whips, the vibrator—the whole goddam magilla!"

He was telling her that she was confusing Eddie with someone from Pittsburgh. Margo put a small trace of anger in her voice. "Harry... Harry I know my customers. I'm not confusing Eddie with Bernie Jefferson. I know Bernie. He talks a lot. You touch him and he comes. This guy is a tough case."

He was pleading now and she couldn't refuse him. After all, he was hustling, too.

"What time? Well... wait a minute. Let me look at my book." She picked a white pad off the night table. Quickly, she computed the time requirements of the two names on the pad; if she skipped lunch, it could work. Besides, Eddie liked to watch. It would give her an excuse to crawl around with Dusty. "All right... between one thirty and two o'clock... Yes, the Belgrave. I know the suite." She paused, then added, "And, Harry I wouldn't do this for anyone else . . Right, 'bye."

He hung up. "I love that girl. She's a real pro."

Phil nodded. "We're rich with professionals. Margo and Charlie."

Harry stood up and smiled at Phil. "Well, that's not a bad parlay."

Phil said, "Giants in their respective fields."

At the door, Harry turned and said, "They're business people. Charlie sets fires; Margo cools them. It's business. What's the difference?"

Phil sighed. "No difference."

Harry's secretary was a shapeless, tough-looking thirty-two. She tried all the latest diets and miracle Swiss cosmetics but the years slipped by and still no husband. She dwelt vicariously in the refuse and misadventures of other lives.

She typed listlessly, pausing to sip cold coffee from a foul-smelling container. A cigarette burned in an ashtray marked El Mirador, Palm Springs; a ceramic souvenir of some loveless weekend. Harry thought the ashtray had been there at least three years, an aging momento of a splash of sun on a battered desk in a dim hallway.

Her name was Harriet, and it caused some confusion; people called her "Harry." She looked at him over the rim of the coffee container. "Good morning."

Between gulps she told him that Jan had phoned earlier

from the airport; she wanted him to remember to take his Vitamin E. And that she would call him from New York.

Harry's office was larger than Phil's and more elaborately furnished. There was a glass window behind him that ran the entire length of the wall. The other walls were covered with pictures of ballplayers and racehorses.

He sat in a black Danish chair, swiveled around and looked out across the hazy skyline. The glass and brick slowly blurred.

The old blue-green stands of Ebbetts Field broke through the yellow haze of the city. Harry could hear the buzz of the crowd. He whispered, "The thirty-nine Dodgers... first base... Dolph Camilli... second base, Pete Coscarot ... Durocher at short, Cookie Lavagetto at third... catching...catching...was it Babe Phelps? Yes, I think so...No, wait... it... it was Mickey Owen! Yes... Mickey Owen... let's see, the outfield... the outfield..."

The stands faded into the murk as the shadowy skyline reappeared.

The buzzer sounded.

"Mr. Greene and Mr. Mirrell to see you."

"Send them in." Harry let the button up.

Phil walked to the window. Eddie drifted down and stood in front of Harry's desk.

"You're all set, Ed. One thirty at the Belgrave, Tudor Suite, twelfth floor." He opened the top drawer, took out a key and handed it to Eddie.

Eddie smiled a nervous smile. "Will you and Phil be there? I mean just to take the ice off?"

Phil turned from the window and asked, "What ice?"

"Well... it's been a long time. I mean... well, Margo might not remember me. It's been a while..."

Harry stood up, came around the desk and put his hand on Eddie's shoulder. "Oh, she remembers you all right. But if you feel nervous, we'll be there... why not?"

Phil watched Harry. He admired his charm, his salesmanship, his ability to cool everyone. But, lately, there was something dark, something malignant.

Harry moved Eddie to the door.

"I hope I'm not putting you fellas out. I know today is a tough day."

"Come on, we're all friends. What the hell, Eddie."

Eddie smiled a small, nervous smile and went out.

Harry came back around the desk, lit another Sherman, took a long drag, then put it down in a grey ashtray marked Carlton . . . Cannes.

Phil turned from the window, walked over to the black leather couch, sat down, and, shaking his head, said, "Our friend Eddie—represents one of the top stores in the country and the man is a pervert."

"You're wrong, Phil. Eddie's not a pervert. He needs a little action, that's all."

"The only action I understand is my own. I know how to manufacture dresses, but that's not enough. I have to become an accomplished pimp—a party to perversion."

Harry picked up the cigarette, took a drag and said, "Eddie's not a pervert and you're not a pimp."

"I don't know . . . I don't know anymore. Listen, speaking of perversion . . . you're not going to use your Swedish cupcake in the show?"

"Ula's Danish and she's a good model. I told her to be backstage at two thirty; she's a good model."

"How can you say that? She moves like a bear. You underwrite her life. You do enough for her. You don't have to put her in the show."

"It's a matter of self-respect. She has to work." Harry paused. "Besides, she'll be a refreshing switch from all those dykes."

Puzzled, Phil asked, "What dykes?"

Harry was surprised at the question. "Half of those models are in love with each other. The other half are in love with themselves."

Phil shrugged. "The only dikes I know are in Norway."

"That's Holland," Harry replied. Then he smiled. "You must have been a champ in geography. Come on, let's get some lunch."

Phil looked at him and said, "You know, I'm going to be sixty and I don't understand: dykes, arsonists, hookers, fraud . . . what's going on? I don't understand."

"It's business," Harry said.

Phil removed his glasses, took out a tissue and wiped them furiously. "Business? Business for what? To become a thief? A pimp? To burn down buildings? What for, Harry?"

"So you can fish." He said it, flat and fast.

It angered Phil. "To fish? A man works all his life and he hasn't got a right to fish? No . . . we're falling into the sewer. We're becoming part of what's ripping the country up. There's thunder on the right, and thunder on the left. The middle is going. There's a vacuum, Harry. And the boots are in the wings. You can hear them! Believe me, you can hear them! Just take the time to listen!"

Harry crushed the Sherman out, shook his head. "Right, left—what the hell's the difference? They'll still need dresses. They'll still need clothes."

Phil replaced his glasses. "How can you say that? You live here. You're part of it."

"I'm not part of it. I have nothing to do with all that. The last thing for me was that Biafra thing. Another lost cause. I just haven't got the fucking strength to get involved."

Phil rose and walked to the window. "Harry, believe me, the boots are in the wings."

The door burst open, and Rico entered, preceded by a stunning Chinese girl wearing panties and a bra. He spun the girl around. "Look . . . no ass. No ass at all. Now watch." Rico handed the model a pair of slacks. She slipped them on quickly, then pivoted slowly. Rico's voice verged on ecstasy.

"Now you see two little egg rolls . . . the pants with the built-in keister."

Phil smiled. "Rico, if you can do the reverse, we're in."

Rico laughed. "The heavy babes shouldn't wear pants." He turned to the girl who still held a final pose. "Okay, Irene. Thanks."

The girl left quickly.

"Irene?" Harry asked.

"Yes. Irene O'Neil. She's a refugee, from Hong Kong. Raised in a Catholic home by Jesuit priests."

Harry smiled. "I saw the picture. The priest was Charles Bickford. I think the girl was Wanda Hendrix. And Bogart masquerading as a monk hustled her out of Sinkiang just ahead of the Red Chinese."

Phil said, "You're a movie nut."

"They help me sleep." He turned to Rico. "We're going to lunch. Get everything set and over to the hotel. We'll meet you there about two."

Rico nodded. "Right. Later." He closed the door gently.

"Egg rolls," Phil said.

"Good idea. Let's go to Chinatown."

"I feel like pastrami."

"That stuff's murder, Phil. They have to fly it in from New York. Come on, we'll have some sweet and sour pork."

They waited for the formica elevator. It always seemed to linger on the fifteenth floor as if it were leery of attempting another descent.

Phil asked, "How's Jan?"

"On her way to New York."

"New York?"

"Her uncle died."

"Sorry."

"Nothing to be sorry about. He was a killer."

The elevator was jammed. Harry and Phil squeezed into the imprisoned flesh. The shiny formica cell threw off its rank oxide odor. They rode down in silence. No one spoke. No one smiled. There was only the sound of straining cables.

The familiar layer of yellow smoke hung over Los Angeles Street. The dead air seemed to reach its confluence in the downtown area, choking everything below.

They walked out of the grey lobby into the cacophony of traffic noises. The paper rubble leaped into sporadic life, fueled by the occasional hot gusts of the Santa Ana. They walked slowly up toward the corner of Los Angeles Street, moving through the crowds of the blacks, the whites, the Mexicans, the models, the worn-out and the done-in. They were mostly the middle-aged and the old: very few young people were in those streets at noon.

"Harry, my eyes are burning."

"Mine, too."

Phil shook his head. "City of the Angels."

Harry said, "There's one marvelous thing about L.A."

"What's that?"

"It's not Buffalo."

"Harry, let me tell you . . . the sea. You remember what the sea smells like? When I was a kid, I hitched a ride on the back of a trolley car, all the way out to Coney Island. I saw the sea for the first time. My God, nothing could blot it out. Nothing could get in the way. Just blue. Just blue and green!"

But Harry was only half-listening. He was tuned into his own thoughts. Dolph Camilli . . . Pete Coscarot . . . Durocher . . . the blue-green bleachers of Ebbetts Field.

Phil said, "Did you hear me? The sea... the sea..."

"Yes, I know. It's blue and green."

They got into the lead cab at the corner. The yellow car disappeared into the stream of flesh and metal.

Chapter 9

Three strawberries growing out of yellow rims pushed their way through the base of the driver's neck. Harry wondered what nourishment they were stealing from the man's body in order to flourish in that hairy garden.

All the windows were down, but the Santa Ana wind provided no relief. Harry loosened his tie and released the top button of his shirt. The heat did not seem to bother Phil. He had his glasses off, cleaning the lenses with the wide bottom of his tie.

The interior of the cab was filthy: eddies of dust, bits of paper, cigarette stubs swam fitfully over their shoes and pant legs. The frozen voice of a female dispatcher droned a steady stream of calls.

They were moving north on Broadway through heavy noon traffic. Now Harry wished he had taken the Lincoln. He had thought of it but decided it was not worth another encounter with Willie.

He pulled his eyes away from the red-yellow growths, shifted his weight slightly and asked, "How's Linda?"

Phil replaced his glasses. "Fine. Fine. She finally became a sailor."

"Does she fish?"

"No. The worms, the hooks are too much for her. But she enjoys the boat."

They were passing the criminal court building. A black man and a well-dressed white business type were coming down the steps of the austere building. The black man was speaking rapidly.

Harry wondered what the man was up for. Murder? Rape? Assault? Or maybe nothing. Maybe he was up for his color. But then why assume the man was up for anything? Reflex—those goddam conditioned reflexes.

Phil said, "You know, that boat is my only luxury."

"Christ, Phil, let's not get into that."

"I didn't mean anything personal."

Harry rubbed his hand over his eyes. "Sorry. I'm worn out. I'm sorry."

They passed the complex of federal buildings and turned right, heading east. Harry saw the first Chinese letters over a small store. He wondered what the oriental characters were advertising. Then quickly, he blurted, "I picked up a kid on the Strip."

"A kid?"

"Yes. A girl . . . thumbing. She said she was twenty, but she wasn't over eighteen. She asked me how old I was." Harry smiled. "I said thirty-eight. I don't know why. It just popped out."

Phil brushed his pants and said, "We're ashamed of so many things. I suppose age is one of them."

Suddenly Harry said, "I miss Jan. Every time she leaves I miss her."

Phil smiled. "Even with the great Dane?"

Harry shrugged. "Ula's alone. This is a tough city to be alone."

The dust swirled up from the floor of the cab. Phil leaned forward, close to the red boils. "Hey, pal."

"Yeah?"

"Don't you ever clean this cab?"

The driver inclined his head slightly toward the rear. "Yeah. I have a maid come in twice a week." He turned back to the traffic.

Harry said, "Never ask. Never ask these guys anything."

They were in Chinatown now, passing pagodas, Chinese theatres, groceries, and restaurants. The people in the streets were almost exclusively Oriental. The heat and smog did not seem to slow them.

"Tell me, Phil. Who played left field for the thirty-nine Dodgers?"

"That's a hell of a question."

"You were a fan. I thought you might remember."

"Well, let's see . . . I may be wrong . . . I'm not certain, but I think it was Joe Medwick."

Harry smiled. "Ducky Medwick. Never throw him a high outside pitch. Always murdered a high outside pitch."

They turned the corner of Main Street. The cab slowed and angled into the curb. There was a large neon sign with three-foot-high Chinese characters. Just below the silent neon there was a sign in English that spelled L-U-M-S.

The driver flipped the flag, leaned back and opened the door. Harry got out first. Phil hunched himself up and slid out. Harry moved to the front of the cab and looked back at him. "Better get a table."

Phil nodded and went inside.

The driver said, "That'll. be a buck seventy-five."

Harry took out a disorganized roll of bills, extracted two singles and handed them to the driver. The man handled the two bills with disdain. "You're a very generous citizen."

"Well, take a good look. We're a vanishing breed."

The driver rummaged beneath his legs and came up holding an empty quart-sized milk bottle. "You see this, Mac? You know what it is? It's a toilet! The way things are, I can't take five minutes off for a piss. So don't make jokes with me!"

The pain on the whipped face pierced like a scalpel, ripping through the skin of Harry's conscience. "I'm sorry. You're right." He took a five-dollar bill from the sticky pack and handed it to the man. "Take a buck for yourself."

The driver made no move for the bill.

Harry noticed Lincoln's sad eyes, as if the murdered president bore witness to Harry's callousness.

The driver let all his breath out and, in a low tone, said, "Stick it up your ass, buddy." He gunned the motor and shot away from the curb.

Harry watched the yellow cab disappear.

The restaurant was on one level. The kitchen was in front; rows of booths lined each wall; white formica-topped tables were scattered down the center section. The place was busy with an even mixture of Caucasians and Orientals. Piped Muzak mingled with the hum of dialogue. The waiters barked their orders in sing-song Chinese and teenage busboys walked rapidly, carrying high stacks of dishes.

They sat in a rear booth, near the rest rooms. From the Muzak speaker, angled from the ceiling directly over their table, came the strains of Patti Page's "Tennessee Waltz."

Phil mentioned Charlie Robbins. Harry cut him off. They discussed the friction between Meyer and Rico. Harry said he would take care of it. Phil curved into Eddie Mirrell and the low logic of hanging onto an account by the virtue of Margo's unique gifts. Harry repeated what he had said before. "It's business."

They finished the meal in silence.

Harry speared the last gleaming brown cube of pork and washed it down with the tepid tea. He pushed his plate away and lit a Sherman, mad at himself for succumbing to the habit, but, in spite of it, inhaling deeply. He looked at all the food they hadn't eaten; in other days he would have asked the waiter to put it in a bag.

Phil sipped some tea and said, "You know, the line has character."

Harry nodded. "All we need is money."

Phil wet the end of a cigar. "Yes. Money." He lit it and puffed; six small jets of flame flared at the tip.

The Muzak carried Jo Stafford's "You Belong To Me." Harry thought, only a Chinese restaurant would carry those vintage sounds.

Suddenly, Phil said, "Three thousand helicopters."

"What?"

"We've lost three thousand helicopters since the war started. In Viet Nam." He sucked the wet end of the cigar. "You know how much money that is?"

"Drop it. I don't want to hear that." The snap in his voice surprised Phil.

"What's the matter with you? I only meant the waste. The incredible waste of money."

"And the men? What about the men?"

"The men? What do you want me to say?"

"Look, Phil. I just don't want to hear that. Fuck the helicopters."

"For God's sake! All I meant was . . ."

Harry cut him off. "I can't listen. I can't hear about war." He crushed the cigarette out and leaned forward. "You remember five or six years ago Jan and I, we . . . we were in Italy. We went to Anzio. There was a ridge where the sand piled up. A dune crested the beach . . . it ran about two hundred feet. In 1944 it was muddy with blood. Now it's covered with bikinis."

"Bikinis?"

"Yes. Bikinis. Cute little buckets sweating into the sand. The same sand where the blood was."

"It shouldn't surprise you Harry. Battlefields have a way of turning into resorts."

"Well, just don't talk about war to me. That's the last joke."

"I've been there, too, remember?"

"I know. I know. But it was different. You wanted to be there. So did I. Those early days in camp, in Louisiana . . . I was fresh off the corner. At night, they lowered the flag; they played taps. I looked at that flag and I swear to you, Phil, I believed it stood for everything that was right in the world. I damn near cried." Harry waved his hand. "But today, it's all bullshit! These kids are dying for the fun of it."

Phil picked up his fortune cookie, opened it, read it. And it wasn't good. Even Confucius was letting him down.

Harry's voice surged with sudden excitement. "Listen, Phil! Listen!" The Goodman sextet leaped out of the speaker. "That's Charlie Christian on guitar! That's 'Air Mail Special.'"

Phil drew gently on the wet cigar, studying him carefully. He saw the pale blue eyes clouding over. It was there. Again. Gnawing.

Harry lit another cigarette. He was smiling. "Jesus, how I wanted to play with Goodman."

Phil spoke softly. "Come on, let's get a check."

But Harry was all alone. ". . . One summer, up in the Catskills. We had a vocalist. Everyone in the band was making it with her. Except me. I had a crush on her. She could hardly stand up at night. But she could sing 'These Foolish Things' and put you in Paris. Before a number, she'd say to me, 'Light on the brushes, kid . . . light on the brushes.'"

"Brushes?"

"Yes. Steel brushes. They give you a soft sound on the snare."

They listened to Benny. The grey smoke of the Tampa and the blue smoke of the Sherman fused into a gunmetal cloud. It wafted gently over their heads.

Harry murmured, "'The winds of March that make my heart a dancer.'"

Phil signaled the waiter for the check. "You know, when we were kids, it all added up. Life was simple."

Harry shook his head. "Not so simple. Those corners were cold and tough."

"Still, it was simple. After school you delivered groceries. Fridays you dumped a few dollars in the old lady's lap. It was simple."

"Well, not anymore. This kid I picked up today . . . She stays on the Strip. I mean all day, Phil. She goes back and forth on the Strip. She wanted to ball me! In the car! Right there! No words."

The waiter handed the check to Phil. He examined the addition briefly, nodded, and gave the man a ten-dollar bill. "Your tip's in there." The waiter thanked him and hurried away.

Harry said, "Kids today . . . I don't know."

"Thank God Linda and I have no children. We've managed to live without that blessing. It's a nightmare."

"Why is it, Phil? Why?"

"Who knows? A few blocks from here ghetto kids are being babysat by Lucille Ball reruns, and we're taking pictures of Mars. Who knows why? Ask David Susskind." Phil got up. "Come on. We have a customer waiting to get laid. And a hundred buyers waiting to see the line; and, in the wings, Charlie the torch man. The flame of liberty."

Harry made no move to get up. He looked straight ahead at the empty space Phil had occupied. "I told her I was thirty-eight. It just popped out. Thirty-eight."

Chapter 10

The Volkswagen camper covered with psychedelic designs was parked on the rim of a ridge up in the hills above Laurel Canyon. In the winter, when the rains cleared the smog, the view would have gone all the way to the Pacific; but now, the yellow haze shrouded Sunset Boulevard, less than a mile away.

A mailbox with the flag still in the up position, and the blackened remnants of a chimney were the only evidence that someone's home had once stood on this choice location. The entire area had been devastated in the fire-storm of the previous summer. The strident sounds of acid rock emanating from the camper frightened a foraging squirrel. The bushy-tailed survivor of the great fire was still plagued by the sounds of civilization. He gave up his noon search and scurried back into the charred woods.

There were four of them inside, including Myra. She was seated at one end of the barren interior, her back to the curved wall of the bus. The boy in the black satin shirt sat alongside. He sucked hard on a joint. Against the wall, on the opposite side a dark-haired, heavy-set girl, in an ankle length muu-muu, smoked another joint.

Alongside the girl sat a blond boy of eighteen. He wore jeans and a T-shirt and waited patiently for the girl to pass the roach. A small transistor in the center of the cabin blared the rock.

The girl in the muu-muu passed the grass. She coughed hard, causing her large braless breasts to jump.

She said, "Oh, shit. It's great shit."

And while the blond boy sucked the grass, she opened his fly with her right hand. The boy inhaled deeply, paying no attention to her exploring fingers.

Neither did Myra nor the boy in the black shirt.

Janis Joplin, alive on wax, shouted furiously at an uncaring square world. The lyric was a syncopated invitation to a very private hell.

Myra passed the hot roach to the bearded veteran. Her words were slurred in grassy cadence. "This groovy guy . . . in . . . in a Lincoln . . . with a phone, and a . . . and a tape deck . . . You know what I mean, Larry?"

Larry didn't answer. He drew hard on the Mexican grass. He was watching the muu-muu girl's hand. It slid up and down the stiff column of flesh, keeping time with the record.

"You know what I mean, Larry? A tape deck, with German music."

Larry sucked hard on the roach and passed it to Myra. She inhaled deeply, holding the smoke down in her lungs. Then, letting go, she said, "You know what I mean? German music... spooky. Sad. Blue. God, it was blue!"

Without missing a stroke, the muu-muu girl asked, "Did you ball him?"

"No. He was in a rush." Myra sucked the sweet smoke and turned to Larry. "You should have seen that Lincoln. It was out of sight."

"I did see it. I was there. Now pass the goddam joint."

She passed the half-inch weed. "He wore a shiny suit and smelled nice."

The Grateful Dead came on with a soft tune.

The muu-muu girl's hand changed speed. She slowed the jerking, keeping perfect time with the new rhythm. She drew on the grass with her left hand, then looked over at Myra and asked, "What happened? I mean, did he say anything?"

Myra started to giggle. "He said... he said... have a nice day." The giggle escalated into laughter. She repeated, between the rising waves, "Have a nice day."

Larry started to laugh. "Jesus! Have... Have a nice day."

The muu-muu girl laughed. "Have a nice day... Oh, shit!..." She went into a gale, and gasped, "Oh, shit... have a... a nice day."

But her busy right hand never faltered. It worked slowly up and down in perfect sync with The Grateful Dead.

Myra was gagging and tears streamed down her smooth cheeks. "Have... have a..." She tried to say "nice," but couldn't.

Larry was laughing hard and mumbling under the gales. "Jesus... Jesus... nice day..."

The muu-muu girl's laughter was shrill and infectious.

The blond boy was smiling, looking down at the busy fingers coaxing him to a climax. He drew the last of the roach into his chest and snuffed out the stub between his fingers.

Myra caught her breath. The gales of laughter were breaking. She coughed, "I'm... I'm not kidding." She fought for breath. "That's what he said."

Larry's laughter turned into a spasm of coughing. He shook his head and, taking an envelope from inside his shirt, began to roll another joint.

The muu-muu girl wiped some tears off her face with her left hand. She said, "Have a nice day... Oh, shit. He must be reading bumper stickers." She looked at Larry and said, "One for us, Larry."

It grew quiet. The rock had changed. It was a guitar, soft and Spanish.

The blond boy looked at the muu-muu girl. His voice was calm, but had a teen-age ring. "Hey, I'm coming."

Instantly the girl removed her hand. She pushed hard on her legs, sliding her back up, using the wall as leverage. She stepped in front of the blond boy, facing him. Then, lifting her dress at the edges she slowly lowered herself down onto him. She put her hand under the billowing dress to adjust, to accommodate. She moved slightly, said "Oh," and slid all the way down. She had the length of it up inside her. The muu-muu covered their flesh and the bulk of the girl's back hid the boy's face.

Larry had the new roach and passed it to Myra. She drew on the grass as she watched the heavy girl swiveling on the blond boy.

Larry got up and walked across to the locked pair and stood over them. The blond boy had his hands on the girl's waist, guiding her up and down. His glazed eyes stared straight ahead, but all he saw was the top of the girl's head. She was looking down, holding the front hem of her dress up.

Larry leaned over and picked up the rear hem of her dress. He lifted it chest high, exposing the joined flesh to Myra. The girl's large, round ass spun out of the boy's dungarees. Holding the dress, Larry looked at Myra and asked, "Okay?"

Myra's voice was indifferent, and she shrugged her shoulders. But the word was clear. It was the cornerstone of their emancipation. It was "groovy."

Chapter 11

Pershing Square is a pedestrian island surrounded by rivers of traffic and shadowed by mountains of forty-year-old stone; a green scar of hopelessness in a forgotten section of a city that never happened. The charcoal-colored statue of General Pershing is stained with yellow-white slime.

The General should have been standing in the Tuileries, facing south, looking across the Seine to St.-Germain—but Fate, and misguided patriotism, had deemed otherwise. Still, old Blackjack stood firm; his stern countenance dominated the Square.

He had won the war to end all wars and would defend this patch of green until the last pigeon had dropped its final load. He was a bronze shield for the madmen, the charlatans, the fanatics, the depraved preachers of doom who were permitted free speech within the perimeter of his dead vision. They stood on wooden platforms, the American flag fastened to their makeshift podiums; under the shield of the General, and the national cloth, they shouted their moral outrage and mad doctrines.

And in the audience: little old ladies living on the small largesse of the city; wizened men, hiding in three-dollar-a-night rooms to escape the barren ghettos of Sunset Village; winos of all ages resting in afternoons of white lightning; young homosexuals seeking a score among the aged; and mini-skirted secretaries eating their mercury-laced tuna sandwiches.

Harry and Phil got out of the car at the north end of the park. The one-way on Hill Street made it impossible to pull up in front of the hotel. They walked diagonally through the angry preachments of the speakers.

The Santa Ana gusted occasionally, whipping the tiny American flags.

The podiums were spaced within sixty feet of each other. One young man in a white robe, with hair down to

73

his waist, was selling Jesus. At the next stall, a brown man with a shaved head, dressed in orange silk, was explaining the true Buddha.

Near the corner of Sixth Street, at the last booth, a red-faced man in a World War I Marine uniform praised Lieutenant Calley.

They were at the corner, waiting for the light. The Marine shouted, "All the heroes of history have been crucified! They have all spent their time on the cross! So shall it be with Lieutenant Calley!"

As they moved through the white crosswalk, Phil said, "What about that?"

"About what?"

"Calley."

"I can't believe we were in the same Army."

Phil nodded. "Hard to understand. We hung the Germans."

"Forget it, I told you. We have nothing to do with it." They walked north for three more blocks.

Over the entrance to the hotel were two flags: one American, the other Mexican. The front steps were busy with buyers: men and women with out-of-town stamped on their faces killing time, waiting for the afternoon shows. They studied the foreign streets, eyes smarting, hair blowing, fanned by sudden spurts of the desert wind. Like soldiers on a point, they would stare for a while, then retreat into the dark lobby.

Harry and Phil made their way up the stairs through the shifting crowds at the entrance. As they entered the lobby, the light drop was sharp. It took a few seconds for their eyes to adjust to the formal darkness of the lobby.

Gales of laughter and bursts of dialogue echoed through the columned pomp of the lobby. The potted palms, tapestried furniture, and turn-of-the-century chandeliers seemed out of place among the mod men, mini- and midi-skirted women. The hubbub was punctuated with the occasional shouts of pages; they called out room numbers that corresponded to the chalked numerals on their signs. The bar to the left of the lobby enjoyed a high tide of ten to one martinis: models, buyers, designers, manufacturers streamed in and out through the dark portal. Predictions of what would sell were everywhere; these were the soothsayers, the fortune tellers of high fashion.

Phil and Harry made their way through the busy lobby, moving toward the elevators. Harry nodded, exchanging brief salutations with buyers. They stopped before a closed set of brass doors, over which an indicator said: LOCAL 1 TO 15. The clock hands over the elevators pointed to one thirty.

"At least it's handy."

Phil asked, "What's that?"

"The hookers. The show. All under the same roof."

"You know, Harry, someone on television—I think it was Eric Sevareid—said that 'ultimately civilization corrupts mankind.'"

"Maybe it's the other way around. The whole country is a colossal madhouse. Got to have my daughter in Switzerland."

"You did the right thing."

"That's what Jan said. No Horse."

"Horse?"

"Yes. The kind that hangs out in toilets."

A pack of men and women burst out of the elevator, shoving, pushing, eager to swim in the excitement of the lobby, their frenetic energy fueled by that out-of-town syndrome of sudden freedom. The bonds were off; they were in another town. By virtue of profession, they had stolen some time: a brief parole.

Harry and Phil waited for the nerved-up herd to pass, then entered the gleaming brass cage. The middle-aged black woman at the controls waited for more passengers. A handsome woman, followed by two young men, walked into the car. They were jewelry buyers. They spoke in that special idiom of carats, points, cuts, precious and semiprecious. For them, Harry and Phil did not exist.

The black hand swung the lever down. The doors closed. She asked, "Floors, please?"

Harry said, "Twelve, please."

The woman pressed the number 12 button. The handsome lady said, "Fourteen." She did not say "please."

They felt the surge of the lift-off; their stomachs floated up to their throats as the elevator rose rapidly and stopped abruptly. The doors opened.

The black woman said, "Twelfth floor. Watch your step."

They walked down a green-carpeted hallway. Small, beveled English lanterns were spaced along the oak-paneled walls. An occasional Toulouse-Lautrec print provided some small relief to the eerie light.

Harry had long since lost count, but lit another Sherman and chalked it up to the tension of the day; tomorrow he would cut down. Halfway down the corridor he tugged at Phil's sleeve. "Center field . . . dammit, Phil, who played center field?"

"You're worried about center field thirty years ago, and I'm trying to find our friendly neighborhood whorehouse."

Harry shook his head. "It could have been Georgie Moore."

They reached the point where the hall forked to the right and left. Phil examined the directional plaque on the wall. "Here. Down here." They took the corridor to the right.

"I know where it is."

"Sure. Your Swedish matinees."

"Danish."

"Is there a difference?"

"I don't know. I haven't tried any Swedes."

They walked another sixty feet, stopping at a door marked TUDOR SUITE. Harry rang the bell. It chimed inside. Almost instantly, they heard Eddie's voice. "Right there!"

Phil mumbled, "Not enough we pimp. We've got to play the overture."

"We do eighty grand a year with him."

Phil sighed. "I suppose it could be worse. He could want to make it with us."

The door opened. Eddie had his jacket and tie off, and his buttoned-down shirt was open at the neck. His craggy-clown face was creased with a rubbery smile.

"Come on in, boys."

The silence of the empty hall was disturbed by two uniformed Mexican waiters turning into the corridor. The thin one, with the pencil moustache, pushed a large portable serving table. His partner was heavy and squat. He walked alongside, a napkin draped over his forearm.

The tray clattered; it was loaded with dishes covered by round, silver lids.

As they passed the Tudor Suite, the thin one, in heavily accented English said, "I don't understand. All day, they eat this fucking bacon. Always well done. You can taste nothing."

The fat one nodded. "The fucking Gringos, they like pork but are afraid to eat it. So they burn it."

The thin one shook his head. "Fucking Gringos, they burn everything. All the time they say, 'creesp . . . creesp.' We have no word—'creesp.'"

They proceeded down the hall.

Chapter 12

The sitting room of the suite was spacious, air-conditioned, insulated from exterior sounds. Floor-to-ceiling windows ran the length of the far wall facing the street. Two large beige sofas were placed opposite each other. Four Louis XIV chairs were set haphazardly around the center of the room.

There was a portable bar at the far end, near the windows. A color television stood on a metal rack alongside the sliding doors that opened to the bedroom; someone had left a brown, smiling teddy bear on the wooden slat at the base of the TV carriage.

Phil was seated on the sofa nearest the bedroom doors. Harry was at the window, his back to the room.

Behind the portable bar, Eddie smiled a nervous smile. "What'll it be, boys?"

Phil lit another cracked cigar and, through the smoke, said, "Vodka on the rocks."

Eddie nodded and looked at Harry. "Harry?"

Across the rooftops in Pershing Square, the World War I Marine still extolled the virtues of Lieutenant Calley.

Harry said, "Nothing, thanks."

Eddie poured the Smirnoff over ice and some Johnny Walker for himself. He came around the bar, crossed over to Phil and handed him the colorless drink. Eddie raised his glass. "Good season, boys."

Phil nodded. "Cheers."

Eddie sipped his Scotch and looked back at Harry. "Hey... what's with you?"

"I need orders."

"Hell, the word's around... you fellas have a hot line."

"It's not on paper, Eddie."

Eddie sat in a Louis XIV, sipped some more Scotch. "You guys are really something. Big homes, kids in Swiss schools, pleasure boats, sitting on a hot new line, and you're..."

Harry cut him off. "None of it's paid for."

"Hell, who pays for anything? It's all the little cards. Charge. Down payments. Friendly layaway plans. You think we'd ever sell a button if we insisted on cash? The system is the cards. The little cards."

Phil coughed, spilling some ash on the beige rug. "What Harry means is, we need cash to manufacture."

Harry followed fast. "And cash for public relations."

Eddie snapped. "What public relations?"

Harry felt the heat rising. "You can't put hookers on the little cards."

Eddie jumped to his feet; his jowls turned crimson. "That's horseshit! Listen, Harry... you want to call it off, say so!"

Phil said, "Eddie... Eddie, please. Harry's a little tense. We're in a very difficult cash position."

The crimson in Eddie's cheeks slid to pink, and his voice reflected the color change. "Well, that's got nothing to do with this. You write this off. The Government pays for the cooze."

Harry said, "Our balls are in the wringer."

Eddie moved back behind the bar. He poured some more Scotch. "I'm sorry to hear that, but don't lay it off on me. We've been doing business for six years. Eighty thousand a year. That's almost half a million. Have I ever asked for a kickback? A bottle of Scotch? A Christmas card?"

"Never," Phil said.

"Okay, then. Once in a while I come in to town. I need a little relaxation. What does that mean?"

The doorbell rang; the chimes sounded almost Catholic. Harry went to the door, opened it and flashed the sales smile. Margo came in followed by a stunning coffee-colored girl.

They were both wearing pantsuits: Margo in pink and carrying a large black tote bag, Dusty in red, holding a small gold lamé clutch.

Harry kissed Margo on the cheek. "Hi, babe." Then to Dusty, "How've you been?"

The Oriental eyes glittered. "Making it."

He put his arms around the girls' waists and moved them into the room. "You girls know my partner, Phil Greene, and Eddie Mirrell."

Margo smiled at Phil, then turned to Eddie. "Long time."

"Yes. A long time." Eddie had trouble looking away from Margo.

Harry kept things moving. "How about a drink?"

Margo said, "Scotch on the rocks."

Dusty smiled. "Ginger ale. I can't drink. It throws me." She looked at Phil. "I like to know what I'm doing. You dig?"

Embarrassed, Phil replied, "I suppose it's better that way."

Dusty giggled. Eddie went behind the bar. Margo lit a Gauloise. Harry watched Eddie mixing the drinks. They stood in silence; the curtain had risen, but the overture had belonged to another play. A madam was needed, a stage manager who could whip through the preliminaries of putting combinations to bed.

Harry glanced at his watch. "It's one forty-five. We better get going. The show is at three on the mezzanine."

Margo took the Scotch from Eddie and smiled. "Handy, isn't it?"

Phil nodded. "Harry said the same thing."

Dusty took the ginger ale and put her arm around Eddie's waist. She sipped the bubbles and smiled at Phil. "You don't have to go. I like an audience. You dig?"

"Thanks, but we have business."

Dusty shrugged.

Harry walked to the door, opened it, and waved his hand. "Have fun, people."

Phil moved past Harry and stood in the hallway immediately behind him.

Eddie and Dusty were going toward the bedroom. He stopped and waved. "See you at three, boys." Dusty smiled as they went inside.

Margo took a final sip of Scotch, set it down, and walked up to Harry. "I've got everything but the whips."

From the hall, Phil said, "Come on, Harry."

Harry put his hand on Margo's shoulder. "Listen, be careful. He's been sick."

"Careful with him? He read Maggie and Jiggs to the Marquis de Sade."

He touched her cheek. "I appreciate this."

"Wait till you get the bill. This is extracurricular."

"Sure it is. I'll be in the bar if you need me."

"Fine. By the way, Harry, that's a nice-looking suit."

The door closed; Margo turned the bottom lock, then slid the top latch into its groove, picked up her bag, and walked into the bedroom.

Eddie, fully dressed, was lying on the bed. Dusty sat in a large easy chair. Naked. Her legs were wide apart, dangling on the long arms of the chair. She sipped her ginger ale and smiled at Eddie.

Margo came in, put her bag down and pulled the drapes, darkening the room.

Dusty swung her legs off the armrests, set her drink down on the rug and got up. Her straight black hair spilled down to her shoulders. She was slim and firm, with small breasts that were topped by large, brown nipples. Her body was not unlike a ballerina's; muscles rippled along her thighs when she moved.

Margo walked up to her and turned around. Dusty's fingers found the handle on the zipper and ran it down. The blouse fell off and Margo stepped out of the tight, pink pants. She had nothing on underneath. Dusty slipped her arm around Margo's naked waist.

Margo smiled ominously, "Get off the bed, Eddie."

Chapter 13

The bar was lively, dark and crowded. Black leather booths with white-topped tables lined the horseshoe shape of the wall. Green-uniformed waiters shuttled back and forth through the crowd, servicing the tables.

The conversations of the people at the booths were restrained; like atmosphere players in a film, they provided a clandestine backdrop to the frenetic action at the bar. Over the bar, a TV set was on.

Bogart was making a heroic stand in the Sahara. All he had going for him was a tired Sherman tank and a fistful of men against a brigade of Afrika Corps Panzers. The preoccupied crowd at the bar were unaware that only Bogie stood between the Germans and Cairo. Except Harry. He popped some roasted peanuts in his mouth as he watched the action on the large screen from a booth not far from the television set.

Phil sipped his vodka and said, "We should check the mezzanine."

"What for? Rico's handling it. Leave him alone. It's his moment."

"You've got to heal this thing with Meyer and Rico."

But Harry was in the Sahara. He was with Bogie. "Phil, you remember *Casablanca*? This scene . . . Rick's club. Closed . . . four in the morning . . . Dooley Wilson's playing that song. Bogie is sitting at the bar, smoking, watching his reflection in the mirror. Everything's been building to this moment; then Bergman floats in behind Bogie. Christ, you can almost smell her perfume . . . She gets close . . . she whispers, 'Hello, Rick.' Bogie doesn't move. Keeps smoking. Bergman moves a little closer. She says, 'You remember Paris, Rick?' . . . Now he takes the cigarette out of his mouth; never looks at her. He says, 'Yeah, I remember Paris. You wore blue and the Germans wore grey.'"

Phil said, "I don't think it happened that way. I think they met downstairs, in the casino."

With a tinge of anger, Harry replied, "Well, that's the way I remember it." Then he softened. "Who wrote those things and where did they go? What happened to them?"

Phil nodded. "I know what you mean. Take John Garfield, in *Four Daughters*. He had a speech about being mediocre. He sliced life right up the middle. Those guys. That time. I don't know, they made you feel something."

"Damn right they did. Eddie G. in *Little Caesar*, dying in the gutter, blood pouring out of that shiny black suit. He raises his arms and screams, 'Mother of Mercy, can this be the end of Rico?'"

Phil was caught up now. "W.C. Fields in *My Little*

Chickadee. He has a line, "That woman drove me to drink and I never took the time to thank her!' And how about all the great Indian pictures? Remember that fantastic shot, thousands of Indians silhouetted on the ridge?"

Harry's fist came down hard on the table. The sound was loud enough to make Phil turn around to see if anyone picked it up. Harry was beaming. "Goddammit, that's it!"

Apprehensively, quietly, Phil asked, "What?"

"Center field! The thirty-nine Dodgers! Indian Ernie Koy! I almost have it all fleshed out: Camilli, first base; Coscarot, second; Durocher at short; Lavagetto at third; Babe Phelps catching. I thought it was Mickey Owen, but it was Phelps. Medwick in left; now, right field . . ." Harry's voice trailed and died.

"We better go."

"Relax. We have time."

Phil relit the cigar, studying Harry through the spurting flame and wondering how much longer he could hold himself together and if Jan recognized the danger, and, if she did, could she help. He didn't think so.

A small fly made a graceful landing on the top nut. Phil watched the fly rub his front legs together. It was an expression of sheer joy at having found so tasty a destination. The fly reminded Phil of Eddie.

They were two cones, one inverted on the other; one vanilla, the other coffee. And they were melting into each other, working slowly on one another, making soft sounds.

Eddie sat in the big easy chair watching the two girls. His eyes raced from point to point, trying to keep pace with the pictures flashing through his brain. He felt as if an oven had been turned on in his chest. He would watch Dusty burrowing, swivelling into Margo; then he would quickly shift his eyes down to Margo feeding on the coffee-colored girl. He tried not to miss anything. He knew the moment was precious. Stolen. He could not stage this play in Cleveland. Not with this cast.

The scene kept coming in and out of focus. It had a drifting reality—it was mirage-like, and Eddie felt a gnawing fear that it would suddenly dissolve. He leaned forward blinking his eyes—making sure these two gorgeous girls were actually only ten feet away.

Dusty withdrew her candy box and slid her legs down to

her part of the bed. She turned Margo over, belly up. Dusty was lying prone, her mouth into Margo. Margo stretched her arms back over her head, spread her legs wide and closed her eyes. Eddie could see Margo's stomach flatten out and grow taut. Tiny muscles in the smooth, flat belly were jumping and pulsating. She moaned softly.

He knew it was absurd; they were paid performers; but he could not chase the thought that Margo was actually enjoying herself. Eddie got out of the chair and started over to the bed.

Bogart walked out of the fort toward the Panzer captain. They were both carrying white flags. The German column was in desperate need of water and they thought Bogie had a hidden well.

Phil was on his second Smirnoff.

Harry was walking alongside Bogie, carrying the BAR low; it would rise to the left when he pulled the trigger. If Bogie needed help, he could chop the German in half in three seconds.

"Harry, it's after two. They've been up there a long time. I hope she remembers Eddie's health."

"Listen, Phil. Margo's gone down on everything but the Queen Mary. She's a total professional. The better the performance, the bigger the order."

A heavy voice with a southern slant boomed out at them. "Harry! Harry Stone! How the hell are you?"

A six-foot-two, fifty-five-year-old Texan stood over them. His skin carried the magenta flush of long-ago rivers of booze. The fleshy face was topped by a grey ten-gallon Stetson. He wore a blue pinstriped suit, a white shirt with a black string tie whose ends slid through the eyes of a silver longhorn steer.

Harry put his hand out and smiled up at the towering bulk. "Hello, Chester. You know my partner, Phil Greene?"

"No. Don't believe I've had the good fortune." He dropped Harry's hand and stuck a large red paw out at Phil. "Chester Seagrave."

Phil put his hand inside the red flesh. "Pleased to meet you."

Seagrave sat down. His sheer bulk pushed Phil two feet up the curve of the booth. He took out a square of Beechnut chewing tobacco and closed large, yellow teeth over the brown cud. "Goddam! The word's around you boys got yourselves one hell of a line."

"You'll see it first hand in about an hour. What are you drinking, Chester?"

"No. No drinks. I quit. Goddam liver's actin' up. Turned yellow as Mao Tse-tung two weeks ago." He shook his massive head. "No. I jest chew now."

Phil asked, "What store do you buy for, Mr. Seagrave?"

"Bowden's."

"That's Dallas, isn't it?"

"Yes siree, the jewel of the prairie "

"I've shipped you quite a bit of goods."

The shrill laughter of two women at the adjacent table washed over them. A waiter dropped a bowl of peanuts and cursed softly in Spanish.

"Phil's the inside man. The engineer. He makes it all happen."

"That's right. I'm inside. I just see names on invoices. But Harry . . . Harry knows the faces."

Chester spat a quick, surreptitious stream of brown juice on the tiled floor. "Hell, I couldn't be a factory man. I like people too much for that. I enjoy servin' the Americun public." He paused, chewing carefully, thinking about his "Americun" public, then quietly said, "Ain't easy anymore."

Harry said, "Nothing's easy anymore."

"Oh, I don't mean business." Chester frowned. "I mean all the goddam meatheads. Commie kids. Pornographic movies. Panthers. Weathermen. And that cock-lickin' Fulbright. I tell you, they're fuckin' up the old Republic."

Harry said, "All they understand is a cloud of tear gas."

"Tear gas, my ass. I say line the bastards up and push some steel into 'em."

Phil swallowed some more vodka. "Well, I for one, can't go along with that."

"We have no choice, Phil. Chester's right, they're ruining the country."

Seagrave spat again. "Goddam right. That's what I'm sayin'. I bet your kids don't go around breaking windows and pissin' on the flag."

"You can sleep on that, Chester. My little girl knows her place."

"What school's she at?"

"Berkeley. Right in the middle of the whole mess."

"Goddam! Berkeley! And she keeps her nose clean. Goddam!" Chester shook his head and pulled his bulk up, jarring the drinks on the table. "Goddam. You gotta be proud of that little girl. Well, boys, I'm gonna take a crap and a shower. In that order. See you at three. Nice meetin' you, Mr. Greene."

"Same here, Mr. Seagrave."

"Later, boys." He lumbered off, crashing into a Mexican waiter who precariously maintained the balance of a drink-laden tray. The waiter hissed an ancient Spanish epithet.

Phil signed the check and signaled to the same waiter who had just called Seagrave "the son of the great whore." The green-jacketed man set his tray down and came over to the table. Phil handed him the bill. "We have an account here. The tip is included." The man examined the check. "It's all right. We have an account. You understand? A charge account." The man stared and frowned.

Harry said, *"Tenemos una lina de credito, comprende?"*

The sun came out. The man smiled. *"Si ... si, comprendo."* He left, moving among the tables toward the smoky bar.

Bogart and the Panzers had been temporarily done in by a cat food commercial.

Flicking the cigar ash, Phil asked, "How the hell can you say those things?"

"What things?"

"Seagrave."

Harry swallowed some Scotch. "The man is a customer. A good customer. I feed him what he wants to hear. What's the difference?"

The shrill voice of a page broke over Harry's last word. "Phone for Mr. Stoner." He sang it. "Phone for Mr. Stoner."

Harry turned toward the doorway and shouted, "Here! Over here!"

The boy waved and moved quickly to the end of the bar and picked up a phone with a long extension cord and started over. As he neared the table he asked, "Mr. Harry Stoner?"

Harry nodded.

The boy smiled. "Just a moment." He set the phone down on the table and plugged the square jack into a wall socket. He clicked the button on the phone's cradle, waited a few seconds, then, into the receiver, "Operator, I have Mr. Stoner." He handed the receiver to Harry. Phil gave him some change which produced a broad smile and a "thank you." The boy hurried off toward the lobby.

Phil heard the hellos, then saw the color drain out of Harry's face.

Harry sucked the air and blew it out. He spoke low and fast. "Jesus Christ Almighty. Get dressed. Don't call anyone. We'll be right up." He hung up and looked at Phil. "Eddie's dead."

Chapter 14

Margo had her pink pants on, but her blouse was open. She straddled Eddie's stomach, trying to pour some Scotch into his lifeless mouth. Eddie was naked, comatose, his face slate grey, his eyes slitted.

Beads of sweat oozed out of Margo's forehead; they traveled down her face to her neck. They swam, like one-celled amoebae, across her exposed breasts. Reaching her nipples, they fell, one by one, onto Eddie's chest.

Dusty was dressed. She wore the same fixed smile as she watched Margo work.

Margo was past pleading, she commanded Eddie, "Come on, you son of a bitch. Drink!"

The yellow fluid ran out of the corners of his mouth, staining the white pillow. Margo put the bottle down on the nearby night table. She leaned over Eddie and, with the fingers of her left hand, pinched his nostrils shut. She covered his mouth with hers and methodically pumped her breath into his lungs. Her sweaty breasts were bunched up under his chin. She increased the tempo, pulling the air into her nostrils and exhaling into the still mouth.

She worked feverishly, picking up a "one-two" rhythm: in and out . . . in and out She heard nothing, felt nothing, except the cold lips covering her own.

After three minutes, Margo felt dizzy. She pulled her mouth away, sat up, and looked down at Eddie. She hoped it wasn't imagined, but the dark grey color had lightened slightly, and the blue flush around his eyes was less pronounced. She raised her right arm and brought the heel of her hand smashing down onto his chest. A low groan slipped through the small opening of his mouth. She wasn't sure, but then another sound came through. It was somewhere between a croak and a moan.

Margo screamed. "He's alive! The prick is alive!"

Dusty widened her smile.

Margo swung her legs off Eddie. She put her ear to his chest and, guessing where the heart muscle was, she began to massage. She rubbed hard in a small circle over Eddie's heart. The beads of sweat coming down from her forehead burned their way into her eyes.

Eddie gasped, then groaned again; but the grey face was definitely a shade lighter.

The cathedral-like chimes floated in from the outer room. Margo stopped the massage, wiped the sweat from her forehead and, in a breathless voice, said, "Get the door."

Dusty went out.

Margo pulled the covers up to Eddie's chin. She leaned over, pinching his nostrils shut again, and clamped her mouth over his icy lips once more. She began anew to pump her breath into his tired lungs.

Harry and Phil brushed past the still-smiling Dusty. Margo heard them and pulled her mouth away from Eddie. She sat on the edge of the bed, breathing heavily, staring down at the rug.

"He's alive."

Her words stopped Harry. He saw her sitting there, hair disheveled, sweat-covered breasts heaving up and down. For a second or two, he had trouble, but then managed the word, "Alive?"

Margo nodded. A bead of perspiration fell from her cheek to her lower lip.

Harry repeated, "Alive?"

Still staring at the designs on the rug, she said, "I worked on him. He's breathing. He's making sounds."

Harry snapped at Dusty. "Get some blankets. Phil, call the desk... Ask for Jack Sorell. Tell him to get the house doctor up here fast and get an ambulance."

Phil went quickly into the living room.

As Harry approached the bed, Margo got up slowly and moved out of the way. He leaned over Eddie and placed his mouth close to Eddie's right ear. "Ed . . . Ed . . . Can you hear me?"

Eddie groaned, but his lips could not form any words.

"Eddie . . . come on, Eddie . . . this is Harry. Harry Stoner. You hear me, Eddie?"

Harry straightened up and looked down at the rubbery lips and half-open eyes. Eddie's face was a piece of grey clay; the saddest clown in the circus.

Suddenly he gasped. His lips moved in slow motion, forming the words with exquisite precision. "Like . . . like . . . pain like a knife . . . too much . . . doctor . . . doctor . . . please . . ."

Harry bent over. "Sure, Eddie. Sure. Doctor's on the way. He's on the way."

Dusty handed Harry a folded blanket. He gently draped it across Eddie, straightened up and turned to Dusty. "Okay. Out!"

She smiled, wet her lips and drifted toward the doorway. Harry walked over to the window.

Margo had a small atomizer of Estée Lauder and sprayed it across her breasts, underarms, around the baseline of her soft hair, then into the palms of her hands. She patted her cheeks, then dropped the vial back into her tote bag and started to button her blouse.

The sweet smell of the French fragrance laced the air. Harry watched her as she brushed the back of her hair with sure, strong strokes. She had regained her composure. The girl in the Modigliani frame. Harry thought she had the resiliency of a paratrooper. She dropped the brush into the tote, took a Gauloise out of the blue pack. Only the slight quiver in her hand betrayed the tension of the last thirty minutes.

Margo blew the smoke at Harry. "He kept pleading with us to prolong it."

"But I warned you. I told you to go easy."

From the doorway Dusty smiled. "He's an out of sight cat."

Harry nodded. "Yes . . . almost out of this world."

Margo shook her head. "Every time I do someone a favor, I get kicked right in the ass."

He took one of her Gauloises and nervously searched his pockets for a match. Margo's gold lighter was right there. She held the flame until the tip of the cigarette glowed. He inhaled deeply and sighed. "It shouldn't have happened."

"How could I know? It was fast." She snapped her fingers. "Like that. It happened fast."

Phil came in, his face chalky. "The doctor's on the way."

Harry nodded. "Okay, girls . . . Out! Game's over."

Dusty spoke through the smile. "See you around."

Margo paused at the doorway. She looked at Eddie, then back to Harry and Phil. An element of guilt fell from her eyes. "I'm sorry." She went through the wide arch.

Harry took a few steps to the corner of the drapes and pulled them open.

Eddie groaned steadily.

Harry blew the smoke against the window pane. "What's the doctor's name?"

"Samuels."

They fell silent. There was another low moan from Eddie.

Phil said, "Well, at least he's alive."

Harry turned from the window. "We should have gotten the order up front."

Phil removed his glasses and rubbed his hand over his eyes. "Thank God he's alive. We can live without the order."

"We needed that order."

Phil moved to him and grabbed Harry's arm. His voice was hoarse with anger. "We're responsible here! We set this up. The man may die!"

Eddie groaned as if he concurred with Phil.

Harry shrugged Phil's arm off. "This is not our fault. If we didn't set it up, someone else would have. Eddie's just another casualty."

In disbelief, Phil said, "Casualty? He's a man. With a family. He may come home in a coffin."

Harry sighed heavily. "I've got a whole hall of men in coffins—row after row of distinguished crosses."

Phil stared at him for a moment, then looked back at Eddie.

Harry said, "Tell Samuels to give him the best—specialist, private room, whatever—and bill us. Stay with him till you're sure it's all buttoned down. I'm going to check Rico. I'll be at the show."

Phil replaced his glasses. He looked down at the windowsill. "What the hell is this?"

"The vibrator. She forgot her vibrator. I'll see you downstairs."

Phil clicked the apparatus on. He felt the blood in his hand start to hum. He whispered, "Business."

Alone in the elevator, Harry felt queasy. A growing icy wave gripped his chest. The numbers on the elevator panel began to swim. A swelling tide of nausea looped through his stomach. He thought it would burst out of both ends. The elevator landed abruptly on the mezzanine floor.

The big ballroom to his right was filling up with buyers. Directly opposite the bank of elevators, there was a door marked Rest Rooms.

There were four urinals to the left with two nearby mirrored sinks; to the right, three metallic stalls. Harry walked quickly into the farthest one.

He removed his jacket and hung it on the protruding hook, then dropped his pants, eased the boxer shorts down around his ankles, and sat down on the cool, black plastic. He put his head down between his knees and felt the blood rush up. He pulled some tissue out of the dispenser and wiped the sweat off his face.

As he held the position, a sharp pain raced through the shell fragments. Harry wondered if he should have them X-rayed again. The last time the neurosurgeon advised against surgery. They were too close to the spinal column. "Just grin and bear it."

He thought: When I'm in the coffin, when all the flesh is gone, they'll drop. They'll take the last bounce. And what a trip: a factory in Silesia to Italy, to me, to a box under a pile of California dirt.

He wondered what the man was doing now: the man who fired the shell. Probably helping pollute the cities of the world with "the people's car" —the little bug that Hitler had promised to the Volk.

There was no feeling in his bowels and the nausea subsided. He urinated as he raised his head. The cold chill diminished. Harry rested his elbows on his knees and examined the scrawled messages on the backside of the door: LBJ SUCKS . . . ROSS HUNTER FOR QUEEN MOTHER . . . A KILO A DAY KEEPS THE BLUES AWAY . . . PHONE ME, I TAKE IT IN THE EAR . . . NIXON BLEEDS PUS.

There was an extremely well done drawing of two males screwing, and alongside, CALLEY IS INNOCENT. Harry thought about the babies in the ditch. He refused to believe that American soldiers had sprayed those children.

He thought of his division, his regiment, his platoon and the murderous beating they took at Salerno. But they came into the town with chocolate bars in their hands and the children swarmed all over them. The thing was that through it all, they held on to their humanity. They, his boys, were really what America was all about.

These kids today, in the jungle, killing babies . . . but then again, forty-five thousand of them died. And for no reason. Maybe that was it. That had to be the answer. The absence of reason had destroyed their humanity. But then . . the Germans, they had reason; they believed. And they pushed children up smokestacks . . . No, it was the man . . . the individual. That was the only answer. It was the man.

He flushed the toilet, got up, fixed his pants, lifted the jacket off the hook, and crossed over to the sink. He pushed rapidly on the soap lever, remembering a long-ago Easter. Jan was away. His daughter was five or six, and he had taken her out to dinner. She had to go to the bathroom, and Harry took her into the men's room. She was fascinated with the soap lever. When they got back to the table, she suddenly asked if she was too old for the Easter Bunny. And he had answered, "You're never too old for something you still enjoy."

But now, drying his hands on the coarse paper toweling, Harry wondered if that was true. There was Eddie, fusing his whole life into a scramble with a couple of hookers. He enjoyed it; and it almost killed him. But, Christ, you can torpedo any truth. There is no dictate, no wisdom, no great oracle's pronouncement that can't be shattered.

What commandment . . . what symbol . . . what high voice in Heaven had the answers? The Gods looked down and you were fucking alone. That's the way it is. All you have is what you know. And you use it. Make them beat you. Make it tough.

He splashed some cold water on his face and dabbed it off with the paper towel.

He looked at himself in the mirror. The reflection seemed soft, blurred. He thought about right field. Who was it? Ripple or Furillo? No... Furillo was later. 1939. 1939... right field... it would come to him.

He touched the handle on the door. He would have to be careful... he'd have to get backstage without running into any buyers; it was bad luck to discuss the line before the show.

Chapter 15

The width of the stage ran about eighty feet from wall to wall, and half as deep. The wide runway snaked out from the center into the audience. A heavy muslin curtain hid the backstage disorder.

High-pitched feminine laughter, shouted jargon of styles, fabrics, accessories, the swelling sounds of thirty people coming up against a curtain bounced off the brick walls.

There were a dozen portable make-up tables at the back wall, with models seated, facing illuminated mirrors. Women armed with combs, brushes and hairpins clenched between their teeth hovered over the girls. They were the dressers. Racks laden with garments were lined up end to end across the center of the stage, and each garment on the racks had a large number attached to it.

Rico flitted nervously from table to table, smiling, chirping, patting, admonishing. Alfonso checked off the clothes on the racks against a list in his hand. A tall, smartly dressed woman stood downstage near the curtain. She carried a hand mike in one hand and a script in the other. Her lips moved silently as she studied the pages. The music from a well-amplified trio out front mixed with the backstage throb. They were playing "What the World Needs Now."

Harry walked down to the apron of the stage, pulled a few inches of curtain apart, and looked out at the audience. The huge room was crowded. The buzz of the buyers competed favorably with the music.

Uniformed Mexican waiters slithered through the milling crowd, carrying trays of drinks and hors d'oeuvres. A large banquet table, set up across the rear of the ballroom, featured trays of smoked salmon, caviar, and cocktail frankfurters encased in heavy dough. Near the doorway, at the corner of the table, two bartenders were dealing drinks.

The musicians, a trio of piano, drums, and alto sax, survivors of a lifetime of bar mitzvahs, sat on a raised platform flush against the right wall. They were filed under "events" at the union. From the mechanical way they played, Harry knew they were probably thinking about their next job.

Satisfied with what he saw, he released the curtain. It was a fine turnout; there had to have been some solid word of mouth about the line. There were no kept secrets; every season, before the showings, there was some advance word; something leaked.

As he walked to the racks, he heard Rico shouting, "Love later, girls. Work now! Work now!"

Alfonso finished checking a rack and started for the next. When he saw Harry he smiled, exposing the curved tooth. *"Como esta, patrón? Todo bien?"*

"Up yours, Al."

"The name is Alfonso."

"What do you want, Al? I overpay my maid."

The smile broadened. "Harry, you're a real revolutionary."

Harry put his hand on Alfonso's shoulder. "You know, a real honest-to-God American can't get a job picking grapes."

"For you, Harry, we'll waive the rules."

Harry squeezed the shoulder and dropped his hand. "Listen, are we okay?"

"Si, señor. No tengo ninguno problemas."

"Good. You're a hell of a man. If we fall on our ass today, you can open a taco stand. You'll be big, Al. King of the tacos."

"Yes. The greasy kind. Let me work now, *patrón*." Alfonso moved away.

Harry noticed Ula at the far end. She was standing in front of her make-up table, changing clothes; a grey-haired woman fussed with her hair.

He walked through the racks toward Rico. The dapper designer was adjusting a belt around the narrow waist of a tall brunette. She was the same girl who had told Harry the line would sell earlier that day.

Rico's voice was shrill. "Be still. Goddammit, Rosanna. Hold still."

"I'm barely breathing."

"You're not breathing. You're panting over Blondie there."

Harry asked, "You all right?"

Rico spun Rosanna around. "Super, Harry. Absolutely super."

He paused and checked the girl once more. "Okay, honey. That's your first number."

Rico stood up on the tips of his toes and looked through the racks, downstage, toward the woman with the script. He spotted her and shouted, "Jackie! Jackie!"

The woman kept moving her lips over the script.

A dresser started to unzip Rosanna.

Rico muttered, "Shit," then screamed and waved his arms. "Jackie! Jackie Ross!"

The handsome face looked up from the script, acknowledged Rico, smiled, and started over.

Harry asked, "You sure you're all right?"

"We're fine. Believe me." Rico studied Harry's face for a few seconds; then in a low, conspiratorial tone, "I know this isn't the time, but that commissar—that fucking Bolshevik—is driving me up the wall."

"You're right. This isn't the time." Harry wished he had gotten more anger into his voice, but he was too tired.

Rico nodded. "Okay. We'll talk later. Listen, you better check the line-up with Jackie. I've got to circulate." He danced away.

Harry watched the tall brunette, Rosanna, clad only in panties and bra, leaning over the blonde model at the next make-up table. She had her arm around the girl's shoulder, feeding a stream of whispered words into her ear. He thought Rosanna's moves were practiced, that she had made the same pitch many times before.

Jackie's voice shattered his diagnosis. "How are you holding up, Mr. Stoner?"

"I'm fine."

"Do you know what Rico wanted?"

"He wanted to be certain you had all the changes."

The woman smiled. "All nailed down." She exuded that special under-pressure confidence that belongs to professionals.

"Thanks, Jackie."

"Thank you, Mr. Stoner. I need the work." She moved off, trying to find Rico.

Rosanna resisted the tugs of her dresser long enough to brush her lips across the blonde's neck.

Harry shook his head and glanced down the far end of the wall. Ula was slipping into a casual print. As he started over, he heard the trio playing "The Lady Is A Tramp." The melody flashed echoes of New York.

Ula saw Harry's reflection in the small mirror. Their eyes circuited, and for a few seconds shorted out the rest of the world. She was absolutely beautiful, but he felt no deep emotional tug for her.

He guessed it was time. A man crosses a time zone with one woman and there's no emotion left for the escapades— a taste, a bite, a whiff, a touch, but no emotion.

He smiled. "Nervous?"

She nodded and the lemon hair glittered.

"What are you wearing?"

She got up and, taking his arm, moved him over to a nearby rack. She touched each garment as she spoke. "Two pantsuits. Three midis. And this." Her hand rested on a small strap of red-striped cotton.

"What the hell is that?"

She smiled, "Hot pants. Rico put it in at the last moment."

He loved what the Scandinavian accent did to "last moment."

"I'm terrified."

"So is everyone else. Just keep your shoulders back and smile. Okay?"

"Okay."

"Remember . . . Shoulders back and smile down at them."

The grey-haired dresser took Ula's hand, moving her back to the table. Over her shoulder, Ula asked, "After the show?"

"Yes. After the show. Good luck."

He started across the stage toward the rear exit. As he walked, images raced by: lacy black panties; red nipples; white, brown and black asses; zippers opening, closing;

changing aromas of perfume; stroking brushes, sliding combs, mouths full of hairpins; Rico kissing, chatting; lipstick following soft curves; Alfonso muttering Spanish to his brown assistant; Jackie's lips moving slowly, memorizing; Rodgers and Hart floating in from the tired trio. The shapes, sounds and smells came and went: models bending over; eyes flashing up; bodies turning, pivoting, straining against the tight-fitting garments.

And caught in the backwash of this fragile carnival: a house, a wife, a distant daughter... a payroll, and sixty-three employees.

He started down the backstage steps, wondering what was keeping Phil: maybe three floors up Eddie was dead; a relapse; killed in action on patrol, seeking a ten-second spurt of excitement; a thrill that receded as fast as a plug being pulled from a socket.

Two ambulance attendants were wheeling Eddie out. Phil caught their last sympathetic comment; it was something about "cunt-crazy Jew bastards." Phil thought, it was on again; it was fashionable again. The anti-Semitic slurs were everywhere. But this time it would be different. The groveling, the cowering old beards were gone with the herring vats of the Lower East Side. That Jew is history. Yes, this time it would be different.

Dr. Samuels sat on the edge of the bed, writing his report with a fountain pen. Phil hadn't seen a fountain pen in years. The doctor had blue-black hair; his face was dominated by a pug nose that belonged to a third-rate welterweight. He was in his middle forties and losing the waistline battle.

"What do you think, doctor?"

Samuels kept writing. "You can never make any predictions with cardiac arrest. We'll keep him in intensive care." He shrugged. "If he's lucky, he'll survive."

The doctor signed the yellow form with a flourish, capped the pen and tucked it inside his jacket. "You know, this is the third case in less than a year." He paused. "I mean, under similar circumstances."

Phil chewed on the unlit cigar. "Well, at least he has a chance."

The doctor rose, snapping his black case. "Why do they

do it? Grown men, having been through an attack... having once been warned. Why do they do it?"

"He told us his doctor back in Cleveland had given him permission."

"Yes... that is to say, normal sexual gratification. From what you told me I hardly think what took place here was 'normal.'"

Phil said, "What took place here was business."

Samuels shrugged. "Well, there are worse ways of dying... believe me. I examine an X-ray. I see the spot. I look at the patient. What do you say to that patient?"

"Happy New Year."

"You're not far wrong, Mr. Greene. You can sing 'Auld Lang Syne.'" Samuels brushed some dandruff off his shoulder. "No, it's not a bad way to go... at the peak of sexual excitement. Of course, it's embarrassing to the family." Samuels paused, watching Phil light his cigar. "Have you notified the family?"

"No. Not yet."

"I think you should."

"I will, doctor. Listen, you have my card. Just send the bill to that address, to my attention. Needless to say, don't spare a thing. Whatever you feel is necessary."

"Fine. Fine. We'll do our best. By the way, you wouldn't happen to have another cigar?"

"Yes, of course. Sorry I didn't think to offer you one." Phil took one out of his inside pocket and handed it to the doctor. "They're not very good. They're from Florida."

Samuels inspected the red-gold band. He nodded in agreement. "Since Castro, it's impossible to get a decent cigar. Damn shame we can't make some sort of deal with him. I don't mean to sound unpatriotic, but I have nothing against Fidel Castro. After all, we do business with Red China."

Phil nodded. "I was thinking of that this morning."

Samuels sucked at the wet end, fueling gusts of flame and billowing grey smoke. He extracted the cigar and examined the glowing end. "Don't burn evenly, do they?"

"No. They don't burn evenly."

They stood there looking at one another, puffing occasionally, trapped in the embarrassed silence that engulfs the survivors of sudden disaster.

Phil asked, "Would you care for a drink, doctor?"

Samuels nodded, "Maybe a few fingers of Scotch."

He followed Phil out to the sitting room. The bedroom was empty. Only the sweet smell of Estée Lauder hung over the room.

Chapter 16

In the ballroom, neat rows of chairs had been placed on either side of the long, red-carpeted runway. The chairs were four feet lower than the runway. Some of the buyers were already seated, looking up, waiting. The others milled around the banquet table, sipping a last drink, nibbling a last dry hors d'oeuvre.

Harry caught snatches of dialogue as he moved through the crowd.

A pretty redhead spoke to a very mod man:

"Rome in January?"

"On the fifteenth."

"Maybe, this time, we'll see the city."

"Why?"

A young beard was talking to a grey beard:

"Here we are, at a fashion show. And men are dying."

"Turn to sex, Richard."

"Sex is not my bag."

"I don't mean the heterosexual kind."

An older, smartly dressed woman conversed with a stubby red-faced man:

"We had the Parisian midis copied down last season—and nothing... absolutely nothing."

"They still want the mini."

"Yes. Anything to show some ass."

Two horn-rimmed, immaculately dressed men spoke in hushed tones:

"And he has this chauffeur who scores for him. I mean the best, Larry. Acapulco Gold."

"And he's cool?"

"Not only cool—he knows his place."

Harry had moved through smiling, nodding, shaking hands, finally working his way to the back of the room.

The overhead lights flashed and dimmed. Strong 1-K lamps threw powerful beams down the length of the runway. The trio sounded a crescendo and the buyers streamed toward the chairs. The drummer played a two-stroke roll that never quite made it. Harry thought the drummer would have been in deep trouble had he tried a one-stroke roll. He had no wrists.

The ceremony of a hundred people settling down took another few minutes. The runway lights dimmed; a lamp from the rear booth projected a wide circle of light on the front curtain. On the final cymbal crash, Jackie, microphone and script in hand, stepped out.

As Harry watched Jackie, his vision suddenly blurred, throwing everything out of focus. He blinked rapidly, then closed his eyes for a long beat. When he opened them, the focus was back.

Jackie's voice, through the amplifiers, commanded the room. "Good afternoon, ladies and gentlemen, and welcome to Los Angeles. We are only twenty-five minutes late, which means we are on time." There were a few appreciative chuckles. Jackie widened her smile. "Before we begin, I should like to present the president of Capri-Casuals—Mr. Harry Stoner."

There was a polite splash of applause.

The beam of the follow-spot stabbed through the room, searching for Harry. The trio drifted into "The Isle of Capri." Harry started toward the stage. He wasn't nervous; he had done this before. The spotlight found him and moved with him up the stairs to the center of the stage. He took the hand mike from Jackie. She slipped back inside the centerfold of the curtain. The trio stopped abruptly in the middle of a chorus.

The overhead lights came up a few points. Harry could see the faces of the buyers. He cleared his throat. "I want to thank you all for being here today. While I don't know each of you personally, through our field representatives and our long association, I feel we are all friends."

A streak of pain shot through the shell fragments.

The faces blurred.

The men of the One Hundred and Thirty-Third Regiment were in the chairs. They were the early ones. The best. The men from Tunisia. Hill 609. They were all dead: sitting upright, staring at Harry.

He clenched his eyes and cleared his throat. A cold chill grew in his chest. Harry looked out again. The buyers were back. His voice wavered. "I sincerely hope you enjoy what we are about to present. Your individual field men will remain with you at the conclusion of the show. They will handle your..."

The soldiers were there again: the socketless eyes, the wounded eyes, the dazed eyes; staring. Accusatory.

Harry's voice tightened. "I am quite proud of Capri-Casuals... but I realize there are more crucial things going on in the world today." He paused, sucking hard at the chilled air. A growing swell, a buzzing murmur, rose out of the audience. Harry continued, "People are... Panzers... We're loving ourselves into wars... too to the 88s... to the beach..." He stopped, gasping for air. His voice trembled.

"We have... faces... men are missing, but the spirit, the spirit of the company... Charlie company... brave men. They believed in something..."

The faces of his old comrades were in sharp focus. He wanted to jump down, to hold them, to embrace them.

Immediately behind the curtain, Rico, Jackie and Rosanna were huddled together.

Rico bit his nail. "My God, he's freaking out."

Rosanna hissed, "It's the pressure. It's the pressure."

Rico said, "Get him off, Jackie! Get him the hell off!"

Harry got a grip on his voice. "Perhaps you're wondering about the name 'Capri.' It has great significance to me... I was on that island in 1945. It was an island of... of sad Italian songs... brave men—they... they stuck together."

The consternation on the faces of the buyers heightened. Their murmurings were more pronounced.

Again, Harry's voice trembled. "A paradise... a paradise... So the name, you see... the name is..."

Jackie came out. She took the hand mike from Harry and smiled broadly at the audience. "What Mr. Stoner means is that the choice of 'Capri' was no accident—rather an inspiration. Now, how about a round of applause for Mr. Stoner!" Their applause started slowly, sporadically; the band went into "Isle of Capri"; then, as if giving vent to their embarrassment for Harry, it grew, building into a loud, continuing wave.

Harry moved down the steps. The spotlight held on Jackie and the runway lights brightened as she announced the first number.

The curtain opened. A backdrop of Paris hid the racks and make-up tables from view. It appeared that the girls were entering the runway from a Montmartre street. They came striding out, casting frozen smiles down at the buyers.

Unnoticed, Harry made his way to the rear of the ballroom. He lifted a Scotch and soda off the banquet table, swallowed, and lit a cigarette. The chill in his chest had been replaced by a burning sensation. He took a second swallow of Scotch.

The trio underscored Jackie's descriptions.

Harry sipped the drink as he watched the action on the runway. The applause following each presentation seemed genuine.

A hand suddenly touched Harry's sleeve. His arm jerked reflexively, spilling the Scotch.

Phil asked, "What's wrong with you?"

Harry looked into the yellow lenses, then down at his Scotch-stained Gucci loafers. "Nothing's wrong. You just startled me. What happened with Eddie?"

"The doctor says he has a chance."

Ula came down the runway in a pink sweater and the red-striped hot pants, drawing a rousing hand from the male contingent.

"What did you tell Samuels?"

"The truth... It's the third one this year."

"What hospital?"

"Cedars. I called Cleveland. I talked to his wife. She'll be here tomorrow."

"How did she take it?"

"She didn't say much. She asked for only some details: my name, the doctor, the hospital, so on—and then she thanked me."

Harry indicated the rows of drinks on the table behind them. "Have a drink."

Phil picked up what appeared to be vodka or gin. He sipped it; then satisfied it was vodka, took a firm grip on the glass. "How's it going?"

Harry dropped the cigarette, crushing it out carefully. "All right. I don't know... I don't... well, Christ, I started talking about the war." He thought about mentioning the soldiers, but decided not to. "Lately, I keep thinking about things that happened . . . I mean, years ago . . . years ago, Phil."

Phil studied him carefully but said nothing.

A black girl in a printed maxi pivoted at the end of the runway. Jackie's voice sold the garment. The trio played "Arrivederci, Roma."

The black girl went off and Ula came on again wearing a beige faille pantsuit. The trio switched into "Moulin Rouge." Jackie chirped, "A lovely Parisian inspiration, combining the subtlety of Cardin with the lines of Balmain." Ula walked the length of the runway but pivoted badly.

Phil grumbled, "She moves like a bear."

"So what? Gives the men something to look at."

"You really enjoy that Swede?"

"Danish, Phil. Danish. It's a place to relax."

"Better off in the steam room."

Ula went off to a smattering of applause.

Rosanna came out in a pink slacks outfit. The trio played something Italian. Jackie droned, "A real Capri-Casual . . . skintight in pink faille. Simple lines, beautifully cut." Rosanna moved gracefully and pivoted expertly.

Phil sipped the vodka. "Now, that would be my speed."

"She's a dyke."

"What's real, Harry?"

"When you wake up and you know you made it again."

As Rosanna moved off, the little blonde was coming on. Rosanna winked at her as they passed. The blonde wore a blue blouse and white hot pants. The trio played, "You Go to My Head."

A page entered the rear of the room and approached them cautiously. He whispered, "Mr. Stoner?"

"Yes. I'm Mr. Stoner."

"There's a lady in the bar would like to see you. She says it's important."

"Did she give her name?"

"No, sir."

Harry looked at Phil, shrugged and said, "Be right back."

Phil nodded, but didn't look at Harry. He was watching the blonde and wishing he was ten years younger.

*   *   *

The TV set was off and the population had decreased considerably. Two men in ten-gallon hats were eyeing Margo.

She sat on a stool in the center of the curving mahogany, her soft, dark hair framing the smooth white skin. Her pale pink suit was creaseless. She looked like a society lady, toying with her afternoon Scotch mist. She wore a simple gold ring on the third finger of her left hand. Whenever she was alone in a public place, she'd slip the band on; it offered some small protection against prowling boors.

She knew the two hayseeds farther up the bar were interested. She lit a Gauloise. Out of the corner of her left eye, she saw the thin one, the one with long sideburns, start over. She blew the smoke straight ahead toward the back of the bartender. She knew what was coming.

His voice was Kansas or Arkansas. "Pardon me, miss, but my friend and I . . . well, we wondered if you'd care to join us for a drink?"

She turned to the man, seeking his eyes, but there were only eyebrows covering sockets with tiny beads.

Her voice was off the tundra. "I'm a Mrs., not a Miss. And my husband will be joining me any minute now. He's a homicide lieutenant on the Los Angeles Police Force."

The eyebrows shot up and a sheepish grin came onto the thin lips. "Well, that's fine. No harm done. It's so dark in heah, I didn't catch that little old ring." He backed away and rejoined his larger friend. The encounter had made him nervous. He grabbed his bourbon and ginger, took a big gulp and, in a hushed voice, "Goddammit, Ruby I couldn't see the little old cunt's ring.

The big man grunted. "Too fuckin' dark in heah."

Margo drained the glass and the bartender was there instantly.

"Can I do that again?"

"Yes, please."

The two hayseeds were still looking, wondering what was keeping the homicide lieutenant.

The bartender did his number and placed the fresh drink in front of her. He showed some caps and said, "Say, that's a very nice perfume you're wearing."

Margo picked up the squat glass and said, "Thank you." She sipped the semi-sweet drink and gently brushed the hot end of the cigarette against the surface of the ashtray, crisscrossing until all the red glow was gone.

He saw Margo looking at herself in the mirror. She was the girl in a Cole Porter tune. But there was a fundamental sadness that cloaked itself in her classic geometry.

She turned just as he walked up to her. She thought he looked chalky and drawn, but it could have been the lighting.

The bartender moved in. "What'll it be?"

Harry said, "Nothing thanks."

The bartender moved off toward the ten-gallons.

Harry hoisted himself up onto the stool and reached for her blue pack of Gauloises. He said, "You sent a royal page, Princess?"

She stared deeply into the faded blue eyes. "I wanted to tell you . . . I'm sorry as hell. It shouldn't have happened."

"Everybody misses."

She tossed her hair. "Not professionals."

"Yes, they do. Good quarterbacks get knocked down, and good nurses get knocked up. Everybody misses."

"Well, I'm sorry. I know how important Eddie is to you." Her eyes riveted into his. She was trying to turn him on but didn't know why.

He crushed the cigarette. "Forget it. You did me a favor. It must have scared the hell out of you."

He slid off the stool and straightened up. "As a matter of fact, I'd like to make it up to you. I'd like to buy you a dinner."

She raised her landscaped eyebrows. "A dinner?" She smiled. "What are we going to talk about?"

"Business. We'll talk about business."

"Yours or mine?" she asked.

"We're all selling the same thing."

"Yes. Trick or treat."

"That's right, honey. Every day is Halloween. Look, I've got to get back upstairs. Now forget it. You pulled him out."

She didn't know why, but she gave him a very hungry look. "I just wanted you to know . . . I'm truly sorry."

"Forget it. Some night, let's have dinner."

"Sure. Some night we'll have dinner."

For a few seconds their eyes locked. He thought he saw

something warm in those soft brown eyes. He touched her cheek, smiled and left.

Margo sipped the last of her drink. She wondered why she had tried to turn him on. Probably because he never regarded her as anything but a machine. She quickly shook that line off. That was deadly. That was emotion. It was too late for that . . . ten years ago. Still there was something about Harry she would like to own. To have inside her. It had nothing to do with sex. It was something else. It reminded her of when she was a little girl in Wheeling, West Virginia, looking into a store window at things she couldn't have. She spun the ice in the empty glass with her forefinger.

The bartender moved in like an actor picking up a cue. "Another one, miss?"

Margo nodded and lit another cigarette.

He mixed the drink and asked, "Does it bother you?"

"What?"

"The warning. Cigarettes. Hazardous to your health."

"Yes . . . it bothers me."

The man shook his head. "Funny. The government warns the people they're gonna die if they keep smoking . . . still they smoke. Funny!"

She blew the smoke in his face. "Yes. It's a scream."

Chapter 17

The grey muslin curtain was down. The lights were up full and the trio was gone. The buyers grouped around the field salesmen who were writing up orders and taking notes. The Mexican waiters cleaned up the residue of drinks and stale hors d'oeuvres. Harry and Phil exchanged thank-yous with various buyers.

Chester Seagrave shoved two women aside. His yellow teeth stopped attacking the Beechnut long enough to crack a stained smile. "Boys . . . you got yourselves a hell of a line."

Phil smiled weakly. "Thank you."

The mod man in horn-rimmed glasses grabbed Harry's hand. "Delicious, Harry."

"Well, put it on paper, Irving."

"Right now, baby."

Seagrave said, "Me too. A'hm goin' up to mah room and write you boys an order."

"We need it, Chester."

Harry took Phil's arm and started to move him toward the ramp leading backstage.

Alfonso and three women gathered up the samples, putting them back on the racks. The models were changing back into their street clothes; the dressers no longer hovered over them. The girls laughed and called out numbers that had not yet been picked up. The backstage atmosphere had the joyous lilt of a hit show on opening night.

Rico beamed and kissed Jackie's cheek. "You know what this is, Jackie?"

She smiled. "It's a smash, that's what it is."

"No. It's graduation day. Now I can move."

"Move? Why? You're doing fine."

"No. Harry's hung up with a Commie patternmaker. I've got to split. I can go with anyone now."

"But they've given you an opportunity. You've had absolute freedom to create, to design."

"Yes, and I designed the best line they've ever had. I'm not taking any crap from a cutter. No, I tell you, honey...I'm going to split."

"You'll stay, Rico." Harry's voice startled him and Rico turned quickly.

Jackie sensed the approaching storm. She smiled at Harry. "Congratulations, Mr. Stoner. The line is a smash."

"Yes. I think we're going to be in fine shape." Harry sucked at the air and blew it out. "Listen, Jackie. I want to thank you for getting me out of trouble. I mean up there, on the stage."

"It's happened before. It's just pressure. Well, thanks for the job. I'm off to the kiddies now." She smiled a last smile and left.

Rico said, "We may as well have it out. I'm leaving."

Quietly, Harry said, "We have a contract."

The shrill, feminine pitch came into Rico's voice. "Contract?" he laughed. "You just try and get a design out of a contract."

Phil said, "You're making a mistake. The line is in. It's a fact of life. We don't need you to make the clothes."

"No. You have Joe Stalin."

Phil chewed on the dead cigar. "Not Meyer. I supervise the production."

Harry said, "Every house in town previews this week and next. There won't be any design requirements for months. Now just simmer down. One solid showing isn't a career." He paused, and softened his tone. "Look, Rico, you're all nerved up. Take some time off. Go to Acapulco with your boy friend."

Rico chewed his lower lip.

Harry continued. "You need a rest. Take a month.. on us."

Rico's voice dropped. It was armistice time. "You will talk to Meyer? I mean, that's a promise?"

"Yes, I'll talk to Meyer."

"Acapulco?"

"Acapulco."

"On the house?"

"On the house."

Rico smiled. "I withdraw my resignation." He wagged his finger. "Temporarily... temporarily."

Harry said, "Good."

Rico looked at Phil. "You'll line up the production schedule?"

"As soon as I get back to the office."

"Fine. I'll check with Alfonso to make sure there's no pilferage. I don't trust these twats." He swished off.

Ula, wearing a simple black sheath, walked up to them. "How did I do?"

"Ask my partner. You know Mr. Greene?"

"Yes, of course."

Phil said, "You were perfect. I thought you moved like a gazelle."

"Thank you. I was terrified." She touched Harry's arm and hesitantly asked, "Can I see you for a moment?"

Harry glanced at Phil, who started to say something, but scratched the thought. Harry said, "A minute, Phil."

They walked to the far side of the stage. Phil watched them go, then felt a light tap on his shoulder.

He turned to a smiling, dapper man with polished black hair and startling black eyes that shone out of brown, Sicilian skin. The neck was too long for the short body. He was a cobra in cuff links. "How you doin'?"

Phil lit the cracked cigar and carefully blew the smoke over the man's head. "Hello, Tony."

"Snazzy line. I wuz watchin'. I seen everything. Snazzy."

"Glad you liked it."

Tony took out a platinum cigarette case. "You got bread?"

Phil blew some smoke. "I think we're all right."

Tony carefully extracted a thin, brown cigarillo. He depressed a button on the head of the case and, through the smoke said, "Big line, big orders ... needs big bread."

"That's right."

He tucked the cigarette case away. "You're lookin' at the bank."

Harry's voice came from a few feet away. "Hello, Tony Loanshark. What's the mob selling money for these days?"

"Same as always. Twelve percent on the unpaid balance for the first month; then it sort of levels off."

"Yes," Harry said. "It levels off at two hundred percent."

Phil said, "Practically a gift."

Tony smiled. "What the hell? Think it over. The bank ain't gonna give you shit—but we'll throw dice with you. Think it over." He walked off in the direction of a black model with a huge Afro hairdo.

Harry said, "Wonderful fellows."

Phil shrugged, "It's a good sign. If they sent Tony, the word's around we have a hot line."

"The mob has money; but the banks don't."

Phil smiled. "Every good banker leaves room for the Mafia."

"Can you imagine living with their hooks into you?"

Phil bit the cigar. "No worse than arson."

"Yes ... it's worse. You remember what happened to Kramer? He fell behind. A guy came into his office and hung him out the window, by his armpits, fourteen stories up. Then put him back in his chair. Kramer's face turned the color of his white-on-white shirt and hasn't changed since."

"And if we get caught burning the plant?"

"A nice, clean cell. Three meals a day. Television and

exercise." He glanced at his watch. "Let's go. You have to be right on the dot with Charlie."

They started toward the rear door. The large backstage area had quieted down; the racks, the dressers, and most of the models had left.

As they reached the door, Phil asked, "What did Miss Denmark want?"

"She wanted dinner tonight. I told her we'd be working late."

At the far end of the stage, the little blonde sat at the make-up table, crying quietly. Rosanna stood behind her. Soothingly, Rosanna said, "It's only for a weekend."

The blonde sobbed at her reflection. "You said it was over."

"I'm trying."

"But you said it was over."

Rosanna kneaded the flesh in the girl's shoulder. "She was very special. I'm trying."

Chapter 18

At the four corners of Pershing Square, the headwaters of the five o'clock rush were bubbling: subterranean pools of cars streamed up, surging out of underground caves, flowing out into the streets, forging a river of stagnant, creeping metal. They rolled toward the interchange where they dammed up, backing and filling, rolling ahead nervously, in small waves.

The pedestrians swam through the metal: secretaries, laborers, executives, blacks, yellows, browns, whites, crossing quickly moving by unseen commands to bus stops, where they stood impatiently, waiting for the growling black carbon with the right number.

Harry and Phil walked up Sixth Street and went into the candy store at the corner. There was a stacked candy counter near the cash register, and a soda fountain punctuated by three black-knobbed spigots ran down the length of the store. The spigots were marked: Pepsi, 7-Up,

Fresca. In the rear were three round, white-topped tables with wire chairs spaced around them. A jukebox against the back wall blared acid rock.

At the counter, two Mexican men and a black girl toyed with their drinks. A section of pornographic paperbacks lined the wall opposite the counter. A derelict, smelling of wine and vomit, perused the positions.

Harry picked a chocolate bar off the counter and asked the teen-age counterman, "How much?"

"Fifteen cents."

He searched his pocket, but came up empty.

Phil took out a half-dollar and placed it on the counter. "Here. Take out the candy and give me a chocolate soda."

Harry removed the wrapper, exposing the chocolate. He murmured, "Used to have picture cards inside. Ball players, fighters... we used to trade them. Zale for DiMaggio; Pepper Martin for Dixie Walker." He stopped in mid-bite. "Dixie Walker! Hey, Phil, that's it! That rounds it out! Dixie Walker, right field!" He took another bite, smiling to himself; then softly, "Dixie Walker. I saw him throw Enos Slaughter out. A perfect strike from deep right field."

A counterman set the soda down. Phil sipped and made a face. It was too sweet, and the soda was flat; it had the texture of water.

The pimples on the counterman's face reddened. "Whassa matter?"

"Nothing. I'm not thirsty."

The wino belched loudly.

The counterman rang up the register, handed Phil the change and addressed the wino.

"Hey, creep. Get lost."

The wino turned and slurred, "Listen, sonny, don't call me a creep, not when you got all these fuck books."

The wino looked at Harry and Phil. "These kids, they don't respect nuthin'."

The faces of the sparse audience in the dark, cavernous theatre were lit in the light reflected off the screen. The theatre could accommodate six hundred, but there were no more than eighty people scattered about. Five teen-age girls, sitting together, giggled nervously at what they saw on the screen. A man sipped Gallo red from a bottle wrapped in brown paper. A sedate woman in her sixties chewed gum rapidly, her eyes transfixed. Three boys in their early twenties were passing grass. The other customers were a cross-section of those who had nowhere else to go and the genuine pornography buffs of all ages, sexes and colors.

The theatre smelled of grass and stale popcorn. Years ago, it had been called The Fox and great films had been shown on its big screen. A background score played on an organ gave a religious ritual air to the action on the screen. The moans and groans of the actors rose and fell in sync with vibrating tones of the organ. Two blondes were going down simultaneously on a sailor. The sailor had his top on, but his pants were down around his ankles. A cigarette dangling out of his lips, he looked down at the tops of their bobbing heads.

Charlie Robbins sat halfway down and three seats into the center aisle. He wore a smart black suit, a blue button-down shirt with a maroon tie and his steel-rimmed glasses provided a fitting accompaniment to his iron-grey hair. His features were small and regular. Charlie was a conservative; he had voted for Barry Goldwater and had not bothered to vote since. He removed his glasses, checked the luminescent dial of his wristwatch, shook his head, put his glasses back on and impassively watched the Danes perform.

Phil walked into the outer lobby, examining the posters and advertising material. Harry went directly to the ticket booth. In the small glass cage, a seamed, sallow-complexioned woman, in her middle yesterdays, sat on a high stool. Her hair was like blue Brillo.

Her voice was low and raspy. "How many?"

"Two, please."

She didn't depress the ticket button. She said, "Ten dollars."

"What was that?"

Boredom and fatigue crept into the rasp. "Ten dollars."

"You're kidding."

"Look, mister. It's five bucks a head. You want a pair or not?"

He shoved two fives across the small counter. "What are you giving away?"

Taking the money, she said, "The name of the attraction is *Denmark Speaks*. It's been here sixteen weeks. It has the world-famous smörgåsbord scene. You can have a private booth for seven fifty."

"Private booth?"

She pushed the tickets across. "We get all kinds."

Taking the tickets, he said, "Do you qualify for Medicare?"

"Very funny. But you're buyin', mister. I just work here."

"That's true." He paused, smiled, then added, "Sweetheart."

Phil was absorbed by a poster showing a mating couple holding a difficult position.

Harry said, "Let's go."

Phil straightened up. "This is really raw."

"At these prices, it better be."

They waited at the rear of the theatre, giving their eyes a chance to get used to the dark. After several minutes, Harry could see shapes and outlines.

He whispered, "Come on. I can see."

"I can't, Harry. I can't see a thing."

"Well, quit looking at the screen. We're late."

"The screen is all I can see."

"Give me your hand." Harry led him slowly down the center aisle. At the halfway mark, he halted, scanning the sparse audience.

He had full vision now, and he spotted Charlie sitting alone, exactly where he was supposed to be.

"I see him."

Harry moved into the aisle and took a seat a space away, to Charlie's left. Phil took a seat a space away on Charlie's right. They neither looked, spoke, nor in any way acknowledged each other's presence.

On the screen, the sailor was completely naked now and lying down on a huge bed. The two blondes were still working on him. Harry noticed the heavy blonde seemed to be enjoying herself. The sailor moaned loudly. The organ groaned with him.

Without turning from the screen, Robbins said, "Nice suit."

"Thanks."

"Silk?"

"Right."

"Hong Kong?"

"Rome."

"Nice, Harry. Very nice."

"Thanks, Charlie."

Phil slipped an envelope out from his inside pocket, reached over with his left hand and dropped it in Robbins' lap. Charlie's eyes never left the screen; but his hands worked quickly and quietly. He slipped the envelope into a prepared space in his shirt-front, then rebuttoned the middle three buttons.

Phil said, "The key. The . . ."

Charlie snapped him off. "Keep watching the screen. Talk without moving your lips. Don't look at me."

Phil nodded slightly and finished his sentence watching the Danes. "The key. The down payment. And the address."

"When is it vacant?"

"After six."

"Any watchmen?"

Harry shook his head.

"Don't shake your head, Harry. Just answer without looking, without moving your lips."

"Okay, okay. Christ, Charlie, we're not passing secrets."

"Listen, you don't pump gasoline with a cigarette in your mouth. I want to retire in my own fashion, without any assistance from the State. Now, what else is in there?"

Phil said, "Shirt factory on the ground floor. That's it."

"How old is the building?"

Phil shrugged slightly.

Charlie snapped. "Don't shrug, Phil. Just answer."

"Well, I would guess the building is thirty-five or forty years old."

"Okay. I'll check it tonight. Meet me here tomorrow. The show starts at one forty-five. I'll drift in with the crowd. You come in fifteen minutes later at two."

They sat in silence for a moment. The sailor had gone to the bathroom. The two girls were working on each other.

Phil said, "They're in good shape. Look at those muscles."

Charlie said, "It's the diet. They eat a lot of fish. They haven't been poisoned by fluoride."

Harry said, "Charlie, I want you to play it safe."

Ice cold, Robbins replied, "You want to forget it, say so."

Phil sighed, "We can't endanger anyone, Charlie."

Charlie went into an old familiar speech. "Fellas, you're not dealing with a pyromaniac . . . a lunatic with a match in his hand. This is a science. A precise, exacting science.

I've set fifteen major industrial fires across this country in the last three years. I've had two firemen overcome by smoke. Both recovered and received citations."

Harry said, "We just don't want anyone hurt."

Charlie answered in a mellow voice. He knew he had them. "Don't confuse morality with technology. Setting the fire is technical; the decision to do so is moral. I can't help you there."

The sailor was back. The heavy blonde sat on his face. Two other girls were sitting on a love seat, smoking and playing with each other while watching the sailor and the heavy blonde. The soundtrack was alive with the Danish equivalent of "Ohs" and "Ahs."

Phil said, "I guess there are worse ways of making a buck."

Charlie said, "They enjoy it. They don't have the same hangups we have. We're an afflicted nation."

Phil persisted, "If there's the slightest chance, Charlie . . . the remotest possibility of someone . . ."

Charlie stopped him. "I'm not God. If someone's number is up . . . that's Kismet. I'll match my record with anyone in the business. But, as I said before, you want to forget it, fine with me."

Harry said, "Take it easy, Charlie. We've never been involved in this kind of thing."

Charlie cleared his throat. "Well, I can understand that. But I want you fellows to know that safety is my cornerstone."

Harry said, "Fine, Charlie, fine. We'll meet here, at two, tomorrow."

Charlie rose. "Enjoy the picture. Nice suit, Harry. Later, boys." He moved to his right past Phil and walked up the center aisle.

The other two girls had come over to the bed. One of them went down on the sailor. The other began kissing the girl who slid up and down the sailor's face.

"Let's go."

Phil had his glasses off. "Wait a minute, I've never seen one of these before."

"Come on. They'll just go to another position. They don't feel anything. It's like watching a cartoon." Harry got up, impatiently waiting for Phil. He couldn't believe Phil was really caught up in the Danes. He thought Phil was delaying, as if there were security in the dark theatre.

Phil got up slowly, his eyes still fastened on the screen. "The guy still hasn't popped."

Harry smiled. "Maybe that's why he's a star."

A voice barked out of the darkness. "Down in front!"

As they started up the center aisle, Phil turned back to the screen. The naked Danes danced in his glasses. Harry tugged at his sleeve.

Phil sighed, "They've come a long way from wooden shoes."

"That's Holland, Phil. Wooden shoes are Holland."

Chapter 19

They came out of the lobby and blinked reflexively, but their eyes adjusted quickly to the failing light. They had reached the street and were standing alongside the box office. The clamor of the homeward rush had subsided.

Harry said, "You have to respect Charlie . . . a real pro; a great technician."

Phil sighed. "A giant in his field."

"Well, it's a way out . . . it's a way out, Phil."

Phil peeled another cigar. "Let's get a cab. I've got to get with Meyer, set things up."

"Go ahead. I'll meet you at the office. I'm going to walk."

Harry noticed the harridan in the glass cage watching them. He smiled at her and she immediately dropped her head into a paperback.

Phil had the cigar going. "You sure you want to walk?"

"Yes. Go on . . . I'll meet you up there."

"You all right?"

"I want to take a walk. Okay?"

"Okay, Harry."

Phil started up the street. Harry watched him for a moment, then went off in the opposite direction. He crossed through Pershing Square, heading south, toward Olive.

A bearded youth in dungarees and T-shirt shouted: "Save the tiger! Save the tiger!" He had a fistful of

pamphlets and occasionally handed one down to a specta-
tor. "We need your help! Save the tiger."

Farther along, a woman dressed in a long white toga
yelled down from her platform: "May Christ save you from
eternal fire!"

Harry stopped. Her line was ironically appropriate.
He whispered to himself, "Amen," then noticed the
woman's hair; it was like blond moss clinging to the
contours of her scalp. Harry suspected "she" was a man
in drag.

Near the southeast corner of the square, a group of men
were picketing. They carried a variety of signs, all generi-
cally the same: ITALIANS FOR JUSTICE; WE HATE THE MAFIA;
ITALIAN POWER; FBI UNFAIR TO ITALIANS.

A stocky, sign-carrying man thrust a handful of leaflets at
him. "Hey, buddy, read what they're doin' to us."

Harry just looked at the man.

"Come on, buddy, read it. This here material will open
your eyes."

"No thanks."

The man grabbed Harry's sleeve. "Listen, everybody's
worried about the Jigs and Spics; they ain't got enough
Cadillacs. Yeah, well, what about us Italians. We made this
here country. We discovered this here country."

Harry shook the man's arm off. "Don't tell that to the
Indians."

The man sneered. "Yeah, well frig dem. And all dere
friggin' tribes!"

"Sure, pal, when I have time."

Harry left the man wondering whether or not he had
been insulted.

As he turned the corner of Olive and Sixth, Harry
thought of another corner: a vital corner, in a town on the
Volturno . . . he was walking point with a replacement, an
Irish kid from Paterson, New Jersey. He told the kid to
hug the wall, but the boy swung wide. An S.S. trooper
leaned out of a doorway and peeled the boy in half, then
swung his machine pistol at Harry—but nothing happened.
Harry emptied his BAR into the German. His body kept
jerking, and Harry kept firing.

Now, walking through the late afternoon heat, he thought
how fortunate these old California streets were, and how
remarkable that in a country that had known continual

warfare for almost two hundred years, there were buildings standing that had never lost a chip.

He remembered them—the big ones: the fifty-ton Pattons trundling through, fifty and thirty-caliber machine guns screaming... spitting, and the long ninety-millimeter cannon revolving slowly, then zeroing in, then the ear-shattering crack; and the chunks of brick blowing up and out, falling into the rubble-strewn street; orange tongues of flame dancing from odd angles; the low roar when the walls bulged and the center of the building fell in... the stench of smoke, dust, burning rubber, and scorched flesh mixing with the cordite of the heavy guns... the house-to-house mutter of automatic weapons, when fingers froze to triggers; frenzy time: new clip, lock, swing it up and bang away, watching the stuff fly, hearing nothing, cardiums plugged by the racket. Hours later, they would still be shouting to each other.

He wondered what the Americans would do if fighting came to their streets. Would it pull them all together? The right, the left, the young, the old, the poor, the rich, the blacks, the browns, the pot-heads and the dropouts... would they fight? Because it wasn't the weapons; they all had the same weapons. The difference was always the people. The Russians... the fucking Russians at Stalingrad had rage and love... and the French had the Maginot line. And that was the difference. And what about himself? Would he fight? He didn't know. There were no "guys" anymore. Guys that had that special thing for each other in that long ago war that thing that had nothing to do with causes. That special thing you never talked about but was there. You could see it sometimes on a professional football team; inside the ten-yard line, when they were dug in, trying to hold. The thing was you always covered the other guy and he always covered you. That's how it was.

But what the hell... today it was every man for himself. And now, by the grace of Christ knows what, people were concerned only with the small perils of getting home.

A few feet from the corner of Hill Street, a newsstand had the late paper clipped to its side. In large blue type, the banner read: B-52's DROP ONE TON BOMBS. Underneath, to the left, a smaller headline carried a sport bulletin: some kid on the Dodgers had pitched a no-hitter. He didn't recognize the name of the pitcher and doubted

that he was that good. He had his own Hall of Heroes...
Enos Slaughter sliding in, spikes high, and Walker's throw
just beating him. They tumbled together in Harry's mind;
Slaughter and the catcher, shrouded in thirty-year-old
dust.

Phil was seated in the center booth of the showroom.
Two well-dressed men were standing over him, looking at
the stack of orders on the table. Phil chewed on the butt of
the unlit cigar and, in a tired voice, said, "We'll deliver,
and on time."

The younger one, a man in his mid-thirties, wearing
conspicuous jade cuff links, said, "It's a great line."

The older man showed a lot of grey at the temples
and wore a concerned expression. "It's going to take a
pile of dough. It's very diversified... rich as hell to
manufacture."

"Don't do my worrying for me, Rudy. Please. The line is
sold. We'll deliver."

The jade cuff links asked, "When do we get our commission checks?"

Phil took his time lighting the stub and blew the smoke
up at the salesman. "The same as always. The end of the
month." He removed a small thread of tobacco from his
lower lip. "What is it with you guys?"

The grey temples said, "Rumors. You and Harry...money
problems."

Phil let a wide smile develop. "I'm really surprised.
You fellows have been in the rag business long enough to
scratch that talk. Has there ever been a season when the
manufacturer wasn't in trouble?" Phil paused, inhaling
the Tampa. He hoped he sounded cavalier, and waved his
hand. "Come on now... go home boys. Chicago, New
York... get out to the airport. Traffic's heavy this time of
day. You ought to get moving. Go on. I've got work to
do."

The younger one smiled. "We have a few hours before
flight time. You wouldn't happen to have any numbers?"

"No. I wouldn't. One casualty a day is enough."

The older man said, "We heard. Eddie Mirrell." He
shook his head, feigning concern. "Too bad. I hope he
pulls out." He lost the concern and smiled. "Well, good
luck. You just deliver. The line will walk out of the stores."

They started for the door. The jade cuff links stopped and turned, "Say, Phil, what the hell happened to Harry?"

"What do you mean?"

"I mean when he spoke to the buyers and started getting into the war."

"What do you think, Jerry? Nerves. Pressure. Come on now, get out of here."

The older one said, "Well, give my best to Harry."

"I will, Rudy. Now, so long, boys."

The door opened and Meyer, carrying a small dish with a steaming glass of tea surrounded by sugar cubes, brushed between the departing salesmen. He walked over to the table and sat opposite Phil. He dipped a cube of sugar into the tea and sucked the brew through the cube.

Phil shuffled the order forms. "Salesmen . . , a shine and a smile . , , let Arthur Miller manufacture a line of clothes. Just once. One season."

Meyer took the cube out of his mouth and dipped it again. He pointed the wet cube at the orders. "Looks good."

"All we need is money."

"You'll discount the orders. You'll have money."

"Not enough."

Meyer looked at Phil's drawn face; and, with the cube in his mouth, he picked up the glass and sipped the hot brew. He set the glass down, wiping his lips with the back of his hand. "Where's Harry?"

"On the way."

"I have to talk to him."

"This isn't the day to talk to Harry."

"I have to talk to him."

Phil removed his glasses and rubbed his fingers across his eyes. "Meyer, there's something going on with Harry. He's not the . . ."

The old man cut in. "Blind, I'm not."

Phil shook his head. "He's not the same man." He paused and drew a breath. "Remember when he was on the road? *There* was a salesman. My God, that man could sell smoke signals to the phone company."

Meyer sucked some more tea. "Now he's an executive . . . a president."

Phil smiled, "You remember those early years, how he

carried us all—how he sold those blouses. My God, the crap we made in those days. Those goddam blouses."

Meyer nodded, "I remember. Even the fabric was no good. We were buying hot goods in the street. Stolen goods. No roll was ever the same."

Phil shook his head, "Still he sold those blouses."

There was a pause during which the only sound was the old man sucking his tea.

Phil pushed the table toward Meyer and got up. "I'll leave these orders with you. Lay out the heavy numbers first." He walked to the door, stopped, and looked back at the old man. "Everything passes. It's like the sea. We're all on a raft."

And with the stubbornness exclusive to the very old and the very young, Meyer said, "I have to talk to Harry."

Phil went out.

Meyer took a fresh cube, dipped it, sucked it, and looked up at the models on the wall. He saw the girl on the Greek beach but wasn't impressed.

The bluish color behind the window reflected the growing darkness as the day began its slow surrender. The overhead lights in Phil's office had visibly gained power.

Phil placed the receiver back on its cradle.

He gave the small stub of cigar an expression of disdain and tossed it into the wastebasket. He looked at the boy in the photo, but his thoughts were not about Spain.

They were thoughts of the sea; of standing in the prow of the small boat, the waves slapping up against the hull, throwing a fine spray across his face; the wind whipping the American flag, snapping it back and forth; the air clean and fresh, with a trace of salt.

He sighed heavily and lifted the receiver. He dialed again; dull staccato beeps buzzed in his ear. He slammed the receiver down, exclaiming to himself, "Busy! Busy! What the hell do they talk about?"

He removed his glasses, cleaned the lenses with his tie, checked them against the light, and put them back on, just as the door opened.

He looked up at Harry. "How's Dixie Walker?"

"He beat the Cardinals with a two out single in the ninth."

Phil replied, "Thirty years ago."

Phil got up and walked slowly over to the photo on the wall and stared at the boy. Harry sat down in the black Danish chair in front of the desk.

Phil turned from the photo. "Would you like to have supper with us?"

"No, thanks. Jan probably left something for me. The maid must be preparing it." He thought about Jan for an instant, then asked, "The salesmen happy?"

"Same as always. Worried. The usual, can we deliver? Meyer is going over the orders."

"What did we write?"

"Close to three hundred thousand."

"With the fire and the discount, we'll just squeeze through."

Phil went up to the window. The dying light had gone from blue to black.

Harry said, "I stopped at Air France. They have connections to Zurich. I want to take Jan and visit the kid."

Without turning, Phil replied, "That's a good idea. See your daughter before we go to jail."

A fresh cigarette burned Harry's throat. "You want to fish . . . the salesmen want commission checks . . . and we've got to get out of bed every day."

Phil turned. "But not to the same overhead."

Harry waved his hand. "Please, Phil, not now. Spare me the 'high living' speech. The way I live hasn't got a goddam thing to do with the business."

"I never said it did. It just takes some of the pressure off when your nut isn't sky high."

Harry took a deep drag. "Well, it's my nut. My pressure. The house is Jan's thing and the monthly rental on the Lincoln is ninety bucks more than a Mustang—that's my thing."

"Except when it reflects on all of us. Like today at the show. You told me you almost blew it."

Harry's face flushed. "That's got nothing to do with my life-style. That's . . . that's different."

Phil sat down on the sofa and stared at his shoes. He heard Harry cough and looked up at him.

Harry took another deep drag and crushed the cigarette out. "The thing at the show . . . that's something else. It's as if I've lost my life somewhere. And it's nobody's fault . . . it's just the way it is. But it's gone. And I'm trying to remember where and when. When I was on that island, Capri... they wheeled me out onto the terrace of a small restaurant. I looked out across the water. It was dusk. An accordion played "Sorrento." The waves sounded like muffled drums, and I thought about the men... the men who made the trip from Louisiana to Rome. The dead ones, not the survivors. They were the best, and sometimes I think I died with them... that somehow I should have. But I didn't. I'm a survivor, and so are you, Phil. We wake up and we go on. And there are no answers. Only that we can't go under. We can't let that happen. We've put in too much time, too much service. It's too late to go under."

In a flat voice, Phil said, "It's a criminal act."

Harry shot back, "What criminal act? To keep people working? You said it yourself this morning. Is that a crime? To hang on to fifteen years of hard work, is that a crime? To have your own business, to be able to let your hair go grey and not worry about some corporate kid throwing you out on the street... is that a crime? Everyone in this fucking country dances around the law!"

He got to his feet and his voice rose. "I've got friends of mine under the sand with bikinis sitting on their heads! Isn't that a goddam crime? What the hell is a crime? You tell me!"

Calmly, Phil said, "So the end justifies the means."

Harry's voice fell. "All I know is that there's nothing heroic about being flat on your back looking up the system's ass. That's what they want."

"Who's 'they,' Harry? *We're* 'they' and there are rules. Rules still exist."

Harry shook his head. "Wrong. Used to. Used to. No more. Listen, I can remember looking at the flag and getting goose bumps. As a kid, alone in my room, listening to the radio and they'd play the anthem... and I'd stand up. Alone in my room at attention. Today they're making jockstraps out of the flag. And maybe that's healthy. Maybe that's terrific. I don't know. But there are no more rules."

He moved close to Phil and dropped his voice. "The only rule is to stay in action."

Phil looked at him for a moment, then replied, "For people like us, there are always rules."

Harry put his hand on Phil's shoulder. "I promise you. I

swear to God, Phil, if anything goes wrong, I'll get you off the hook."

Phil's face reddened and his voice trembled. "Harry, I love you more than any man I've ever known. But don't ever say that to me again. We've been together too long for that. Don't insult me."

He stared at Harry for a long beat, then walked to the door, opened it and turned. "Meyer wants to talk to you. Good night, Harry."

Chapter 20

The huge plane came down smoothly, and eight minutes ahead of schedule.

Jan collected her two Gucci bags and waited in line for a cab. The stagnant humidity of the New York summer night made her uncomfortable. The air was heavy; red stains rimmed the clouds with the threat of rain.

The driver suggested she let him take the Triborough Bridge. But Jan said no and spelled it out for him: Queens Boulevard to the 59th Street Bridge; then west to the Plaza. The driver complained, "It's only a buck more my way, lady, and you save a half hour."

Jan said, "Fifty-ninth Street Bridge, please."

He dropped the flag and the car growled into life. She noticed the ruins of the World's Fair along the Expressway; then, paralleling Queens Boulevard, row upon row of housing projects. She shuddered at the thought of what life must be like in those antiseptic cubicles: the bitterly cold winter nights; the men trudging through the slush and snow, staggering into those tiny caves.

She realized how insulated their own lives were in Beverly Hills, how apart they were from urban reality.

She was stunned by the skyline, by the endless maze of antennas, all shapes, all sizes, as if an asylum of mad sculptors had been turned loose on the rooftops. They were like silent misshapen creatures waiting for the men who lived below to come home and push the button, activating their tubelike arms. The worn-out men would sit and watch their comic-strip heroes perform surgical magic and incredible feats of criminal detection. And there they sat, stupefied, distracted only by the commercials that sold them the good life.

Jan turned the window down and the humid air rushed in. She watched the antennas, stretching into infinity. Maybe she was wrong, maybe they served a purpose, maybe without those antennas the whole country would be shooting horse. But she couldn't absorb the mass of it, the totality of it. She hardly ever watched the thing and was very selective about what programs Audrey watched when she was a child. The whole idea of that big eye in the living room was repulsive to Jan. She felt it was obscene. It was like having the anus of the world spewing its diarrhea onto your rug. But for the dwellers of these cliffs, it had to be tranquilizing; the ultimate narcotic.

Now, riding through this middle-class ghetto she thanked God that she and Harry had beaten their way past all this. Harry had made it happen—but at a price, and lately the sum total of that price was increasingly evident. He was tough, but he was peeling, and the rawness was beginning to show. She loved him but couldn't reach him. She sat up nights, listening to him twist, turn and mumble in his sleep.

She remembered three weeks ago; it was almost four in the morning when his voice had wakened her. His words were loud and clear: "Red... Red... Patterson... What happened... What happened... I told him... The kid went wide... What happened... Sliced him... What happened ... The kid..."

Then Harry shouted: "I told him! I told him!"

She had put her arms around him, kissed his face and massaged his chest and he woke, and they curled into each other and made love wordlessly—out of a nightmare, they slipped into lovemaking. It was quiet and beautiful. That was three weeks ago. But that's the way it happened. Sporadic. Without warning.

The cab was now out of the residential section and passing through an area of factories and warehouses. The factories reminded her of the business. She wondered how Harry's day had gone and how the line had been received. She lit a cigarette and thought perhaps her idea to extend her stay was wrong. Perhaps it would be better if she went home right after the funeral. She missed him, and he was alone. Well, she'd phone him as soon as she was settled.

As they neared the bridge, she saw an enormous billboard advertising Off-Track Betting. She thought of the lotteries in the banana republics and how the poor always platformed the system. The billboard reminded her of the stories Harry told her about his father. The gambling—the world of "if."

They pulled up to the front entrance of the Plaza. The driver got out and removed the bags. She gave him a three-dollar tip and his face turned sadly gay. That was the best his face would ever do. She had made amends for taking the less expensive route.

Two Puerto Rican bellmen escorted her to the small suite. She tipped them each a dollar and immediately began to unpack.

She didn't want to be alone, and once everything was on hangers she called a girl friend and made a dinner date. She showered, and came out in a silk peignoir, her hair in a towel wrapped about her head like a turban. She crossed to the sealed windows.

The park glowed softly in the early evening light; turn-of-the-century lamps illuminated the rise and fall of its contours. Jan still marveled at its appearance of classic tranquility. The hansom cabs at the corner were antique reminders of a different time, a time when one could stroll the park without fear of sudden violence.

She crossed to the large mirror over the mock fireplace, removed the turban and shook her damp hair. She had the jet-lag feeling of misplaced time and wished Harry were with her; but he was three thousand miles away fighting some strange personal demon that defied understanding.

She started over to the small, blond desk; as her hand went to the phone, it rang.

The operator asked if she was Mrs. Harry Stoner. She said "Yes." The operator said, "Your party's on the line."

His voice was tired and the words seemed forced. She answered his question. "Yes. It was a 747. You know, it's funny . . . I was just about to call you." She asked how the show went and said, "That's marvelous. You must be thrilled." But he didn't sound thrilled. She said, "Harry, you sound exhausted. You shouldn't be there so late. Please go home. Carmella has something prepared—your favorite, linguine with clams." There was sudden silence on the line. "Harry? Hello? Harry, are you still there?"

He had his feet up on the desk and was tilted way back in Phil's chair. "Yes, I'm here. Listen, Jan. How would you like to ball me? Right now. Over the phone. Veterans like us can do it with words." She asked him if he was all right. Harry said, "Yes, I'm fine. What about you? What are you doing tonight?"

Jan sat down on the tapestried bench. "I'm going to dinner." He asked her with whom. She said, "Some friends . . . to a French restaurant." He asked her the name of the restaurant. She said, "I don't know. It's on the East Side . . ." He wanted the name. "I don't know. There are lots of French restaurants in New York." He said nothing. She asked, "Harry, are you all right?"

He swung his legs off the desk and tilted forward, resting his head on his elbows. "Sure, I'm all right. I'm terrific. I've had a big day. Listen, Jan. There's a jungle full of rusty helicopters, Columbus discovered America, and New York's loaded with French restaurants." The shadow of madness silhouetted his words.

There was a pause, and his voice turned soft and throaty. "Jan, you remember that time in France, in St.-Tropez, we made love like a couple of kids. My God, that was a sweet time."

Sadly, she sighed. "Harry . . . that was six years ago."

She suddenly wanted to be off the phone out of reach of his voice. She needed a cigarette and began to tap her foot against the leg of the desk. "Harry, please. Go home now. I've got to get dressed. Please go home. I'll call you tomorrow. 'Bye, Harry." She hung up before he could say any more. The sound of the receiver falling onto the cradle triggered the questions: Why was she so abrupt? Why couldn't she communicate with him?

Harry said "Good-bye" into the dead line. He replaced the receiver, lit a cigarette and stood up. How amazing it was that he still cared about a woman with whom he had not had a thoroughly honest talk in almost twenty years. Whether that was love or habit was anyone's guess. It was easier to tell with animals: an animal died in the zoo and its mate would refuse to eat. They would have to keep it

alive with intravenous feeding. You didn't need Dr. Frankfurter to analyze that. You could call that love.

Harry got up and made his way into the factory. One
lone, naked bulb cast harsh tones through the room.

The racks were there; but, shorn of their gaudy garments, they looked forlorn and purposeless. The shiny
black sewing machines were like cooled-off Thoroughbreds,
waiting quietly for the next race. As Harry moved past the
last rack, he remembered this morning; the tall brunette,
the studied lesbian, Rosanna, flashing her smile, flicking
her tongue, straining for femininity. He thought she,
Rosanna, was the tall trademark that stamped the product
of their efforts. And it was desperate; and misleading.

The old man leaned over the pattern table. He sucked
his tea through a cube of sugar in his left hand; in his
right, he held the stub of a pencil and made small nota-
tions on the paper patterns. A Camel burned in the red
ashtray.

Meyer looked up as Harry entered. "Hello, boss."

Harry sat on a high stool opposite Meyer. "Don't call me
boss."

Meyer put the pencil down and picked up his cigarette.
"But you are the boss. You built the business."

"Don't call me 'boss.'" Harry inclined his head toward
the patterns. "How does it look?"

"You'll need money."

"We'll get money."

Meyer dropped the Camel onto the wooden floor and
crushed it carefully. "I don't want to talk about the line."

Harry sighed. "I need you. I need Rico. What do you
want? What do you want me to say?"

Meyer sucked some more tea. "I'm old. I can't be in a
playpen with fairies. Even talented fairies. You can't give
me dignity from the fairy. I understand that. A cutter you
can always get. A designer is something else. Tell me what
to do?"

"You have a job here. Till we go out of business or till
you die."

Meyer dipped the sugar cube. "You need Rico. Tell me
to get out. Go on, Harry, tell me."

Harry loosened his tie and unbuttoned his top button.
"I don't want you out."

The old man moved around the table. "What do you

want, Harry? Come on, tell me. I'm an old stone. I don't talk. Tell me. What is it you want?"

Harry leaned over and picked up a small square of black faille. He thought about the old man's question, looked up at the neon tubing and said, "More."

"You mean money?"

"No..."

"What?"

"Another season."

The old man smiled. "And that's everything? Another season?"

"That's right. It is. The average life in this business is seven months. We've survived for fifteen years—that's something. Goddammit, it's *everything*."

"So it all comes to survival? That's all you want to be, Harry? A survivor?"

Harry got off the stool, looked out of the dark window, then turned to Meyer. "Yes. That's the best you can get, and if you do—well, that's something. That's a hell of a thing."

Meyer smiled. "That's all you see? Survival? No dreams? No hopes?"

"Yes, there's hope. When the smoke clears some goddam fish will crawl up out of the MGM lake and start it all over again."

"So it all comes to a fish, in a lake at a movie company?"

Harry drew in some air and then blew it out. He'd been doing that a lot lately. Jan called it hyperventilating. The old man waited. "Yes, that's right."

Meyer walked back to his stool and sat down. "I'm sorry for you."

Harry leaned over the table. "Sorry for me? You've been running all your life—from pogroms, from Nazis—bent over a machine... what the hell have you got?"

Meyer dipped the cube and sucked the sweet fluid, then placed the cube back in the saucer. "What have I got? I have my craft and I have a woman, Harry. A woman. Old, but still lovely. I enjoy being with her, looking at her, talking to her. It's sweet. And it's every day... every day."

Harry nodded. "And what happens when that's over?"

The old man shrugged. "I guess whoever is left—will remember."

Harry was near the door. His voice wavered. "Well, okay. That's . . . that's something."

The grey head nodded. "Yes, it's something! Now let me work. We spoke. I'll deal with the fairy. Go home. Go to your mansion. Go speak Spanish to your cook. Go to your mansion."

Harry snapped, "There's no mansion. It's a lot of red tile covering a mortgage."

The old man waved his hand. "Go home, Harry."

Meyer picked up the cutting machine and lined up the paper patterns, setting them over a ream of fabric. He pushed the start button; the high whine of the machine covered the sound of the door closing.

Chapter 21

Audrey put her book down and looked out at the lake. It was almost dawn, and a grey, luminous mist spread over the water. The snow-capped peaks of the distant mountains still reflected the fading moonlight.

At nineteen, Audrey had her mother's handsome broad features, curvy form, and large, well-shaped breasts. But her eyes were the same pale blue as Harry's.

She was tired; she had been studying all night. Cramming. The term-end test was that afternoon.

Audrey respected the money it took to keep her in this special scholastic atmosphere. She particularly did not want to let her mother down. She knew that Jan was the prime mover in her being sent to Switzerland. Her father was the fun person; he bought the candy, the toys, and read the books, but she could not recall ever being really intimate and confidential with him.

She remembered that when a friend of Harry's died the widow had asked Harry to go to her son's school with her. The boy had been shattered by his father's death and was unable to concentrate on his work. Harry met with the boy's teacher and told her it was wrong to pressure the boy, that if the child was left back it didn't matter. The boy would get to the front of whatever war we were fighting one year later. The pressure to keep up was nonsense.

Her father meant well, but never got involved. She thought that Harry had always wanted a son; someone to take to a baseball game. She could not confide anything of an intimate nature to him; but her relationship with Jan was excellent. They were like sisters.

She had told Jan of the deteriorating scene at Beverly Hills High School, that she had gotten into some hard drugs. It had begun to frighten her, but it was join in or be left out.

Her father still thought she was a virgin. He still cautioned her about being "easy," about losing respect. He hadn't the vaguest idea of what she knew and what she had already done. And perhaps it was better that he didn't. After all, what difference would it make? What would Harry say? It would only annoy him, make him wish she had been the missing son, the companion at Dodger Stadium.

Audrey stretched her arms over her head and thought about the German who had invited her skiing the following weekend at Gstaad. He was very good for her. He accepted her unusual sexual demands without questions, without dialogue. She liked that, for as soon as intimacy began, as soon as history began, she turned off.

She wondered if that was a problem and should be mentioned to Jan. But why? She was on the pill. She took care of herself; and sooner or later she would meet somebody who would make it all work.

The sound of the phone frightened her. She checked the small clock on the night table; it was ten minutes to five. Automatically, she ran the hours back in time, to Los Angeles. It would be about nine o'clock in the evening. Hesitantly, she picked up the slender white phone.

The heavily accented voice of the operator asked, "Miss Audrey Stoner?"

Audrey said, "Yes."

"This is the overseas operator. I have a call from a Mr. Harry Stoner, in Los Angeles."

Audrey said, "Put him on, please."

A wave of fear crept into her chest. She thought something had happened to Jan. Her father knew the time difference. Why would he call at this hour?

When Harry heard her voice his face brightened. "Hello, Audrey? It's Dad. Sorry to wake you. It must be..." Harry checked his watch. "...It must be five in the morning. No. No. Everyone's fine. Mom is in New York. An uncle of hers died. I don't think you'd remember him. Listen, honey...I miss you. I wanted to talk to you."

Audrey's large breasts sagged as she sighed in relief. "You didn't disturb me, Dad. I was up...studying. I have an important exam later today. Political science." She listened as Harry said that no test was important enough to lose a night's sleep over. Audrey said, "I don't mind. Really. It's terribly important and extremely complicated." Harry asked her what it was about. "Well, Dad, they give us individual problems. Mine is: Suppose Bulgaria declared war on Guatemala..." Harry repeated the names of both countries. "...Yes, that's it, Dad. Bulgaria and Guatemala. Well, what international ramifications would occur? Who would line up with whom? The crisis...the power blocs...you know, Dad...the geopolitical reactions."

Harry's smile broadened. "My, that's some problem. I guess the coffee beans would smell of herring, or something like that." He listened. The smile disappeared. He forgot; she took everything seriously and had a very small sense of humor. He stammered, "No...no...I was just kidding; yes, it is. Very complex. Listen, honey. Tell me about the chocolate. How's the chocolate?"

She didn't believe the question, but she asked, "What chocolate?"

He pursued it. "Well, the Swiss, they're famous for their chocolate, aren't they?"

Dully, she said, "Dad, I don't eat chocolate."

He changed gears. "Well, you're right. It's murder on your teeth. Listen, honey. Mom and I are planning to come over, not this weekend, but the following one." The cold tone on the other end stopped him. He listened for a moment, then defensively said, "Oh, I see. Skiing. Yes. Yes...I know they have it all year round...going with friends...well, okay. We'll try something else."

He listened to her small apology, leaned back, swiveled around and looked out at the lights dotting the tall buildings.

"It seems to me a visit from your parents ought to be as important as a weekend of skiing."

She tried to get some warmth into her voice. "That has

nothing to do with it, Daddy. This is something I've planned for a long time."

"You've been away all summer. We miss you. We want to see you."

Audrey clenched her fist; she wished she hadn't picked up the phone. She said, "Daddy, please understand. I can't postpone this particular weekend."

He wasn't certain they'd come over anyway and didn't pursue it. He sighed. "Well, what about the holidays?"

That one was out of the blue. Unexpected. She fielded it automatically. "What about them?"

"Well, are you planning to come home for Christmas?"

She reached for a cigarette. "I wasn't planning to." He asked why not. She said, "I just thought I'd spend the holidays here. With my friends." She couldn't find a match and it added to her frustration. "If you want to know the truth, Dad, I don't want to come home."

Harry leaned forward in the chair. "What do you mean you don't want to come home?"

She let it fly. "I don't want to come home because there's absolutely nothing there for me."

He tried to hold on to his anger. "I don't understand, Audrey."

She broke the unlit cigarette. "I hate that house. I hate that city. I hate that whole goddam life-style!"

He could not contain his anger any longer. "Let me tell you something, Miss. It's this goddam life-style that permitted you to go to Europe!"

She felt the perspiration gather under her arms. "I'm aware of that. I know how hard you work, but I can't help the way I feel."

Neither of them spoke; both searched for words to cancel the echo of their anger.

"Hello? Daddy? Are you still there?"

He sighed. "Yes. I'm here."

She brightened her voice. "Dad, why don't you and Mom come over here for Christmas? You can meet my friends. We'll be together and it will be a holiday for you both."

Harry looked up at the picture of Stymie flying in the stretch. After a long pause, he said, "Do you miss me, Audrey? Do you love me?" It didn't sound like a question; it sounded like a plea.

"Yes, Daddy. I love you." And she supposed she did.

Harry was sorry he asked. The answer sounded unfelt, conditioned, Wearily, he said, "All right, we'll try to come over for the holidays."

She felt the worst was over. "Fine, Daddy. Please let me know for sure. I'll plan something interesting for us."

He mumbled. "I will. I'll let you know."

"Swell. And give Mom my love . . . And, well, I didn't mean to upset you."

He tilted back in the chair. "That's okay. You get some rest. That's quite a test ahead of you. My God, Bulgaria and Guatemala. Good luck with it. Yes. I'll tell Mom . . . stay well. Yes. 'Bye, Audrey."

He hung up, leaned forward and rubbed his hands slowly over his face. He knew he had lost her. That, possibly, somewhere along the line he had failed her. That her affection for him was without trust, and without respect. They were father and daughter but not friends. The baby was gone: the hugs and kisses, Babar, and the big dolls and the Sunday mornings at the park, and the swings, and the carousels, and taking her to school, and the way she used to look at him when he was about to leave on a trip. There had been a purity, a perfection to the love he felt for that child. But it was over. Gone. The years had erased it all. The voice on the phone a minute ago was a stranger's. "Life-style . . . life-style." Bullshit! The same pressures were in the ghettos. It was time. Time. Put a Geiger counter on it. Bottle it. Einstein it. Theorize it. Add. Subtract . . . Nothing helped. It moved inexorably; a silent thief. Even death didn't stop it . . . it still played with you in the coffin. "Life-style . . . life-style."

Chapter 22

Los Angeles Street was almost deserted; its rhythms were confined to daylight. The night sounds were minor key; only the distant echoes of daytime dissonance could be heard. The heat had subsided with the sun, but the sensual warmth of the Santa Ana kept the night air heavy and close.

Harry came out of the grey lobby carrying his jacket over his arm. Two winos were sitting on the curb, sharing some white lightning. Across the street, huddled in the hallway of a building, two black hustlers were discussing their next play. They waited, every night, hoping for a tired businessman who might want some fast action. They had accosted Harry many times, but had long since given up on him. But he knew their arithmetic. They'd ask for ten and settle for five. Enough for a fix. A Lincoln for a gram. The blue math of their daily trip.

As he started up the corner toward the phone booth, he thought how the price had changed. How once, the price of doorway hookers was tobacco, ordinary tobacco. He remembered a night like this night, with a hot desert wind blowing.

It was Casablanca, late November 1942. But there was no Rick's, no Bogart, no Bergman; and they weren't playing "As Time Goes By." Harry was on a last pass. They were moving out to Tunisia in twenty-four hours. He was wandering through the narrow Moorish streets, not far from the waterfront and sipping cheap Algerian wine from a bottle wrapped in an empty Red Cross doughnut bag.

He walked in an almost catatonic state. It was dreamlike, devoid of time, place and reality. A low hum hung over the city, pierced occasionally by the wail of a siren. Huge searchlights, probing the low-hanging clouds, swept back and forth like the projected fingers of some ominous God, waiting to snatch something out of those leaden skies. Jeeps, motorcycles, and command cars whizzed by racing against a phantom stopwatch. Open trucks loaded with stone-faced infantrymen trundled through the narrow alleys. They moved slowly. There was no rush to get where they were going. Free-French troopers walked by speaking rapidly in that pretty language. Tall, black Senegalese legionnaires bargained with streetwalkers in the eternal sign language of streetwalkers and soldiers. A smell of smoke and incense drifted over the ancient streets.

As he passed the British-American bar he heard Fats Waller's voice, ". . . Every honey bee, fills with jealousy . . ." It was a popular bar and he thought about going in but he knew he'd get drunk and wind up in the arms of an

MP and be hustled back to his camp. He didn't want to risk losing this night, although he had no idea of what he was seeking.

He stopped in front of a mosque and lit a Philip Morris, sipped some more wine; it was half gone now and he was feeling the kick. He walked leisurely down the street and noticed the sign, "Air France"; as he passed the doorway a tired-looking girl who could have been twenty or forty grabbed his arm.

The hall bathroom, on the second floor of a small hotel, was roach-infested and most of the windows had been knocked out by the concussion rings of aerial bombs and the heavy French naval guns that had opposed the initial Allied landings. A radio down the hall played a blue wail in Arabic.

She sat on the toilet seat, and he stood over her sipping the wine and looking down at her busy head and swiveling mouth. Either she was very good, or he had been out of action too long, or a combination of both; but she was getting there.

Suddenly the bathroom danced. Dust fell from the ceiling; the roaches scattered wildly and the sky lit up over the waterfront. Her mouth slid off and she glanced up at him, squeezing his balls and smiling. "Italian plane, ees notheeng." Her mouth clamped back on. Considering the roaches, the falling plaster, the concussion of the bombs, it was a tribute to her long experience that he came.

She wiped her mouth with her sleeve and gave him "that look." He had paid her in advance, a pack of Camels, but the look was unmistakable. It was the look that transcended all languages, all nationalities. It was the "tip" look.

He gave her the rest of the wine, an almost full pack of Philip Morris, and a handful of coins. She whispered, "*Merci, cheri*," and left.

Then the let-down hit him. That depressed feeling that comes after bought sex. It was worse than masturbation.

Three roaches crawled around the sink and he was leery about washing off in the water that would come out of that pitted tap. He zipped up, turned and looked out the shattered window.

The low-flying Savoias were in a V formation and the searchlights had them. The thud of the five-inch and the crack of the three-inch fifty naval guns began their mixed thunder. With the first bursts, the formation broke and scattered in frightened patterns, climbing and diving to escape the lights and the shell fire. Harry clearly saw one of them shear off the tail of another. They came hurtling down, crashing into a warehouse; sheets of flame shot skyward. Then there was a low rumble and the whole building erupted in a great maroon ball of fire, silhouetting the grey naval vessels anchored nearby.

He watched the action for a long time, until the flames were small and the guns had quieted. The low-key hum of the city could be heard again; and from down the hall the sad Moorish wail drifted out into the sultry African night.

The desert winds blowing on the corner of Los Angeles Street felt the same as the hot winds that blew over Casablanca that long-ago night.

The small fan in the phone booth whipped the heavy air around. It had no cooling effect; its currents only raised the day's dust up from the floor and flung it around the booth. Harry shut it off.

He had the hospital operator on the line and asked for a report on Eddie. She said that no information was to be given out on the condition of Mr. Mirrell other than to immediate members of the family. Harry then asked for Dr. Samuels. He waited through a series of clicks and transfers. Finally a cold, mannish voice said, "Fifth floor, Mrs. Parks." Again, Harry asked for Dr. Samuels. There were some more clicks and then the heavy, studied voice came on.

"Dr. Samuels speaking."

Harry loosened the top button of his shirt. "This is Harry Stoner. I was with Mr. Mirrell when he was stricken."

The doctor released a stream of official reasons for not continuing the conversation.

Harry said, "Wait just a minute, doctor . . . my partner, Phil Greene, was with you in the hotel. He made all the arrangements."

Samuels relented and stated the present condition of Mr. Mirrell in precise medical terminology, none of which Harry understood. He tried to punch some meaning into the Latin but Samuels merely countered with more of the same.

It lasted for two or three minutes, back and forth. But

the heat of the booth and the frustration of dealing with Samuels got the best of Harry and he exploded.

"Now you wait! Wait just a goddam minute! I understand English. I even understand Spanish, but I don't understand double-talk in Latin! It's really simple, doctor; I'm trying to determine if Mr. Mirrell is improving, if he's recovering."

Another stream of medical jargon flowed out of Samuels, but this time Harry held on to his temper.

"Yes. I understand. The life signs are strong. But I'm asking you if he is out of danger."

While Samuels answered, Harry cupped the receiver and said, "Fucking doctors." He then uncupped the speakers and said, "Thank you... the prognosis is promising ... that's easily understood. Yes... yes, my partner phoned Mrs. Mirrell. You've spoken with her?"

Samuels said he had and she was expected tomorrow afternoon. Harry thanked him and said he'd check again tomorrow, that he would probably come down. Samuels assured him that everything humanly possible was being done. Harry thanked him again and hung up.

He walked fifty feet to Seventh Street and had a taco and Fresca in an all-night sidewalk stand, then started back down Los Angeles Street toward the parking lot.

The black hookers were still in the doorway. They smiled at him and he nodded back. He felt like saying something encouraging to them; that was a hard hustle they were on.

As he approached the shack, he heard the cold clipped tones of Vince Scully describing the antiseptic action of Dodger Stadium.

Harry thought it would be almost impossible to go nine innings in this dead air; the curve would hang and you'd have to stay with the fast ball, and sooner or later, they'd knock the cover off.

Willie was reading a two-year-old *Playboy*. He had the centerfold turned vertically, carefully scrutinizing the glossy, made-up nudity of the Playmate.

As Harry reached the open door of the shack, Willie looked up and grinned. "Jest look at this action." He turned the magazine for Harry's inspection.

The girl looked back, smiling at the camera. She was a redhead with deep green eyes, her body turned sideway;

her left breast jutted out as if it were held up by an invisible wire. Her ass was the same color as her breasts—vanilla white. They stood out in bold relief against the tan of her legs and back. Her body was curved into a difficult position, but she held it, as if the entire Hefner dynasty revolved on her round ass and stabbing tits.

"It's all make-up, Willie."

Willie folded the magazine and placed it on a small shelf. "Make-up, mah ass. You cain't make that up."

It appeared that Willie had more to say, but Harry didn't give him a chance. "Long day, Willie."

Sensing that Harry had no time for his aesthetic opinions, he grew sullen. "Damn straight, it's a long day. I been sittin' here for twelve hours breathing this dirt." He started out of the shack toward the parked cars. There were only five left in the lot. As he neared the Lincoln, Willie turned and shouted, "Ain't no damn air conditioning in that fuckin' shack!"

Harry wished he had given him a few more minutes to expound on the virtues of the Playmate.

Willie moved like a tired club fighter. He slouched to his right and rolled on the balls of his feet. He seemed to be expecting a sudden left hook to come whistling out of the darkness.

Harry checked his watch; it was nine fifteen. He heard the powerful engine rev up and the squeal of the tires. He moved away from the shack and took a dollar bill out of the soggy roll.

Willie had the car turned around, pointing to the street. The headlights flared into Harry's eyes. Willie roared up, slammed the brakes, and threw the gearshift to P. The nose of the big car dipped under the impact of the abrupt stop.

As he slid out of the driver's seat, Harry handed him the bill. Willie's dropped right eye glinted in the streaking light coming from the shack. He pocketed the bill and said, "Ain't no tapes missin'."

"I just asked you to keep an eye on them."

"Yeah, well, ain't no one stealin' nothin' heah. Sheeit! You slip me an ace and everything's cool."

Harry dropped his jacket onto the back seat, climbed in, flipped the air conditioning on. Willie stood alongside, squinting down at him. Harry smiled. "You know, Willie, you're wrong about me. I'm on your side. I told you this morning. Right on!"

"Right on to what?"

Harry gave in to an uncontrollable urge. And, in a voice like Uncle Ben's in *Salesman*, he said, "To Biafra! Come to Biafra, Willie! There's a fortune to be made!" He flipped the gear lever to D, stepped hard on the gas, and screeched out of the lot.

Willie ducked the dust and watched the taillights disappear. As he started back to the shack, he muttered to himself: "Motherfucker... Goddam crazy Kike! Goddam Jews run the whole motherfuckin' world. And talkin' shit... all the time talkin' shit!" The tirade calmed him down. Willie had no way of knowing that he had leveled his anti-Semitic venom at a man whose theology had been cross-lit by Roman Catholic candles and the flashing numbers on the tote board.

Harry was in the fast lane, northbound on the Hollywood Freeway. He was angry at himself for the tension with Willie. After all, Willie showed up every day and nothing was ever missing. And he was honest. Willie was the same pain in the ass at Christmas as he was in July. Yes, he was honest; and he looked like Ezzard Charles.

Harry thought that sooner or later he'd reach Willie; he'd bridge the gap. Maybe they'd shoot a round of pool together. That's it. They'd play eight-ball or Chicago, and he would let Willie win. Afterward, they'd have a pizza or a hamburger. Whatever. But they'd work it out.

He pulled off at the Highland Avenue exit and saw the large, illumined cross above the freeway. He thought it had no serenity, no dignity, no reason for being there. It had the latent menace of hooded sheets and the decay of roadside Jesus signs. He wondered what righteous citizens had taken it upon themselves to plant that symbol of Christianity in so rank a place. But then, nothing was above the hustle. They had Jesus doing his number on Broadway at thirty dollars a pop; all the beards and long hairs and the sharp operators behind the lights, drooling over the grosses—and he remembered the crucifixes his mother had planted everywhere.

Harry turned right on Sunset and Highland, and drove past the small bars and dome-shaped eastern temples that studded the lower Strip. Those mystical religions that preyed on the lonely, blue-haired women, who used the guru's triple-talk to heat up their empty beds.

The car was comfortably cool now and Harry switched the air conditioner to Low. At the corner of La Cienega and Sunset he took advantage of the long, three-way light, put the gear lever into Park, leaned over and opened the glove compartment.

He groped through papers, pencils, Kleenex, Jan's hairbrush, and finally came up with a small vial of cologne. The traffic light had gone from red to amber, but Harry ignored it. He sprayed the cool liquid around his face and neck; he opened the top three buttons of his shirt, spraying his chest and underarms. The light went green and the horns behind him complained. But Harry took his time. He sprayed his hands, then dropped the vial onto the back seat. The horns had swollen into an angry chorus. Harry put the car in gear and crossed La Cienega just as the green went to amber. A convoy of furious citizens were stuck with a long red and leaned on their horns for relief.

The traffic thickened and slowed to a crawl. The Lincoln was now in the heart of the Strip, whose neon pulse throbbed, flashing multi-colored signals, summoning up its nocturnal animals. And they were there: prowling, sniffing, hunting, seeking a score.

Harry watched them as they milled and swirled past Gazzari's. It was a mélange of costumes out of an Edith Head nightmare: tourists in loud Hawaiian shirts; flower children in printed maxis; Hell's Angels in gleaming black leather; groupie girls with thigh-length minis; blacks in huge Afros wearing caftans; a few teenagers in hot pants; acid-heads in dungarees, barefoot and barechested. They swam back and forth in front of Sneaky Pete's. A confused, psychedelic stream, staining the once-proud boulevard. Harry thought the pavement must have ached for the patent leather of Valentino and the high pumps of Theda Bara.

Rolling slowly west, he saw a blonde girl in jeans standing in front of Cyrano's. She carried some copies of The *Free Press* under her left arm and had her right thumb in the air. Harry flashed his right blinker and pulled up to the curb. He reached over and opened the passenger door. The pretty face wore a sweet smile.

Chapter 23

Myra ran the few feet to the open door, jumped in, and dumped the newspapers onto Harry's jacket in the back seat.

"You put in a long day, mister."

"Every day." He eased the car back into the westward flow of traffic.

"It smells nice in here."

"Jade."

"What?"

"My after-shave lotion, I put some on."

They stopped for the light at Doheny. Two helmeted policemen had a pair of youths spread-eagled against a wall. The spinning light of the prowl car threw crimson splashes across Myra's face.

"Where are you going?" she asked.

"Nowhere."

"Really?"

"Really."

She sucked the tip of her forefinger, studying him. "Listen. You remember the pad I told you about, at Manhattan Beach? The one I share with the pilot?"

"I remember."

"Well, he's away tonight. You want to take me?"

He glanced at her for a second. "Sure. I'll take you."

The traffic had thinned; they were into Beverly Hills. He increased his speed and reached down for the car phone. Myra watched, fascinated, as Harry gave his station number to the mobile operator; after a brief pause, he pressed the Talk button.

"*Bueno. Carmella? Si, buenos noches. Por favor no me espere. No necesito cenar. Si. Gracias, adiós.*"

He replaced the receiver on its cradle.

Myra said, "That knocks me out."

"What?"

"The car phone. It's trippy. Say, was that your home?"

Harry nodded.

"Is your wife Spanish?"

"No. That was the maid. She's Mexican."

"A maid... hey, you must be swinging... I mean lots of bread."

"We're all right."

She pulled her lower lip into her mouth. Her top teeth closed over the full curve.

They were passing the softly lit orange walls of the Beverly Hills Hotel.

"How come you speak Spanish?"

"My father worked in a Puerto Rican neighborhood. When I was very young, I helped him after school."

"What kind of work?"

"Pharmacy."

"You mean a drugstore?"

"That's right."

"That must have been kicky... with all those drugs around."

He smiled. "No. In those days, the only drug I knew about was Milk of Magnesia. The least excuse, and they'd shoot it right up your can."

Her laughter was cute and contagious. She shook her head and repeated, "Milk of Magnesia."

He stopped for the light at Bedford, looked down, picked up a cassette, checked the label, and slipped it into the tape deck. It was "Mack The Knife" with Lotte Lenya singing in German.

The light changed, the traffic was sparse. Harry moved the red needle up to fifty.

Myra said, "You know I made a porny."

"What?"

"A porny. Two weeks ago. You know, a blue movie. It was a gas. They paid me fifty dollars."

She spoke in sudden bursts. Harry thought she sounded like Wonder Woman in the old comic strip.

"Can you imagine? Fifty bucks."

He nodded. "That's a lot of money."

"It was a gas. We were in this bedroom... me and two boys, both gay. And all the time this bull-dyke is on her knees, holding the camera... fixing lights. I mean, we're naked and there she is... I started to laugh and she says 'Cut.' Just like in the movies... 'Cut.' Well, she tells this one boy to lay down and I sit on him. The other boy is behind me, playing with his friend. We start to groove, and all of a sudden the dyke pokes the lens right into us. Well, I burst out laughing, fell off the boy and sat on the floor. I couldn't stop."

They passed the huge medieval walls of U.C.L.A.

Harry asked, "What happened?"

"Oh, the dyke got mad. But she paid me. They finished with the two boys. It was trippy. Really trippy. Hard to believe people actually pay to see that junk."

He glanced at her. "How old are you? The truth."

"The truth? I'll be nineteen in November."

"What about your parents?"

"My mother's dead."

"I'm sorry."

"She was killed... on the Hollywood Freeway. By a drunk. Head on. The cops said she never had a chance. My father collected some money."

"Do you see your father?"

"Once in a while. He sells Wonder Bread. He has a route in the Valley."

And there it was: Wonder Woman's father sells Wonder Bread.

"Say, do you mind if I change that music?"

"No. Go ahead."

She slid over toward him, pulled the cassette, switched the radio on and found some soft rock.

She leaned back and said, "Why do you listen to that?"

Harry saw the big, green sign indicating the Freeway, and slowed to the right. "Why do I listen to what?"

"To that German music."

He took the pack of Shermans out. "Because it's right out of the Berlin Zoo."

"I don't understand."

"Forget it. Look, will you light one of these for me?"

Myra took the pack, searched for the lighter, found it and pushed it in. While waiting for the lighter she grew pensive and the sound of her words turned blue. "I hate zoos. Those animals—they look at you with such sad-sad eyes. It's like they're asking you why they're there."

The lighter popped. Myra extracted it and nudged the tip of the cigarette into the glowing red circle. She got it going and replaced the lighter. For a few seconds she watched the grey smoke curl and weave, then almost to herself she said, "I read somewhere that animals, especially the big cats, the lions and tigers, always return to a place of beauty, a place they remember."

Harry swung the Lincoln onto the southbound ramp of the San Diego Freeway and pressed the gas pedal to the floor. The big car leaped forward, shooting ahead into the access lane. He threw the left blinker, slanting toward the fast lane; he gained the lane and held the needle at seventy. Myra handed the glowing cigarette to him as he pressed two buttons on the door panel. Obediently, the front windows slid down. The rush of warm air filled the car.

He took a deep drag, exhaled and said, "Tell me, if you could have anything in the world, what would you want?"

Without the slightest pause she said, "To ball Mick Jagger."

"Mick Jagger?"

The wind caught the tips of her hair. "He's very groovy. Do you know his music?"

He nodded.

"Well?" she asked.

"They all sound the same to me."

"You're wrong. Mick's got his own sound."

He tossed the cigarette out. "Listen. You know who Louis Armstrong was?"

She repeated the name, then paused for a few seconds and smiled. "Oh, sure. He's that old black man. He used to make faces. I saw him once when I was little. On the Ed Sullivan Show."

"Well, he may have made faces, but let me tell you . . . If Mick Jagger could whistle, just whistle Armstrong's intro to 'West End Blues,' I'd give him an A in hip."

"I never heard that song."

"You should. You should hear it sometime." He threw the right blinker and began to ease over toward the outside lane. "Why did you want to ball me?"

"Well, you smelled nice. You looked nice, and I was a little stoned."

He steered up the Century Boulevard ramp. Two hundred feet overhead, a jet screamed into the east-

west final approach. Harry wondered where it was coming
from and how many of its passengers dreaded the moment
the giant wheels kissed the ground. And how many looked
forward to that moment, relieved that the sealed journey
was over.

The Lincoln moved west on Century, heading toward
the coast highway. He reduced the speed; the rush of the
wind diminished; the sound level of the music came up.

As they reached the Pacific, the heat of the desert wind
decreased.

Myra snapped her fingers in time with Three Dog
Night. She looked over at him and, with that same total
innocence, said, "I have some great grass. You dig grass?"

The cool air felt refreshing.

"I haven't had any in years." He smiled. "We called it
Gage."

"Gage?"

"That's right. Gage. A long time ago...I played the
drums. We used to smoke it. We called it Gage."

Myra's long, blond hair, caught by the Pacific, danced in
and out of the car. She turned the music up, slipped off
her sandals and pushed her feet up against the dash. She
leaned her head on the open window frame, looked up at
the starless black sky, and softly whispered, "Gage..."

Chapter 24

The red New York skies leaked a thin, dirty, odorless rain.
It streaked the windows of the small French restaurant on
East Fifty-third Street.

It was past midnight and only a handful of customers
still lingered in the small, elegant room. Jan and her girl
friend, Lisa, were toying with their Crème de Menthes;
Lisa's husband and their bachelor friend, a TV program-
ming executive, were sipping Martel brandies. They were
sitting at a window table, Jan and the TV man on one side,
Lisa and her husband facing them.

Lisa's husband, Sam, was a dentist to the very rich, and
all through dinner he reveled in his secret Novocained

conversations with the famous and the affluent. The television executive's name was Spencer Harris. He kept his leg pressed against Jan's throughout the dinner. She was fascinated with his hands; they were formless and heavy; like two lumps of pale clay that had oozed fingers. From the lines around his eyes and mouth she guessed he was in his late forties. The irony of sitting next to one of the powers responsible for the garbage spewing out of the tube did not escape her. She felt as if she were having dinner with one of those infamous Nazis who was still at large.

The two men conversed without let-up, but neither one actually listened to the other. Lisa and Jan chatted about furniture, clothes, diet and children, and the benefits of Swiss schools. But it was forced. The voices of the men dominated the table.

Spencer talked about Neilsen numbers, ratings and demographics: he broke the country down by sex, by age, by region, by income, by religion, by color. He was elated that a show called "Space Spies" had finally penetrated women over thirty-five in the southwest. On the second brandy he confided how he had a hush-hush but excruciating meeting with the president of the network, a Major Lewis.

It was hush-hush because it involved the canceling of a show. It was excruciating because it was a hit show. A long-running situation comedy about captured American soldiers. And now, five years and over one hundred segments later, the Major decided it was not really nice to make fun of American men that had been captured and penned up.

A third brandy just fueled the diatribe. Spencer grabbed Sam's arm and said, "Can you imagine that hypocritical son of a bitch? After five years he wants 'Brophy's Bums' knocked off the air."

Sam nodded in feigned sympathy; he was thinking about a twenty-five-hundred-dollar cap job he had lined up for next week.

Spencer sipped some brandy. "Can you imagine, Sam? For five years 'Brophy's Bums' has been beating that pratfalling bull-dyke on the other network. How do you replace a show like that?"

Spencer increased the pressure on Jan's knee and dropped

his left paw onto her thigh, squeezed it and said, "We own thirty million eyes from seven thirty to eight every Tuesday night for the last five years and suddenly the Major gets conscience."

Spencer looked at the women, expecting a comment, but neither Lisa nor Jan spoke.

Sam picked up the cue. He said, "It isn't just your business, Spencer. I deal with the same hypocrisy. That goddam coon-shouter, Helen Cates, needed an inlay. I charged her seven hundred bucks and she complained. I had a running battle with her business manager for weeks. And I happen to know she pays her eighteen-year-old resident faggot that much per week for the pleasure of his company."

Spencer nodded, sipped the last of his brandy and concurred. "That's the trouble with the whole country; misplaced values."

Jan stared at the light rain streaking the windows and wondered what she was doing there. Lisa touched her hand.

"How long are you staying?"

Jan looked at her. "I think I'm going home right after the funeral."

Spencer draped his left arm around her shoulder. "Listen, forgive us for having bored you with all this shop talk. But I think I've got a terrific idea. I have to fly down to San Juan for the weekend on business; why don't we all hit the old runway together?"

Lisa and Sam exclaimed in unison, "Terrific!"

The TV man followed it up quickly. "I mean, it's all on the house. Al Gross, the comedian, is playing the Sheraton down there and we're building a show around him for a mid-season replacement; buy him cheap, too. He's left all his money on the crap tables. Hell of a buy. The guy's really hurting. A very funny man. A bit of a prick, but very funny."

Lisa said, "Why not? Harry won't mind. I mean as long as he knows we're along."

Sam added, "It would be damn selfish of Harry to deny you a sunny weekend with old friends."

Lisa smiled. "It would be pure male chauvinism."

Spencer's arm slid off her shoulder and his shapeless

hand closed around her wrist. "Come on, Janet, what do you say?"

She shook his hand off and said, "I won't be here for the weekend."

Spencer shrugged. "Folks, we have a very sick lady in our midst."

Jan made it as cold as she knew how. "I'd really like to go now."

In the back seat of the Mercedes, Spencer pressed close to her side. Sam drove with Lisa sitting alongside him. As they neared the Plaza, Spencer whispered in her ear, "The hell with San Juan. I can send my assistant. Let's sneak off to Grossinger's, a short ride upstate. We can leave right after your uncle's affair."

No one had come on this way with her since she was a young girl and she didn't know how to handle it. She stared out at the wet streets.

They pulled up to the Fifth Avenue side of the Plaza. The TV man jumped out and said, "If you change your mind, phone my secretary. It's the all-color network. You can see our letters from your window."

Jan ignored him and turned to Lisa and Sam, thanked them for the dinner and promised she'd phone.

Spencer got into the front seat and the big white Mercedes shot away from the curb.

The small suite seemed like a cell. Jan stood at the sealed window watching the rain fall. She checked the time; it was one fifteen; that meant ten fifteen in Los Angeles. She went to the phone and dialed the single digit marked Long Distance. She gave the L.A. number, then her name and room number.

It rang seven times before Carmella's voice came on. "*Bueno? Bueno?*"

"It's me, Carmella. Is the *señor* at home?"

The Spanish was rapid. "*No. El señor no esta, él avisa que no llega. No quiere cenar.*"

Jan said, "Please, Carmella. Speak English."

Carmella apologized in Spanish, then went to English. "The *señor* call. He say, no wait me for dinner."

"Did he say when he'd be home?"

Carmella asked her to speak slowly.

Jan spaced the question. "Did—he—say—when—he'd —be—home?"

Carmella's voice brightened, "No, *señora*. He no say."

Jan sighed. "*Gracias, Carmella.*"

She hung up and went into the bedroom, took off her clothes and hung them up methodically, then checked the simple black dress she would wear at the funeral tomorrow. She hung it back up and slipped her silk peignoir on, went out to the sitting room and put on the light, then cracked the door of her bedroom, so that there was a trace of light.

Harry was probably having dinner with Phil. She'd call him at eleven in the morning, about eight o'clock his time.

She picked up the phone on the night table, dialed the operator, and left a morning wake-up call. She'd be certain to get him at eight. She'd tell him she was sorry she had been so abrupt with him and that she was coming home tomorrow night.

The funeral was at one. She'd book an evening flight to L.A. That gave her lots of time. She thought about trying Harry at Phil's house . . . no, he'd think she was checking up on him. No, she'd let it go. Tomorrow morning—eight o'clock his time.

She turned on her side and the TV man was right: out of her window, in the distance atop a great glass skyscraper the three letters glowed in the misty rain.

There it was. The ministry of propaganda. She thought someone ought to call "Brophy" and tell him to start looking for work.

Chapter 25

The waves curled and crested, breaking angrily against their eternal enemy of sand. A spill of light splashed across the veranda. Soft rock fused with the rhythmic roar of the surf.

Harry was stripped to his boxer shorts; Myra wore his shirt. The high quality Mexican grass had placed a euphoric blanket around them and they were giddy and beautifully stoned. Harry laughed as he watched the slow rhythm of the Pacific.

She had her arm around his waist and giggled, "This is laughing grass, right? I mean it's the first time I've seen you laugh . . . right?"

He slammed his fist on the railing and stammered, "No . . . no . . . it's . . . it's not the grass. It's the sea . . ." He gave in to a quick burst and struggled on. "The sea . . . my partner wants to smell the sea; fish, worms . . ." He gusted again, then caught his voice. "Clams, oysters . . . Phil, the fisherman, the man who stood between Franco and Sam Bronston . . . the fucking Coney Island trolley hopper." He surrendered to the grass again and doubled up. He hadn't laughed like this in years.

He gasped for breath and stumbled on. "His . . . eyes . . . they . . ." He burst again and started again, "They . . . they burn. His heart burns and his . . . his factories burn . . . and the Lincoln Brigade went up in smoke." Harry got the last word out and succumbed to a long whoop of laughter.

Myra watched him bend over and hold his stomach. For a long minute the gales wracked the length of his body; then the cadence slowed. Short bursts came and went, winding down into chuckles and, finally, a series of gasps.

The wind whipped around them. Myra shivered, "It's cold." She put some pressure on his waist and moved him toward the sliding glass doors.

The room faced the sea and was dominated by a large, circular water bed. A bookcase ran around the far wall and nautical decorations were everywhere. A fishing net was stretched across the ceiling with an enormous starfish at its center and a tiger-skin rug, complete with glazed eyes and gaping jaws, covered eight feet of floor space. The room was lit by a single lamp, shaped like an old-time whaling ship's lantern; it was fixed to the near wall and angled down toward the bed. The sheets and blankets looked as though they had been through a blender.

With Myra guiding him, Harry staggered to the bed and fell on it, face up. The water sloshed under the impact of his weight and Myra climbed over him and sat up on her haunches, looking down at him. He was smiling, trying to decipher the lyrics coming out of the stereo. She leaned over, her long hair covering his face, and kissing his forehead. She then raised up and said, "Turn over."

From far off, he said, "Why?"

The innocence was there again. "Please. Turn over."

Harry shifted his weight to his left elbow, angled to the side and collapsed face down. He felt her fingers tracing the ridge of his shoulders; then, moving lower, they touched the first scar and stopped.

He pronounced it carefully. "Italy."

"In a fight?"

"In a war."

"In Italy?"

Harry nodded into the sheets. "In Italy."

She grappled with that; then, in a factual tone, said, "We never fought a war with Italy."

"Yes, we did." He turned over heavily and looked up at her.

She smiled. "You're older than thirty-eight."

"Got another joint?"

Myra stretched over toward the night table. The shirt ran up her back, exposing her ass and a small patch of blond fur in front. She got the grass going, sucked hard, blinking her eyes, and held the smoke down in her lungs. She exhaled, coughed, and passed the joint to Harry. His face glowed as he drew hard on the grass. He held the smoke briefly, then laughed it out.

Myra had drawn herself back up into a sitting position. "Come on. Tell me."

"What?"

"How old you are."

"Twenty-five hundred. I helped Moses part the Red Sea." He paused, dragged and laughed. "And there was Kamu, Kamu swimming against the fucking tide." His voice suddenly lost the hilarity. "I wonder if Audrey knows . . . I wonder if she knows they killed Kamu."

Myra laughed. "Hey—you're on a trip."

He drew some more smoke, coughed and with speed and intensity said, "Listen . . . Listen, we're looking across the Jordan. Me, Moses and Albert Speer, and Moses asks: 'Tell me, Al, did you know about them?' And Speer starts to scream . . ." Harry tried for a German accent. "'I nefer asked Keitel! I nefer asked Goebbels! I nefer asked Himmler! The camps were not within the perimeter of my activities!'"

Harry dropped the German accent and smiled. "And Moses, he's cool. He says, 'It's okay, Al . . . you still make the best chariots this side of the Jordan.' And old Albert, he says, 'Well, after all, I do my best.'"

Myra took the joint from between his fingers and inhaled deeply, holding it, then blowing the consumed smoke down at Harry. She giggled, "I think you're freaking out."

His right hand fell on her knee and his voice was high-pitched. "Listen, kid . . . listen. We're in first class on the 'Enola Gay.' Me and Ray and Ruby and Oswald and Tippett and Sirhan and Jack and Bobbie and Malcolm and King and Medgar . . . and the stewardess is Marilyn . . . and she's smiling at everybody . . . and then the Captain's voice crackles on, and it's Eichmann, with a southern accent."

Harry tinged his voice with a trace of the South. "Good afternoon, ladies and gentlemen. I should like to point out that high-rise on the port side is the new Mai Lai Sheraton: forty stories, three olympic-sized swimming pools, six massage parlors and an eighteen hole golf course."

Harry dropped back to his own tone. "Then Ruby jumps up and yells, 'What about the ditch, you schmuck!'"

Myra laughed, gave him the roach. He sucked hard on it and held the smoke, then blew it out. He raised up on his elbow.

His voice raged, "This Egyptian broad finds me in the bullrushes. She says, 'Cuban Pete, you're just in time for the fourth at Bay Meadows.' Only she's Peggy Lee and they're playing the 'Jersey Bounce.' The rhythm that really counts." He dropped back, flat onto the bed. She took the joint back. It was quiet for a moment, only the sound of the waves and the soft rock. Harry's eyes searched the ceiling, then he said, "Myra, how would you like it if the last thing you heard was 'fasten your seatbelts and observe the no smoking sign'?"

She smiled.

His hand left her thigh and his eyes left the ceiling and he looked up at her. "I have the Tablets. I'm coming down with the Eleventh Commandment."

"What does it say?"

"It says . . . it says, 'No Parking This Side of the Street.'"

She leaned over and placed her lips against his ear. "Come on. Let's make it again."

Harry shifted his weight and, using his elbow for support, sat up and swung his legs over the side of the bed, his feet touching the tiger skin.

Myra looked at his scarred back, then took a last drag, reached over toward the oyster-shell ashtray, and crushed the joint out. Moving close, she put her arms around Harry's neck. "Come on. Let's do it."

"No, no. Look, let's play a game."

"A game? What kind of game?"

He turned and faced her. "A game-game. Now, the game is . . . name famous people. That's it. Name famous people. You start."

"Just anyone?"

He nodded. "Anyone famous."

"Dead people, too?"

"Why not? Sure, dead people, too."

She smiled. "Okay. I'll start. John Lennon."

"Mo Purtill."

Her forehead wrinkled. "Mo Purtill?"

Harry slid down onto the tiger skin and looked up at her. "Yes. Mo Purtill. He played drums for Glenn Miller."

The frown was still there. "Glenn Miller?"

He waved his hand. "Look, kid. I'll name one, then you go. I won't know yours, and you won't know mine. What's the difference? We trust each other. Let's play."

She tossed her blond mane. "Okay. The Rolling Stones."

"Henry Wallace."

"Strawberry Statement."

"Hermann Goering."

"Goering? Was he a singer?"

"Yeah. A soprano. Come on, play."

"Steppenwolf."

"Fred Allen."

"Joe Cocker."

"Cookie Lavagetto."

"Bob Dylan."

"F.D.R."

"The Mashed Potatoes."

"Myrna Loy."

"Mary Hopkins."

"Durante."

"Blood, Sweat and Tears."

Harry smiled, "Churchill."

"Peter Fonda."

"Fiorello La Guardia."

"Crosby, Stills, Nash and Young."

"Abe Reles."

"Doors."

"Rommel."

"Grass Roots."

His voice grew louder. "Jack Teagarten."

"Jefferson Airplane."

He slurred, started, stopped, then laughed. "Heinrich Himmler. Fucking Heinrich Himmler."

She laughed. "Moody Blues."

"Gabriel Heatter."

She paused, thinking, eyes closed, then smiled and blurted, "The Hollies."

Harry got up on his knees. "Pierre Laval. They shot him."

"They shot him?"

"Yeah. They shot him. Come on, play."

She put the tip of her finger to her lips, thinking, then brightened. "Jimmy Webb."

Harry slammed his fist down onto the tiger's head. "Carl Hubbell."

Myra was stopped. She looked through the glass doors to the sea.

His voice was heavy and loud. "Come on, kid. Play the game."

She looked back down at him. "Uh...let's see..." Then quickly, "Eric Burden and War."

"Good. Joe Stalin."

"Jimi Hendrix. He's dead, you know."

"No, I didn't. Uh...uh, Helen O'Connell."

"Three Dog Night."

"Beau Jack."

"Jethro Tull."

Harry thought for a second, "Major Bowes."

She balled her hands into fists and beat the bed. "Uh...uh...Oh, shit...shit...uhm, Jerry Lee Lewis."

He shot back, "Eddie Arcaro."

She slammed the bed with her fists and bounced up and down; her breasts jumped in and out of the shirt; the water sloshed in the bed. "Oh, shit...dammit...dammit..."

Harry's shout was laced with desperation. "Come on! Come on! Names, kid! Names! Play the game!"

She grew frightened and defiantly said, "Che Guevara."

"Good kid! Terrific!" He coughed, then yelled, "Ava Gardner."

She struggled, then managed, "Eldridge Cleaver."

"Martin Bormann."

She fired back, "Dustin Hoffman."

"Bob Feller."

"The Grateful Dead."

"Fats Waller."

"Uh . . . Nixon."

Harry laughed. "That's very good. Nixon! That's excellent. Okay, my turn. Jimmy Lunceford."

"Agnew."

"Christ, that's even better! Okay, Rodgers and Hart."

She began to bounce up and down again. She pressed her hand to her forehead. "Oh, fuck . . . what's that Frenchman's name?"

"What Frenchman?"

"Oh, shit . . . that actor. He has a funny nose." Her hand came off her forehead and she shrieked, "Belmondo!"

Harry beamed, and with pure admiration, said, "That's great, kid! Now, let's see . . . yeah, Laurel and Hardy."

She stared at him.

"Come on, play, kid!"

She started to unbutton the shirt.

"What are you doing? The game's not over!"

She shook her head slowly. "I'm stuck. I can't think. I hate this game. I want to . . ."

Harry shouted. "Stuck! Stuck! How can you be stuck?" He crawled over to the bed, putting his hands on her thighs. The shirt fell off her shoulders; her breasts tumbled out. She was naked now, looking down at him, the ends of her hair in his eyes.

Desperately, he asked, "Let me help you." His hands slid down to her ankles and closed tightly around them. He stared up into her grey eyes, but they were glazed tunnels that mirrored nothing.

His voice was hoarse, and the words gushed. "Joe Lewis! The Hindenburg! Orson Welles! John Garfield! Goebbels! Timoshenko! Gabby Hartnett! Mezz Mezzerow!

Meyer Lansky! Count Basie! Billy Daniels! Willie Pep! Ted Atkinson!"

He caught his breath. The sweat pouring down from his forehead made his face glisten in the streaky light. "Whirlaway! Armed! Gallorette! Those were racehorses, baby! Real racehorses! Thoroughbreds. Mungo! Daffy Dean! Ace Parker! Tuffy Leemans! Sid Luckman! Mel Hein! Ruffing! Mark Clark! Whitlow Wyatt! Franco! J. Carrol Naish! O'Hara! Hammett! Steinbeck! Odets!" He gasped, fighting for breath.

He released her ankles and slid his hands up to her thighs. "Pittsburgh Phil! Cerdan! Luke Hamlin! Chamberlain! Glenn Gray! Akim Tamiroff!" He raised his hands and clenched his fists. "Christ...Christ..."

Myra was frightened now. She put her hand on his shoulder, but he threw it off.

"Goddammit! Uh...uh...Popeye! Lulu! Daddy Warbucks! The Phantom! W. C. Fields!...Uh, Jesus!...Oh, Christ!..."

Harry looked at the dead eyes of the tiger. His voice broke and lowered. "Joe Penner...wanna buy a duck? Wanna buy a duck?"

She put both hands on his shoulders. "Hey, you okay? You want something?"

"Yes. Yes...I want something. I want to see the girl in the Cole Porter song. I want to see Freddie Fitzsimmons throw a knuckle-ball. I want to see Ray Robinson throw a left hook. I want to see Vito Tamulis throw his change. Just once more, I want to see Stymie closing in the stretch. I want to see the hookers on the Via Roma. I want to see a lucky mortar hit an 88. I want to see Barney Ross in tough. I want to see DiMaggio with the hitting streak on the line. I want...I want to hear Lena Horne at the old Cotton Club. I want to hear Billie Holiday sing 'Fine And Mellow'...I want to walk in the kind of rain that never washes the perfume away." Harry fought off the sobs and gulped the air. His eyes riveted into Myra. "Christ Almighty, I want to root for something...I want to love something...an idea, a dog, a cat, a song, a somebody...an anybody, an anything..."

Harry fell back prone on the tiger skin, panting, and shivering as the Pacific breeze closed over him.

Myra watched him unflex his hands. She saw the goosebumps on his arms. She pulled the blanket off the bed and covered him. Kneeling over him, she said, "You're on a real bummer. Are you okay now?"

He looked at her thrusting breasts, the red nipples. "I'm all right. Sure, I'm fine. Got a daughter your age in school."

"You like me?"

"I don't know, kid. I don't know..."

Myra crawled under the blanket and curved her naked body tight against him. She slipped her right hand under his shorts and took the shrunken flesh between her thumb and forefinger. She started to play. And there was life. She felt its comma-like shape start to rise. And that was the thing. The groove. To bring them from lifelessness to throbbing excitement. To watch them flush and pant and scream and curse, and then grow weak.

He had psyched out; a bad trip, and he had spilled his madness all over her, and he owed her one and she would drain him; draw the juices out of that scarred body. He was old; but there was something groovy here. There was something heavy here, in this blue-eyed, grey-haired silk suit, who played sad German music.

Chapter 26

The medicine chest was filled with a cosmetic cross-section of international air travel. Harry brushed his teeth courtesy of TWA, shaved with cream by Aerolineas Peruanas, used cologne by Sabena, and dried his face with an Air France towel.

Leaving his shirt unbuttoned at the neck, he slipped his jacket on and tiptoed into the bedroom. Myra was asleep on the tiger-skin rug; she seemed more innocent and younger than the awake Myra. She shifted her weight slightly and murmured something about Italy.

Harry opened the glass doors and stepped onto the veranda. He took a deep breath and thought that Phil was not wrong. Despite the Santa Ana condition, the air was fresh and clean. The early morning sun backlit the sea, changing the color of the waves from black to green. A flock of seagulls were breakfasting on sand crabs and, farther up, two dogs were locked in violent intercourse.

Slowly his eyes swept the low hills, the wide, flat beach, and the gentle rolling surf...

Beach red! Beach red! Point blank artillery! Taking frontal fire! Naval shelling negative! Repeat negative! They're running Goliaths! They're dropping Butterflies! Heinkels! Dropping Butterflies! Where's the air, goddammit! Mosquitos! Yes! Panel's out! Bravo and Charlie Company into minefields! No chance! No chance! We need air! Beach red...

But the sand was beige, and the sky was blue and the seagulls were feasting. And Harry lit the first Sherman of the day.

He turned his back to the sea and looked through the streaky glass doors at the sleeping child on the tiger-skin rug. He had used her in place of Frankfurter, but the result was the same. After all, who can explain dead soldiers at fashion shows, and peaceful streets under heavy armored assault, Ebbetts Field in mirrors, big red horses flying in the stretch, and dead actors at four in the morning in Rick's Place, and sad Italian songs, and Linda Darnell in the desert...

They were the uncoded IBM cards spinning out of Harry's memory, piling up in the tray of his consciousness. And there they waited for some undiscovered calculus, for some ultimate mathematician who could run them through a computer and formulate an answer.

Harry exhaled and the Pacific grabbed the smoke. He thought about Meyer, and how incredible that after seventy years of battering, those grey Russian eyes could still see life through a cube of sugar.

He tossed the cigarette over the railing, went back inside, quietly walked over to the night table and picked up his tie.

"Hey, good morning." She was leaning on her elbow. The covers had fallen, exposing her breasts.

Harry smiled. "Good morning."

She blinked. "What time is it?"

"Go back to sleep. It's early."

She yawned and said, "Where are you going?"

"Work."

"Hey... what's your name?"

He smiled. "Cuban Pete."

She laughed the question, "Cuban Pete?" She stretched her arms over her head, the firm globes of her breasts thrusting out. "No kidding... come on, what's your name?"

"What's the difference?"

"No difference. Will I see you again?" It sounded genuine.

"Sure."

"Good. You know where I am."

"Yes. On the Strip."

"Right."

Harry took a roll of bills out of his pocket; they were damp and stuck together. He extracted a twenty from the pack. "I'd like you to buy something for yourself."

The blond mane shook. "You don't have to do that. What we did has nothing to do with bread."

Hesitantly, he said, "I know that... I just... well, it's something I want to do." He put the bill on the night table.

"Please. Take that back." She paused, then repeated, "Come on, please. Take it back."

"Okay." He said it softly and picked up the bill.

They stared at each other. She began to say, "Hey... it was groovy..." but the words drifted away, and she gave a slight shrug.

The heat was noticeably stronger on the street side of the house. Harry opened the rear door of the Lincoln and took out the small pile of *Free Press*. He stacked them neatly at the front door of the beach house, walked back to the car, slammed the rear door shut, and slid into the driver's seat.

He turned the engine over and pushed all the buttons: windows up, air conditioner on, FM radio on. The blue car moved out into the light morning traffic.

He had enjoyed Myra in a strange way; he kept thinking of her as Wonder Woman; that he had made it with Captain Marvel's girl friend. He couldn't tell how it had registered with her. He thought, her contemporaries would have doubled his output; but maybe he took something off her fast ball; a change of pace.

Driving along the coast highway he thought again about

that wide beach and low hills, how it would be all right for the LCIs and the LSTs, but once the ramps went down . . .

The announcer's voice punctured his thoughts. He turned the volume down. ". . . With Santa Ana conditions still prevailing. At seven A.M., the temperature reading at Los Angeles International Airport is seventy-nine degrees; seventy-nine at the Civic Center, with Burbank and the Valley registering eighty-two. Moderate to heavy smog is predicted for the entire Los Angeles Basin. Children are advised against strenuous activity. The fires in the Santa Cruz mountains are still raging out of control. In Washington, the President stated that Welfare is the number-one problem in the nation. In Saigon, a military spokesman stressed that the new ARVN offensive in the A Shau Valley is being waged without American participation, excepting Medevac helicopters, which are being used to evacuate the wounded."

Harry switched off the San Diego Freeway onto the Santa Monica fork going downtown. He thought he'd get off at Robertson, go into Beverly Hills to the club and take a steambath.

Chapter 27

Harry stood naked in front of his locker; the silk suit was in a lump on the bench. Other men, in various stages of undress, exchanged good mornings, and compared muscle tone and the general condition of their respective healths. They were the exercise freaks, the health club addicts, trying to prolong their heartbeats with handball. They ate organic food, had quit smoking, drank little alcohol, swam and ran every day.

Harry thought them absurd: their grand passion in life was the avoidance of death. Still, every month two or three names would be listed, in black borders, on the bulletin board.

He spotted the young Mexican face coming toward him and called out, "Julio!"

Being born in L.A. hadn't straightened Julio's accent

out; the flavor was still Yucateca. "Good morning, Mr. Stoner."

"Good morning. I'd like to have the suit cleaned and pressed; same with the tie...and a shoeshine."

Julio nodded and picked up the suit, tie and shoes. "What about your shirt?"

"I have a fresh one in the locker."

"Okay, Mr. Stoner. Everything right away."

"Thanks, Julio."

Julio went through the green arch toward the steam room area. Harry walked to a nearby table that supported a huge pile of white towels, took one, fastened it around his waist, then draped another around his neck.

Lights bounced off the white tile. Naked, sweat-covered men moved to and from the steam room. To the left of the large room, the sounds of four-wall handball could be heard. The archway to the right opened into a small gym and the sounds of men groaning and straining under weights mixed with the rapid staccato of bag-punching. At the far end, the vapor-covered window of the steam room could be seen. The entire complex smelled of sweat and evergreen leaves.

Harry came out of the locker room and walked over to a round table which held a large, cylindrical coffee dispenser, an ice tray of fresh orange juice, and a black phone with a long extension cord. He picked up a cup and held it under the spigot of the dispenser, sat down and sipped the tasteless brew. He pulled the phone close to him, lifted the receiver, flashed the button up and down rapidly and said, "This is Mr. Stoner. Yes...good morning. I'd like seven three six, six five eight four. Thank you."

Phil's wife answered.

"Linda? Hope I didn't wake you. Good. How are you?" He listened to her usual complaints; the woman seemed to be under continual attack by all manner of disease. "Well, you'll get over it, honey...probably just an allergy." Then followed quickly, "Is Phil awake? Good. Yes, I'll hang on." He sipped some more coffee and glanced up as two men came out of the handball court.

They were soaked with perspiration, faces flushed, chests heaving. The short one said, "Those pricks were lucky; we deserved to win."

The tall partner replied, "Well, we beat them regularly, Judge. A win once in a while keeps them competitive."

The judge shook his head. "That's got nothing to do with it. When you win, you win; when you lose, you lose."

Harry listened to Phil, then replied. "No, I'm not home. I'm at the Club. I won't be coming to the office. I'll meet you at the theatre, at two." Phil asked if something was wrong. "Nothing's wrong. No... No Danish matinees." Phil asked about Meyer. "Yes. I talked to him. Well, I don't know. Meyer is Meyer. He said he'd work it out. Yes... that's right.... Right, Phil, 'bye."

He then asked the operator to dial his house number. After several rings, Carmella answered.

"*Bueno?*"

Harry said, "*Buenos días, Carmella ¿qué pasa?*"

"*Nada pasa, señor.*"

Harry asked, "*Hay algo telefonos?*"

There was a pause, then Carmella said, "*Sí. La señora llamada anoche, tambien esta mañana a las ocho.*"

Harry sighed. "*Gracias. Yo llego por la noche.*"

She said, "*Muy bien, señor. Adiós.*"

Jan had called last night and this morning. Well, he'd think of something. He'd tell her something. He walked wearily, heavily, toward the steam room.

The vapor was thick and the odor of evergreen overpowering; one side of the room was frosted glass; the other three walls were tiled; two wooden benches were riveted into opposite sides of the room; an upper berth, hooked into the far wall, appeared to be unoccupied.

Below, three old men were seated on the bench opposite Harry. One of them was completely hairless, but endowed with enormous purple balls. He read from a financial digest to a heavily lined man with sagging rolls of grey flab, who looked like a tired elephant. Farther up the bench, the third man sat reading the Los Angeles *Times;* a white blanket of fur covered his chest and shoulders and he was not circumcised; his foreskin looked like an anteater's nose.

The three men had been in the steam room for quite a while; their papers were soggy; rivulets of sweat streamed down their faces onto their chests and collected in their large belly-buttons.

The man with the purple balls spoke excitedly. "It's gonna break nine hundred."

"Good," said the elephant.

"I tell you, Charlie, it's gonna break nine hundred."

"Good."

"You were worried, you were crying...four months ago, you were crying...Sell! Sell! Who told you to hold on?"

"You did, Harvey. You said 'hold.'"

"That's not what I said. I said, 'would you cut off your cock for a pimple?' That's what I said."

"That's right, Harvey. That's what you said."

"Sure, I did. Now, look. Look at the Dow-Jones. Almost nine hundred."

Harry stared up at the ceiling. His eyes clenched shut. He raised his arms, soaking up the vapor, trying to come down, trying to relax; but the harsh voice of the man with the purple balls drove right through him.

"Charlie...Charlie, lookit Oxy. Oxy is rolling like a sonofabitch. The fucking Arabs signed a new agreement. Didn't I tell you?"

"Yes. You told me."

"You don't have to be a genius. Just ask yourself...who are those fucking sheiks gonna sell oil to? You can't pump oil up a camel's ass!"

The elephant shrugged. "Well, I thought maybe the Russians...maybe the Arabs would sell to the Russians."

Harvey's gleaming head shook, sending a fine spray of sweat over his companion. He exclaimed loudly, "The Russians! The Russians need more oil like they need more poets. It had to be Oxy!" His purple balls moved up and down in agreement.

The other man wiped the folds of grey skin under his neck and asked, "Okay. But now that we held...you think we should sell?"

"Of course, sell! Now we get out! The war ends. Money gets tight. The market will tumble. Now we get out. We get out and we buy eight percent water bonds."

The elephant nodded.

The furry man with the foreskin seized the break. "Hey, boys, listen to this." He read carefully from the folded paper. "'The U.S. Public Health Service Agency for Disease Control stated that gonorrhea in the United States has now reached epidemic proportions. Among teens and subteens in urban Los Angeles, it has become so virulent that the California State Legislature has declared a Venereal Disease Awareness Month. The once-chic Sunset Strip has become a veritable distribution . . .'"

Harry sprang to his feet, grabbed the paper and threw it against the wall. His towel fell. He stood naked over the three men. The words were slow. "Listen, you bastards, I came in here for some steam and not your early morning bullshit! Now, get the hell out of here! I mean it! Just get up and walk out!"

Confused and frightened, they stared at Harry for a few seconds. His face had turned red; the beads of sweat on his cheeks were like drops of blood.

The elephant rose first, his large, tired face staring at the tiled floor. He was followed by Purple Balls. The man with the white fur and pointy foreskin moved last; he reached the door, held it open and said, "Look, mister, if you want privacy, build a sauna in your house." Without waiting for a reply, he let the door close.

Harry sank back down onto the bench and spread both towels out, lay back, stretched out and watched the tiny beads of water form on the ceiling, hold, then drop—one by one.

Suddenly, from the top tier, an X-ray rose up: a specter, a wraith, a ghost of Dachau; a small shiny head resting on a skeletal body. His eyes had the artificial brightness of low-grade fever and he pointed with a finger that had no flesh.

His voice was a low, sandy growl. "Vitamin EEEEEEE." He wailed the "E". "Vitamin EEEEEEE, that's what all the trouble's about."

Harry did not move. He lay there, welded to the sweating bench, staring up at the remnant of what was once a man.

"You should have told them: Vitamin EEEEE." He dropped the bony finger and fell back down, into the vapor.

Chapter 28

The phone was answered on the second ring. "Doctor Vogel's office."

"Yes. This is Harry Stoner. I'd like to speak to the Doctor. No...I have to speak to him...Yes, thank you."

While he waited, he still tossed it around, but Vogel's cheery salutation made the decision. "No, Jerry, it's not exactly an emergency. I got involved, last night...a very young girl."

Vogel said, "How soon can you get over here?"

"Twenty minutes. I'm a few blocks away at the Club. Right. Thanks, Jerry."

The office was oak-paneled and spacious. The furniture was all leather, all large, all sumptuous; numerous degrees spotted the walls. Piped FM floated in; the lighting was indirect and soft. It could have been the bar in a conservative men's club. There was a fake bookcase from floor to ceiling behind the doctor's desk.

Harry sank down in an easy chair. He never felt comfortable with Vogel; his hair was too long, his gold-rimmed glasses too mod, and, if he had ever lost a patient, there was no trace of it in the unlined thirty-eight-year-old face.

"A little off campus activity?"

"It just happened, Jerry. It wasn't planned."

"When were you exposed?"

"Exposed?"

"When did you fuck her? How long ago?"

Harry shrugged. "I guess about eight hours ago."

Vogel pressed the button on the small speaker. "Marion, will you prepare an injection...wait, hold on...Harry, you ever have a negative reaction to penicillin?"

Harry shook his head.

"All right, Marion, I want one million units G type. Right. Thank you."

Vogel opened a small gold-filled box and took out a long, slim cigarette. "Harry?"

"No thanks."

Vogel spoke through the smoke. "I've tried to quit so many times, I can't remember. How about you?"

"I still use them."

Vogel shook his head. "Poison."

"You know, Jerry, I'm probably over-reacting."

Vogel cut him off. "No point in taking a chance. I meant to tell you, I enjoyed dinner the other evening. Jan is an extraordinary lady."

"Yes. Yes, she is."

The door opened and a Vargas girl came in.

Harry thought she made Willie's Playmate look like a boy. She was stuffed into a starched, white nurse's uniform and her red hair fell out of the white cap in perfect disarray. She set the stainless steel tray on the desk. Harry could see the small jar of creamy fluid, the capped hypodermic needle, the alcohol and a tiny ball of cotton.

She paused, looking down at Vogel, a waitress waiting for the order.

Vogel smiled, "Thank you, Marion."

Her picturesque machine revolved out of the office.

Vogel said, "Lovely girl. She wanted to be an actress, but gave it up."

Harry asked, "Why?"

"I guess she was a lousy lay." Vogel got up, came around the desk, and picked up the tray. "Over by the window, Harry, and drop your pants."

But Harry didn't move.

Vogel stopped and looked at him. "Come on. I don't mean to rush you but I've got them back-to-back today."

Harry said, "I don't want the shot."

"What?"

"I changed my mind. I don't want it. I'm sorry, Jerry. I heard some guy talking at the club and it set me off; but I don't want it."

Vogel's voice took on an official tone. "Look, Harry, it's a good precaution and if you're worried about any records I'll show it as a Vitamin B-1 shot. I mean on the bill."

Harry got up, walked to the window and looked out through the slits in the venetian blinds. He watched the activity on the street for a moment, then turned.

"I don't want it. The girl was all right. If I didn't get anything in Naples, I'll never get it."

Vogel shrugged and went back around his desk and set the tray down. "I made time for you, Harry."

Harry walked back to the chair in front of Vogel's desk and dropped into it. He took a deep breath, then exhaled.

And, in a flat, dead voice, said, "I saw soldiers."

Vogel's eyes flashed a quizzical look. "Soldiers?"

"Yes. I saw them. Yesterday."

Vogel sat down and smiled. "They have a parade downtown?"

The question negated an answer. If it had been the old man, Dr. Fisher, he would have told him. But not Vogel.

Harry sighed. "Yes. They had a parade."

"Well, that's nice. Parades are always nice."

There was a momentary silence, then Harry got up and took out a cigarette and lit it. He exhaled, shook his head and said, "I feel worn out, Jerry. It's like I'm going on nerve."

Vogel looked up quickly, but his expression remained unconcerned; calmly he asked, "When did you have your last check-up?"

"I don't remember. I saw Dr. Fisher last November. He took some X-rays of my back."

"Your back?"

"Yes. Shell fragments; both he and the neurosurgeon decided to leave them alone."

"But you haven't had a thorough physical in years... is that correct?"

"Yes. That's right."

Vogel flipped through the pages of his appointment book. "How's next Tuesday at ten? We'll do the whole number."

Harry took a deep drag. "Fine. That's fine."

Vogel made a note on the small appointment card, stood up, and handed it to Harry.

Harry tucked the card in his pocket. He looked at the boyish face and asked, "What can it be, Jerry?"

"What can what be?"

"This feeling. Sometimes, it's as if I'm almost floating."

Vogel shrugged. "Without any tests it's impossible to answer that question. It could be anything. It could be nothing."

"But what could it be?"

Vogel sighed. "Probably nothing more than general fatigue." He smiled. "We'll go down the list on Tuesday." His smile broadened. "Besides, by then we'll know whether you caught yourself a case of clap."

Harry nodded. "You know, Naples... Naples was the clap center of the E.T.O. I made everything in sight, even a Chinese girl." He paused and went on. "No one could figure that one... what a Chinese hooker was doing in Naples in 1945. I never caught a cold."

"Harry, what's the E.T.O.?"

"European Theatre of Operations."

Vogel smiled. "That's a nice suit, Harry."

"Yes. Jan bought it for me. Well, thanks, Jerry. Thanks for the time."

Vogel came around the desk, put his hand on Harry's shoulder, and moved him toward the door. "Take it easy, Harry, and give my best to Jan."

Chapter 29

Coming down in the elevator, Harry wondered why he hadn't been able to mention the blurred vision, the dizziness, the spots. It was the thing Vogel said about the parade. He couldn't get past that line.

He left the Lincoln in the parking lot and started through that very special mixture of noontime Beverly Hills: the super-chic housewives, who would have been perfectly in tune walking down the Via Condotti in their Gucci leather, Pucci dresses, and Bulgari jewelry; theatrical agents, better dressed and better-looking than their actor clients, a few children; a familiar movie face; Mexican maids, clutching their shopping lists; and attorneys and accountants—the new generals of capitalism, the money magicians who, by sleight of law, slipped their clients' wealth past the government.

The air was heavy and gritty. Harry knew if it was this dirty in Beverly Hills, it would be brutal downtown.

He walked east on Little Santa Monica and went into

the Broadway hot dog stand. They advertised genuine Brooklyn hot dogs, and old time egg creams. It wasn't true, but the service was fast and you could eat standing up.

Harry slid his tray along the counter, moving with the progress of service. He ordered a hot dog with mustard and sauerkraut and a Fresca with no ice. He couldn't order an egg cream, not after growing up on the original.

For those who cared to eat standing up, there was a chest-high wooden counter that faced streetside windows. Two men were crowded in alongside Harry. The older one was dressed very mod—double-breasted blue jacket, red banlon and plaid bell-bottoms. His face had a yellow cast, as if he had permanent hepatitis. He reminded Harry of a used up nightclub bouncer. The younger man was dressed in a conservative, dark grey pinstripe. The length of his hair was halfway between the establishment and the generation. Harry recognized him; he was the creative head of a film studio that had been in the headlines. They had been through a long and agonizing proxy fight and had finally been absorbed by a giant cereal company.

The studio chief spoke rapidly through a thick French-fry, spraying the residue over his assistant. "Fuck Warner's. Those assholes have all that parking lot money and haven't made a hit yet."

The yellow face frowned. "But, Sid, it grossed eight million."

"Look, Franklin, if they want that Sally Superstar running through the Spanish canyons with her tits out, fine. But I'm not going to make that picture."

The mod man shrugged and, through the sauerkraut said, "Shit. You can't quarrel with that gross."

The handsome chief raised his voice. "I'm not getting in bed with that cunt. Period." He bit off another inch of French-fry. His voice lowered but the annoyance was pronounced. "I don't understand you, Franklin. We were on the way to becoming a high rise. These cereal people pulled us out. We got to make family pictures." He paused, looking out onto the street, then almost to himself, "Something... something creative... a remake... a remake of *Peter Pan*."

The yellow-faced assistant instantly stopped munching his hot dog. "*Peter Pan!* That's terrific, Sidney! Terrific!"

The studio chief turned to Harry. "Would you please pass the mustard?"

It might have been the dull pain in his back; it might have been his resentment of their ability to crush a career between bites; but Harry ignored the request and continued to sip his Fresca.

Again, the handsome mogul asked, "Say, mister, would you mind passing the mustard?"

Harry took a napkin from the dispenser, touched it to his lips, turned and started out. He heard the assistant say, "A kook. A creep. Must be stoned."

The old street-corner juices bubbled and the anger flashed. Harry spun around and grabbed the mod man's shoulder and pulled him up close with his right hand. Harry's left hand dropped from the man's shoulder and drew back, ready to hook into that sallow face. Then, ice cold, he said, "Were you talking to me?"

The studio chief kept eating, not wanting to get involved. The assistant's face had lost some yellow and picked up some grey and in a shaky voice he said, "I didn't say anything to you."

Harry stared at the man for a moment. "I'm glad to hear that." He released the man and walked out. The assistant stared after Harry for a few seconds, then went back to his hot dog.

He muttered to the studio chief, "Christ, you don't know what's walking the streets anymore."

The handsome chief said, "Peter Pan . . . when she flies out over those kids . . . maybe we use 3-D—maybe we get Bacharach to do the score, and Streisand to play the lead . . ." The mustard oozed out over the hot dog.

Harry drove slowly down Sunset Boulevard, mad at himself for grabbing the man with the yellow face; but he knew why he had.

It was their power: their power over insecure people who spent half their lives waiting for a phone to ring.

That was one of the marvelous things about having your own business. For fifteen years he had had no one to answer to, no one to crawl to. Sure, the usual crap with the bank, the unions, but still those elevator doors opened onto the tenth floor and every inch of it was your own. It was that freedom, that independence that grew in impor-

tance with the passage of time. That's why it was too late
to go under, too late to grab a line and hit the road for a
commission check, too late to fall back on someone else's
largesse, too late to kiss someone's ass for permission to
stay alive.

Harry kept the needle at twenty-five, moving cautiously
on the wide, treeless boulevard. He wondered why there
were no trees; they probably could not breathe the Los
Angeles air.

He pushed the button; it was still on the all-news
station. "... the noted Russian author has been recommitted
to the State Asylum in Moscow. In Washington, a spokesman for the president denied any inordinate profit was
made on the sale by the president of swampland in
Florida... Locally a brushfire fueled by gusting Santa Ana
winds has now engulfed the hills above Santa Barbara... the
fires in Northern California still rage out of control..."

He stopped for a light and picked up a cassette, checked
the label and slipped it in. Armstrong's voice growled,
"And the cement's just for the weight, dear..."

He passed the corner of La Cienega, the same corner he
had picked up Myra from the day before.

He thought under different circumstances it could have
been Audrey standing there with her thumb in the air.
The difference was money, but then who knew what the
weekend action in Gstaad was like? The sex was there.
The pot was there. The put-down of everything was there.
Only the location was different.

And maybe Myra was on a straighter track than his own
daughter. Myra didn't put down anyone's "life-style." She
accepted things the way they were. He was certain that
Myra thought the Lincoln, the Spanish maid, the silk suit
was a pile of nothing. But she didn't put it down. She said,
"groovy." What was sad, and what was lousy, was the loss
of innocence. The big shrug. Let it all hang out. Fuck it.
Everything was "groovy": the airline captain, the veteran,
the pot, the aimless days on the Strip, and her mother's
dried blood on the Hollywood Freeway, and a father
floating around the Valley, hustling Wonder Bread. But
somehow, some fucking how, she held herself together.
That's why the big shrug. There was no other way to
handle it.

He could see her now, walking along the beach pleasantly

stoned on the second joint of the day, the Pacific playing with her long hair, her toes touching the creamy surf. Accepting. Even the mad confessional he laid on her. Maybe in the deep recesses of her subconscious she had understood.

At Vermont and Sunset he slowed, looking for a place to park near the hospital, but the cars were bumper to bumper. He slid the car into a piece of yellow curb with large black letters written on it: PASSENGER UNLOADING ONLY.

It was close to the main entrance and he thought the hell with it; let them write a ticket.

The lighting in the fifth-floor reception room would have been more appropriate in the lounge of an expensive whorehouse. Years ago, a jewelry salesman had taken him to an apartment on Madison Avenue with similar lighting where the girls wore nurses' uniforms, cut in front to permit full view of their breasts.

He studied the lighting for a moment and thought it had been cleverly designed to mask what lay beyond those swinging doors.

Beams of sunlight streaked through prismatic windows, throwing Picasso shadows onto rose-colored walls. Hidden ceiling pin-spots bounced pools of white light off the grey floor. The sunlight and the incandescent light coalesced into a soft, sensual mauve.

The air was manufactured and heavily laced with something that smelled like iodine.

The floor nurse was a pleasant-looking woman in her fifties and her hair was grey, not blue. She said, "Doctor Samuels left an hour ago. What patient are you enquiring about?"

"Ed Mirrell."

She examined a master chart on her desk, then looked up and said, "I'm sorry. Mr. Mirrell is not permitted any visitors."

Harry said, "I spoke to the doctor last night. He said Mrs. Mirrell might be here. I'd like to see her. I'm a close friend of the family."

The woman nodded. "Mrs. Mirrell is in the private waiting room. Down the hall to your left."

Harry walked down the green corridor past doors, some open, some closed. He saw men and women with tubes and jars dangling over them, staring out of Demerol eyes into nothing: no Linda Darnell, no posters of Lugano.

He reached the end of the hall, turned left, and went through the swinging doors marked PRIVATE.

She stood looking out of the beveled window, silhouetted in the sliced light. She turned as the doors whooshed closed.

She was very thin. Blue circles rimmed her large brown eyes; she had even features and close-cropped auburn hair. Her face had that special tranquility that comes with utter desolation.

Softly, he asked, "Mrs. Mirrell?"

She forced a smile. "Yes?"

He walked up to her and put his hand out. "I'm Harry Stoner. I was with your husband when he was stricken."

Her hand fell into his, rested there for a second, then fell out.

Harry took out the red-white box of Shermans. "Do you mind if I smoke?"

She shook her head, and he lit the cigarette, blowing the smoke off and away.

"I missed the doctor. I was hoping to . . ."

She cut in. "My husband is doing as well as can be expected. I want to thank you for your help and concern. It was very kind of you."

"There's nothing to thank me for. It happened fast. It was a shock. Fortunately my partner, Mr. Greene, and . . ."

She interrupted. "Yes, I know. Mr. Greene phoned this morning. I know all the details."

There was a hard edge to her words; somehow she knew what had really taken place, whether it was by instinct or history; she knew. They always knew.

He spoke compulsively. "Well, you see he hadn't been feeling well . . . I guess it was that long train ride. We asked him to go upstairs . . . we . . . we had a suite . . . I mean in that hotel for last-minute meetings . . . and we thought we'd bring the samples up to the room. That way, Ed could rest and still be able to conduct his business."

She stared vacantly at him for a moment, as if she were

waiting for an interpreter...as if he had spoken in a foreign language.

She turned and went back to the window, looking out through the fingers of sunlight.

Harry searched his mind for some new evidence, some new statement of fact that would put a trace of doubt in her mind. But nothing came to him. There was a long moment of silence.

She finally turned and walked slowly up to him. In a tone of calm madness she said, "You know, my husband is really a very nice man. A gentle man."

Harry nodded. "If there's anything I can do. If you need anything, please call me."

She looked into his eyes and said, "Thank you, but there is nothing. Eddie has everything he needs."

They stared at each other, the odor of the strong tobacco hanging over them.

"Well, okay...you have my number."

She nodded but her eyes never left his. It wasn't accusatory. He thought it was hopelessness and she was trying to push into him.

He forced a smile and said, "Eddie's tough. He'll make it. I'm certain he'll pull through."

She turned away and walked back to the window. He wanted to say something else, but there was nothing left to say. He walked to the swinging door and went out.

Tucked under the left windshield wiper was a brown envelope. Harry extracted it, and opened it. It was a five-dollar fine, the kind you could mail in.

He got into the car, leaned over and opened the glove compartment and tossed the ticket in, then turned on the ignition, the air conditioner, the tape deck. He moved the gear lever to D and eased the big car out into the eastbound lane.

And Louie sang: " . Sunday morning on the corner ...there's a body oozin' life..."

Chapter 30

Harry parked on the fourth level of the huge brick complex, took the elevator down, and came out on the Hill Street side.

As he crossed the corner, Harry thought he would have to hold Phil together, stifle any doubts. Charlie was an egomaniac; the slightest trace of mistrust and he would refuse the assignment.

Phil spotted Harry, took the cigar out of his mouth and walked toward him. They met halfway up the street.

"You're late."

"I stopped at the hospital."

Phil nodded. "I called earlier. I spoke to his wife."

"She told me."

Phil was surprised. "You saw her?"

They started walking toward the theatre.

Harry said, "I wanted to try and convince her that the thing happened legitimately. I don't think she bought any of it."

As they walked, Phil said, "You look awful, Harry."

"Yeah. Well, I had a bad night."

They were close to the lobby when Phil replied, "Me, too. I couldn't sleep. I kept thinking about this thing; I feel like we're a couple of criminals."

"We haven't burned anything yet."

"Harry, I tell you, I can't go through with this." He removed his glasses and wiped his running eyes with a tissue. "We can work something out; I'm sure we can."

"Like what? What can we work out?"

Phil replaced his glasses. "I don't know . . . maybe Tony . . . maybe the Mob."

He took Phil's arm and moved him toward the box office. "Forget the Mob. They're killers. If we fell behind, they'd go after Linda. Besides, I'm not going to spend a year of my life working for the shylocks."

Phil chewed nervously on the cigar. "Well, why don't we think about it? We have time."

"Let's hear what Charlie has to say."

Phil went into the outer lobby; Harry walked up to the glass cage. The blue Brillo hair sparkled under the hot lights. The cracked face looked up from her paperback.

Harry knew she recognized him. "I just can't help myself. I can't stop thinking about that last position."

She ground her teeth and pursed her lips. "You want a booth?"

He smiled. "No thanks, sweetheart. I'll rough it again."

Only after he slid the ten-dollar bill through the small opening did she punch the tickets.

Charlie Robbins was in the same seat.

On the screen, the sailor was on his back. The heavy blonde sat on his face and the other one was going down on him. Charlie remained impassive; he could have been watching *Mary Poppins*. He gave no sign of recognition as Harry and Phil moved into the aisle. Harry squeezed past him, leaving one seat vacant between them. Phil did the same on the right. The three men watched the well-equipped Danes.

"You're late, boys."

Harry shrugged.

"Don't shrug. Just watch the screen." Charlie slipped his hand inside his jacket, removed the white envelope and dropped it in Phil's lap. "Don't look down, Phil. Just slip it into your pocket."

"But . . . it's your retainer!"

"I never take something for nothing . . . even though that's become common practice in this country."

Harry asked, "What's wrong?"

Charlie spoke rapidly, with clipped precision. "You're in violation of every fire ordinance in the Los Angeles statutes: faulty sprinklers; no access to fire-escapes; extinguishers dried up; combustible goods strewn all over the place. I've never seen the likes of it. And you fellas were worried about me. My God, you're flirting with a major disaster! I have to wonder about the quality of inspection. It defies belief!"

"Where does that leave us?"

"Don't look at me, Harry. Watch the screen."

Charlie removed the steel rims and cleaned them with

his tie. The Danes were coming. The soundtrack could have been, "*Tora . . . tora . . . tora.*" Charlie replaced his glasses "With all those violations, the insurance would never pay off. I'll give you a list of regulations to conform with. Fix everything up and I'll burn it."

"But how long will that take?"

"Six months or so. You can't light up new equipment. Each item bears the date of installation."

Phil sighed, "Well, that's that."

They sat in silence. An abrupt cut had changed the action on the screen. The little blonde was keeling on the bed, her small round ass up in the air. She laughed and babbled in Danish, while the heavy girl guided the sailor into her. The organ played the William Tell Overture.

Charlie had his glasses off. "Of course, I could start the fire down below in the shirt factory."

Phil coughed on the cigar, then managed, "Shirt factory?"

"Why not? I can get in there without any trouble. The access door is off its hinges. I'll funnel the fire up the back end of your place. Should work out fine."

Phil said, ". . . And the shirt man? I mean, he has nothing to say about it . . . right?"

Harry spoke quickly at the screen. "Don't worry about the shirt man. He'll do fine. Be a blessing. He's probably scrambling, too."

"Harry's right . . . should pay off handsomely for the shirt man. I'll do a force-funnel job; actually, the shirt man will sustain little damage, but the fire will really flash in your place. Hell, it'll be all over in three, maybe four, minutes." He replaced his glasses.

The pain in Harry's back had increased. He shifted in his seat.

"Don't move, Harry. Watch the screen."

The sailor was deep into the little blonde's ass. The big blonde was underneath, helping with her fingers.

Phil was sweating despite the air conditioning. He wiped his face with a tissue. His voice was hoarse. "When would you do this?"

"That's up to you."

Harry said, "But, Charlie, no matter how you handle the fire, we still have the same problem with the insurance."

"No, we don't. Without getting too technical—by starting the fire below, the type of blaze I create will reach sufficient centigrade to make the condition of your equipment academic. Besides, the origin of the fire will throw the suspicion off you fellas. You may get a reprimand, but they'll have to pay off."

On the screen, the sailor slid out of the little blonde's ass and they went into another complicated position.

After a moment, Charlie said, "I can't watch any more of this. I'll be in the lobby, browsing."

He got up, moved past Phil, and disappeared into the darkness. The organ played something from *Die Fledermaus*.

Harry said, "Let's go."

"No. I'm staying."

Harry sighed. "They just go to another position. They never reach a climax. We've been here two days and the guy still hasn't come."

"I don't care. I want to see it. Go ahead. Browse with Charlie. Go on, Harry."

Again he thought that Phil was stalling, reluctant to face what was ahead. It could not be the Danes that were keeping him . . . but then, it was a long trip from the olive groves of Jarama to *Denmark Speaks*.

He touched Phil's sleeve. "Let's go."

Phil stared at the screen. "No. I want to see it." Then he turned to Harry, his glasses reflecting the naked bodies, and with a sarcastic bite said, "I find it fascinating. I mean the things people will do for a krona . . . or a buck. It's really something, Harry."

Phil turned back to the screen and the Danes danced in the thick lenses of his glasses.

Harry got up slowly, moved past him and went up the aisle.

His eyes flinched against the bright sun, and yellow spots flashed, and behind the exploding spots the street activity went soft. Feeling dizzy, he walked to the side of the lobby and leaned up against the wall. For several minutes he gulped the air in and blew it out. Gradually, the spots cleared and the dizziness subsided. Harry looked around and saw Charlie. He was at the opposite side of the lobby, apparently paying close attention to a pornographic poster. Harry walked over to him and stood alongside, studying the same poster.

Charlie spoke without moving his head or lips. "Don't look at me and speak out of the corner of your mouth, on my side."

Harry said, "I want it understood; anything goes wrong and you never heard of Phil Greene."

Charlie said, "If anything goes wrong while I'm working, there won't be any questions. All they'll find is a cinder.

"I mean after the fire, Charlie."

"I'll give you the drill, Harry. First they'll go to the shirt man. Then they'll come to you. It's your building and you're the president of the company. You're clear. You have a successful line. You're in production, and you're only using that building for a few items. They'll never go to Phil. It's a walk-over, Harry. Believe me, I've handled a lot tougher than this. I've burned tax files in skyscrapers crawling with alarm systems."

Harry sighed. "Okay . . . how's Sunday? Phil goes fishing Sunday."

"Sunday's fine. This is Tuesday. That's enough time to prepare. I'll do it Sunday night. Maybe one . . . or two in the morning. Mail that retainer and the key to me." He shot a quick surreptitious glance at Harry. "Same suit, Harry?"

"Yes. Same suit, Charlie."

He turned abruptly and Harry watched him go, a sedate, middle-aged businessman walking through the busy afternoon streets.

Chapter 31

Harry waited for a moment, then moved away from the poster out to the sidewalk and headed toward the corner.

Fifty feet from the entrance to the garage, a bearded man stood on a platform, close to the curb. He was the same man Harry had seen yesterday and he shouted the same slogan. Occasionally, he would stop and hand pamphlets down to passersby. As Harry neared the makeshift platform, the man pointed at him. "Help! Mister, we need your help! Save the tiger!" Harry examined the small features behind the foliage. "Come on, mister, take a pamphlet."

"Are you connected with the Panthers?"

The man looked perplexed. "Panthers?"

"Yes. The Black Panthers. Are you connected with them?"

"No. No. We're not political."

"What are you?"

"Ecologists. We're trying to save the tiger."

Thinking an argument was in the making, some people had begun to gather.

Harry asked, "You mean the animal?"

"Yes. That's right. This regal beauty, this magnificent specimen is being systematically destroyed by encroachment; by shootouts; by actresses in tiger coats. We are murdering one of nature's unique gifts to mankind. A work of art, whose conception is beyond the realm of any Michelangelo." The man thrust a pamphlet at Harry. "We must save them!"

Harry accepted the pamphlet. "What can I do?"

"Just read the pamphlet, mister." He had a crowd now and turned away from Harry and began to shout, "Only five hundred and fifty-six left! Save the tiger!"

Harry tucked the pamphlet into his pocket and walked into the triple-tiered parking complex. He asked the attendant to bring the car out onto the Wilshire side.

The dull ache in his back, the black theatre with the writhing white bodies, the grass hangover, the crunch of the last thirty-six hours were like fingers closing around his brain. He was in a cocoon, weightless, apart from the traffic streaming around him.

The hum and throb of yesterday's activity was greatly reduced. Two black women operated the machines; they were sewing the first samples under production conditions.

Rico watched the progress of the styles coming through: from the cutting room, onto the patterns, then to the sewing machines, then to the presser; and finally being draped on Rosanna's slim figure. Rosanna was the sample model. Her figure was the mold for the entire line.

Each garment had to be checked every step of the way to ascertain whether it was produceable en masse. This

was the machine test of what up till now had been mostly
handwork. The line presented at yesterday's show had
been carefully stitched, piece by piece, and having sold,
would now have to stand the trial of manufacture from raw
bolts of fabric all the way to finished goods on the racks of
department stores throughout the country.

Rico checked the first slack outfit on Rosanna and seemed
satisfied except for a slight tuck near the waist. He knew
that fractional pinch had not been in his original design.

Rosanna stepped out of the pants and handed them to
Rico. He took them, shook his head and walked toward
Meyer's cutting room.

The old man studied a set of paper patterns, the eternal
Camel burning in the red ashtray.

Rico walked up to him, draped the pants across the
cutting table and said, "See anything wrong?"

Meyer's eyes traveled slowly from the waistband to the
bottom of the tapered leg. He then traced the lines of the
slacks with his hands, first one side, then the other. His
orange fingers stopped just to the left side of the waistband. He shrugged his shoulders.

"Let me check the pattern."

As he moved down the long table he asked Rico,
"What's the number?"

Rico tapped his foot. "6024."

Meyer flipped through the six thousand range of patterns, extracted number twenty-four, walked back with it,
and placed it over the waistband.

"I missed a line."

Rico smirked. "Then you admit it?"

Meyer smiled and puffed the Camel. "Admit? What kind
of word is 'admit'? I killed someone? I lost a patient in
surgery? I missed an eighth of an inch on a curve. And
you, my boy... you have the artist's eye. You caught it. So
you know what we'll do?" He blew some smoke over Rico's
head. "We'll fix it. Together we'll fix it. What else is this
time for? To see if the hands were sure." He crushed the
cigarette out and smiled. "Am I right or wrong?"

It took Rico a moment to answer. The calmness, the
logic, the immediate acknowledgement of the error surprised him.

"Well, I suppose you're right. It is the trial and error
period."

Meyer shrugged. "What else? Listen, Rico, this little eighth of an inch should be your only surprise. You'll see the designs you liked the best won't sell. The ones you don't care for; they'll be the hottest numbers. This isn't the toothpick business. Each garment is a guess. Nothing more. Harry built a good sales force. They'll get the goods into the stores . . . but to guess what the women will buy . . ." He laughed. "That's like expecting a warm winter in Siberia."

He turned to a green metal cabinet nearby and took out a bottle that bore no label and was half full of a thick red fluid. He set the bottle down and looked at Rico.

"Tell me . . . you ate lunch already?"

"Yes. I had some cottage cheese and toast."

"Good. Then you can have a drink with me."

He went over to the windowsill and removed two glasses and placed them on the cutting table and unscrewed the cap on the bottle.

"What is that stuff?" Rico asked.

Meyer smiled. "You could call it brandy. I get it on Fairfax . . ."

"But it has no label."

"So who needs a label? This isn't a product. It's a tradition. If you want a label . . . you can call it Slivovitz." He poured the red liquid into the glasses and picked one up. Rico stared down at the glass meant for him.

"I don't think so, Meyer. I'm more of a wine man. I really don't care for brandy."

"Come on, Rico. This is an occasion. A toast to your talent. Your designs are a cutter's dream. They're like paintings. Come on, drink some Slivovitz with an old man."

Rico had come into the room expecting the usual storm, and he couldn't deal with Meyer's enthusiasm. His hand went for the glass as if he were about to pet a rattlesnake.

Meyer stretched his hand out holding the glass; Rico raised his and as they clinked, Meyer said, "To the new season."

Meyer tossed the drink down in one gulp.

Rico sipped cautiously, then swallowed. He grimaced and coughed. "My God! What the hell is that?"

"That drink, my boy, is the fluid of courage. That drink in sufficient quantity throws away fear . . . that drink in the old country kept away the Cossacks, the poverty, the terrible God of the Jews... It made it all a Disneyland."

Rico sipped some more. "I'll say it's fuel. You could run a Mack truck with this stuff."

Meyer nodded and moved close to Rico. He put his large hand on the slim designer's shoulder. "Rico, I promised Harry. No more fights. I'll do my work; if you're happy. Fine. If not. I'll go. But no more fights. Okay?"

Rico stared into the grey eyes and sipped some more Slivovitz. He had worked with other cutters and knew this old man was blessed with expertise. It was just that cutters were the traditional outlets for designers' problems. He knew he had been unfair. He finished the drink without grimacing, and quietly said, "Okay. No more fights."

He picked the pants off the table and started for the door. He opened it, then turned back. "You're a good cutter, Meyer."

Meyer smiled. "No, I used to be good. But the thing is, I still enjoy my work. And I can still recognize quality."

Rico nodded and went out.

Harry pulled the Lincoln up to the small shack, but Willie was not around. He slipped the car keys under the upper visor and headed for the lobby.

The elevator doors slid open and Gloria smiled on cue. "Good afternoon, Mr. Stoner."

"Good afternoon, Gloria."

"Your secretary has some messages."

He nodded. "Anyone around?"

"Alfonso is down in the shipping room. But Meyer and Rico are here, and a few women making samples. But it's pretty quiet."

His secretary typed laconically, the container of cold coffee at her side. Her eyes caught the suit; they didn't dwell, but they swept up the fact that it was yesterday's.

She kept her voice nonchalant. "Your wife called..." She took a beat, then emphasized the word, "Twice." She handed him the two pink message slips. "And Meyer would like to see you."

In a tone as neutral as hers, he thanked her. In his office, he tossed his jacket on the couch and sat down behind his desk. He rubbed his thumb and forefinger over his eyes and as they closed, naked bodies crawled.

It had been painful, sitting in that theatre. There was a strange, sickening parallel between those meshed bodies and the newsreels of naked women running in front of grinning German guards in the death camps. A similar smear of human degradation stained those disparate films.

He unbuttoned the top button of his shirt, loosened his tie, tilted back in the chair and stared up at the ceiling, wondering whether Phil was still sitting there in the dark. He felt a consuming sadness for Phil.

Phil was a man of old-fashioned principle, a man crowding sixty and still defending Madrid, still holding some mythical moral line. Some last-lost cause.

But they didn't show "morality" in any passbook. What would Phil do if they went under? Hit the street at sixty? Look for a job? Where? The top houses had long-term contracts with their production men. And there were no in-between houses. Only the top and the bottom: those fly-by-night schlock houses where you came back from lunch and they were out of business.

Harry sighed heavily and tilted forward. Maybe when it was over he'd move Alfonso up, give him more responsibility, take the load off Phil. Let Phil get out on that boat, drop a line and watch the sea. After sixty summers, he deserved it.

In any case, no matter how things broke, Phil was out of harm's way. Still, the sadness remained. It hung in the room like a blanket with no edges; it could not be folded.

Harry looked up at the photograph of Stymie. It was a frozen-frame of poetry. The big, chestnut horse was flying in the stretch, all four feet off the ground, muscles rippling, chest straining, powerful shoulders hunched, nostrils flaring, skin glistening like wet satin, the jockey huddled into his neck. It was a picture of honesty, of effort, and courage—the kind of courage you can always see in a great Thoroughbred on that final curve, when they turn for home.

And even Stymie lost. All the great ones lost, but you respected the honesty of their effort. Harry remembered how he had worshipped that kind of courage, that kind of honesty; and how it seemed that in those days there *was* room for losers. What was important was the effort, the consistency of past performance.

But that was another time. Today, it was a new ball

game every day. They had been doing business with the same people for fifteen years—the mills, the unions, the bank—successfully fulfilling their obligations for fifteen years in a business that had a life expectancy of zero.

Still, at the bank that record meant only fifty cents on each purchase order. The same deal they could have had if they walked into any bank that morning. Effort and history didn't count anymore. The only thing they respected was the bottom line in the asset column.

He looked down at the two pink message slips and pressed the buzzer on the phone. His secretary came on the intercom:

"Yes?"

"Try my wife at the Plaza."

Chapter 32

Jan prowled the room, giving it all a last-minute check. She was packed. The funeral had been brief and devoid of outbursts. There were no tears, no widow, no children, only a small group of relatives, none of whom had been close to the dead man. Jan had exchanged some pleasantries with an elderly aunt and some remote cousins, but she declined the ride out to the cemetery, explaining she had to make a plane that afternoon.

She returned to the hotel at three. She was booked on the eight o'clock American. She was on edge and troubled all through the funeral service. She had tried Harry last night, then early this morning, then twice at the office.

Last night, she had thought he was having dinner with Phil, but he certainly should have been home this morning. He must have been out all night. Balling some buyer; or maybe . . . something happened to him. She didn't like the wan color in his face and those purple scars, and lately he'd been smoking those goddam cigarettes one after another. She sighed, no . . . if anything had happened she'd have heard. No. He was out, screwing around.

She crossed to the window; the light was going from grey to blue and the lamps in the park were on. The light rain of last night had picked up intensity, the pavement glistened and the hansom cabs had canvas covers thrown over them. The ring of the phone startled her.

She walked quickly to the white desk and picked up the phone. The operator asked, "Mrs. Jan Stoner?"

"Yes. Speaking."

"Go ahead. Your party's on the line."

Harry crushed the last of the dark cigarette out. He drew a deep breath and let it out through his teeth. "Hi, babe."

"Where are you, Harry?"

"The office."

She had a flash of relief; there had been no accident, no sudden illness. "I tried to get you last night and again early this morning."

Harry lied best when he lied fast. "I had dinner with Phil, and we received a call in the middle of dinner. A buyer, an important buyer, had a heart attack at the hotel. I had to handle the whole thing."

"All night?" Her words were threaded with a needle.

But he came right back. "Yes, all night. I left the hospital at two thirty and didn't have the strength to drive home. I checked into the Biltmore."

Jan thought it was too original to be totally false. But she went after it. "You bastard! You were out with one of those lollipop models! You were screwing around!"

He went on the offensive and almost believed what he was saying. "Goddammit, Jan! Don't start that crap! Not today. You want details? Okay! We fixed this buyer up. He passed out with two hookers sitting on him. It wasn't pretty and it needed fixing. Now for Chrissake, lay off!"

She listened and wanted to believe him, and there was no point in pushing it. She was up against the clock anyway; it would be a mess getting out to Kennedy in this rain.

"How is the man?" she asked in a softer tone.

Harry sighed. He was past the roughest part. "You know doctors, they give you a lot of Latin. His wife is with him, and he's got the best."

"Does she know what happened?"

"I think so."

Jan bit her lip. "Christ, what a thing."

Harry crumpled the two pink slips, tossing them at the wastebasket and missing. "When are you coming home?"

"Tonight. I'm making the eight o'clock. It arrives at ten thirty. I was going to stay, but I missed you." Her voice dropped and sounded throaty. "I missed the hell out of you, Harry."

That last hurt, and he asked gently, "What flight?"

Hurriedly she said, "Don't bother, please. I'll take a cab."

"I want to pick you up. What's the number?"

"American, Flight Number Five."

He clenched his fist, leaned back in the chair, looked up at Stymie ... and wanted to say more ... he wanted to reach her.

"Jan ... Jan ... listen. We have to go away. We have to have some fun. I called Audrey yesterday, and if everyone thing's okay, we'll go over there for Christmas. If it all works, we'll take a month ... and if the line sells ... if we have no trouble. I'm going to move one of our salesmen up, Rudy, the guy in New York ... he's good and if he wants to live out here, to be sales manager ... if that works ..." He stopped suddenly.

"What is it? ... Go on."

He tilted forward, sighed and said, "All of a sudden, I sound like Marty."

"Marty?" she asked.

"Yes. My father. He was always saying 'if.'"

"Harry I wish you would start seeing Frankfurter. He did help you there for a while."

"I saw Vogel this morning. I'm going to have a check-up next Tuesday."

"It's high time you did."

The doorbell of the suite rang. "Hold on. I think the bellmen are here." She set the phone down and went to the door. The two bellhops picked up her bags.

Harry lit another cigarette and thought, If I could tell her the truth. I spent the night having confession with a blond priestess who lit grass instead of candles. He drew hard on the brown cigarette, exhaled and she was back on the line.

She said, "I've got to hang up. I'm leaving right now. I love you ... And, Harry—"

"Yes?"

"I don't really give a damn where you were last night."

He shook his head. You could never sell them; not after twenty years.

But he ignored it and said, "I'll be at the gate. Have a good flight and don't eat that crap on the plane. We'll have a light supper at the Bistro."

The bellhops were leaving. She said, "We'll see. I may be too tired. But we'll see. 'Bye, Harry."

" 'Bye, Jan."

He dropped the receiver onto the cradle and placed the cigarette in the ashtray marked Carlton-Cannes.

He stared at the curling smoke and thought of that hotel and how much fun he and Jan had that summer in France. It was four or five years ago.

He rented a small Peugeot and they drove up the coast toward St. Tropez, the blue Mediterranean sparkling off to their left. They stopped in a small restaurant by the sea and ate mussels cooked in white garlic sauce and washed them down with cold, white Cassis. They stayed the night in St. Tropez in a small pension . . . They made love: on the floor, standing up . . . sideways . . . backwards . . . every way . . . and all the time the sound of the sea came through the open shutters . . . and from a discotheque French rock and every so often a love song by Françoise Hardy.

In the morning they had hot French bread, jam, croissants and an enormous pot of coffee; then got into their bathing suits; Jan wore a black bikini. They walked out onto the beach and all the kids rolled their eyes over her. She walked a few feet ahead of Harry and he watched the kids admiring her and he thought there was no beauty, no sensuality, like a mature woman who had kept it all together. You look at her and you can read all the nights . . . and all the moves, and all the secrets that were locked up along the way.

They swam and sunned and laughed and drank wine and he could taste her . . . that special feline thing she had . . . but that was five years ago. Why? Why was there always a long gap between sweet memories?

The buzzer sounded. He pushed the intercom button and picked up the phone. "Yes, Harriet, what is it?"

She sensed the annoyance in his voice and figured he had an argument, on the phone, with Jan.

"Meyer would like to see you."

"Okay."

Meyer came in carrying a pantsuit outfit. The end of his cigarette burned perilously close to his lips. He put the cigarette into the grey French ashtray alongside Harry's smouldering Sherman. He held the outfit up.

"Look, Harry! Just came off. Look at this quality!"

"Off the machines?"

Meyer nodded and smiled. "At twice the price it would be a bargain. Harry, we'll be looking for factory space. These goods... these clothes. Rico... Rico did some job." He draped the outfit over a chair. "We talked... we had some Slivovitz. It's all right. Now there's peace."

Harry smiled. "You got Rico to drink Slivovitz?"

"What's so surprising? Half a glass he drank... we're going to have a season."

Harry blew his breath out. "We have some serious problems, Meyer. We need money."

The old man waved his orange fingers. "Money? It's always a problem... we're used to it. Phil called me. He wanted to check with me what's happening... he told me he's going to the bank first thing tomorrow."

Harry's voice tightened. "When did he call?"

Meyer shrugged. "A half hour... forty-five minutes... I don't know... he was going home. You should both take some time off. There's nothing to do till we run all the numbers."

"Did Phil ask for me?"

"No. He just said he was going home and to the bank in the morning."

"The bank's a waste of time. He'd be better off going out on his boat." He changed his tone suddenly. "What do you want, Meyer?"

The old man smiled. "Only to tell you that you have quality here. And I know you and Phil are worried... but when you have goods like this," he picked the slack outfit off the chair, holding it up, "when you can manufacture this kind of quality, money will come. Quality attracts money."

"Not true. The only way people sell you money is if it's insured, collateralized. That's the only quality they're interested in."

"Harry, believe me, for this line you'll get money."

"Yes. We will."

Meyer picked up the despair in Harry's tone and the

grey in the leathery cheeks seemed to darken. His voice
trembled. "Harry, listen to me. I've been alive a long
time . . . better to fail than to put your soul in the garbage
can. A business you can start again but you can't pick your
soul out of the garbage."

The pain suddenly sliced through the German steel, and
Harry shivered slightly. He thought Phil must have told
Meyer. That's why the old man came in. Harry said, "Go
back to the cutting room. Please, Meyer, leave me alone."

"All right; I'll go back to the cutting room. But I want a
minute. I want to tell you something. Listen to me. This
you don't find in history books. I was five or six. We lived
in a shtetl. A small village in Bessarabia. On a quiet
Saturday right after services the Cossacks came; on horses,
slashing, shooting, killing. One big officer leaned down,
picked me up and threw me into a pile of manure, and I
lay there. Safe. Years later this same officer was the
commander of his troop. They were stationed in our
village. I was then maybe a boy of twelve."

Harry tried to evade the grey eyes, but they held him.

"I tugged at the sleeve of his uniform. He looked a
hundred feet tall. I told him I was the boy. The child he
threw out of the way. I asked him why he saved me. And
he said, 'I didn't save you, kike. I saved myself.'"

Harry sucked at the cigarette and said nothing.

Meyer turned and went to the door. He opened it,
looked back and said, "You see. Even that murderer had to
hold onto a piece of dignity. A little boy he couldn't kill.
That made up for the rest of the slaughter. In that murderer's mind he kept his humanity."

He went out, closing the door softly.

The phone rang instantly. He hoped it was Phil. Harriet
said, "There's a lady on the line. She says it's personal.
She won't give me her name."

He thought it might be Mrs. Mirrell. "Put her on."

The voice was mellow and warm. "Hello, Harry." It was
Margo. She spoke fast. "I called you for two reasons . . . I
didn't want to disturb you. But I was anxious to know
about Eddie."

Harry said, "He's hanging in. The doctor says the
prognosis is promising."

Margo was stretched out in the sun, on her terrace.
"I'm glad to hear that. Listen, I thought if you weren't

doing anything tonight...well, I make a great linguine and clam sauce."

Harry smiled. "That's my favorite dish. How did you know?"

"I didn't. It just happens to be one of the few things I know how to make. I thought we could have dinner here. And then relax."

"You must be kidding, Margo."

"Well, why not?" she asked.

"Because you'd feel nothing. And I'd feel like a 'John.'"

That was the last thing she wanted to hear. But how could he know that? Softly she said, "That's not what I meant." Then hesitantly, "We will have dinner some night?"

He sighed. "Yes. Some night, we'll have dinner."

"Okay. Call me, Harry." She said it sadly.

The connection clicked off. He held the receiver for a moment before replacing it.

He thought, Christ, even Margo needs a pair of arms. But somehow her pain was a fact, simply a fact.

Chapter 33

The late afternoon sun was strong, but the Santa Ana had stopped gusting. It hung over the city, motionless, invisible, mixing with the smog; a silent, hot message from the desert.

Willie saw Harry come into the lot and started toward the Lincoln. Harry waited at the shack and thought that Willie seemed to be dragging himself, laboring. The car rolled up slowly, very different from the usual whoosh, surge and sharp braking.

Willie eased out of the driver's seat and held the door open for him. Harry got behind the wheel. He didn't tip Willie, nor did he greet him.

Willie said, "I missed you when you came in. I went for an Alky Seltzer."

Harry looked up at him. "It's all right."

He moved the gear lever to D, but Willie's hand remained on the door.

"I don't feel so good. I pissed blood."

Harry stared at the black face—the flat nose, the dropped eye and the thin red lines streaking through the whites of his eyes. Harry said, "Blood?"

Willie nodded. "Woke up my usual time. Six fifteen. I went to piss and it was red. It looked like cherry soda. And I got this here pain on my side. My left side."

"Well, why didn't you stay home? Go to the doctor?"

"I went to the clinic." He pronounced clinic as if it had a final "K."

"What did they say?"

"They didn't say nuthin'. I went to the emergency man in the clinic. He took a test of my urine. He said to call him in two days."

There it was again. A man works twelve hours a day in a fucking parking lot and pisses blood and call back in two days.

Harry wanted to say something reassuring, but the word "clinic" kept bouncing around his brain, and he could not pull his eyes away from the streaking red lines in the whites of Willie's eyes. He gripped Willie's wrist and squeezed it as if the applied pressure would evoke some life in his own vocal cords, but no words came.

Willie stared down at him waiting. Suddenly and quickly, Harry blurted "Fucking clinic . . . goddam fucking, clinic!" Willie took his hand off the door frame, turned, and moved back toward the shack.

Harry eased the car into the Los Angeles Street traffic, tapped the visor down against the late afternoon sun, and steered north, toward Wilshire Boulevard. He cursed himself, thinking that Willie's ulcer or kidney stone could have brought them together. Had he been able to say the right thing, they could have crossed that Rubicon of bloody urine. He laughed hysterically as an image flashed of himself and Willie side by side in a rowboat sailing on a thin stream of blood.

He felt giddy, light, as if he were floating. He felt a tongue of dizziness licking at a spot just behind his eyes.

He drove trancelike, both hands choking the wheel. It was a run through the house of mirrors: faces whipped by, then flattened, squeezed and passed. They were followed by voices:

"You used to love baseball, Harry...Those green eyes with their soft lights...He's breathing, he's making sounds...The Father, The Son...First base, Dolph Camilli...War must be something else...God is a four horse win parlay...And here comes Stymie...The fucking thing is over, Sergeant...It's still early, Harry...Hey, it was groovy...Three thousand helicopters...Kamu died ...Nice suit, Harry...I don't eat chocolate, Daddy...You're not dealing with a pyromaniac...Remember Paris, Rick? ...We were never at war with Italy...Killed on the Hollywood Freeway...The boots are there, Harry...He sells Wonder Bread...You always know a man when he's down on his luck...Even the murderer needed dignity. ..Nice suit, Harry...What's E.T.O. Harry?...Denmark Speaks...I pissed blood...He's a very nice man...Even the murderer had humanity...Every day is Halloween..."

The big car bounced off the curb and slid to a stop. Harry closed his eyes and leaned back. He let his breath out, opened his eyes and looked out of the window. He was at Roxbury Park and the kids were playing little league baseball.

He took off his tie and tossed it in the back seat. He got out of the car and dropped his jacket on the front seat. He locked all the doors, turned and headed toward the diamond.

He was seated on the bottom bench of a bleacher unit alongside the third base foul line.

He remembered the radio's warning, that morning, about "strenuous activity," but the children were oblivious of the poison hanging over them. Harry guessed the ages of the children to be ten or eleven. The diamond was scaled down to conform with their physical capabilities.

The team at bat were in blue-white uniforms which carried the label "Brownies." The team in the field, the "Angels," wore green-grey. The Angel pitcher was a blond boy who took no windup. He had just thrown a strike and was looking in for the next sign. He nodded, reared back, cocked his arm and threw.

The umpire called it a ball. All the Angel infielders shouted their objections to the close call.

Harry agreed with them. He thought the pitch had caught the inside corner. The face of the pitcher clouded with the injustice of the call. He kicked the mound, looked in for the signal, nodded, and threw a high inside fast ball. The batter ducked, but the ball struck the bat and bounced across the third base foul line.

Harry jumped off the bench and fielded the ball. He held it in his right hand and turned it over slowly. He saw the imprint "Big Leaguer." His fingers gripped the red stitches and squeezed. He made no move to release the ball . . .

The pitcher shouted, "Hey, mister, throw the ball!"

The boy shouted again, "Hey, mister, come on, throw the ball!"

Harry started to wind up like Johnny Van Der Meer: double pumping, kicking high, swinging his right arm in a great arc, coming down and snapping his wrist as he let it go . . .

The ball sailed over the pitcher's head. "Why did you do that, mister?"

Harry started to the mound.

"Hey, what are you doing, mister?"

The boy's eyes showed some fear as Harry placed his right foot on the rubber.

Harry looked in to the plate . . . It was Ebbetts Field and Enos Slaughter was on deck . . .

"Come on, mister, we're playing here. This is a league game."

Harry turned his back on the plate . . .

No rush . . . let 'em sweat . . . Durocher said, "You threw a lotta pitches in the seventh . . ." Lavagetto asked, "Gettin' tired, Harry?"

"Someone should call the cops. He just threw the ball over Stevie's head."

Harry saw two left-handers warming up in the Cardinal bullpen. He turned to Coscarot "The hop's still there, Petey . . . the curve's breaking down. I'm not going out. It's the ninth, I got it in . . ."

"He won't listen. Does anyone know him?"

"No. I've never seen him before."

"Somebody should call the cops."

"Is he Danny's father?"

"I don't know."

Harry saw the signal go down to the bullpen...Durocher, Cookie and Pete were silent; they pawed the ground and looked at the stands. They were announcing Hugh Casey. Harry pleaded, "My stuff is still good...my stuff is still good..."

"Well, say something to him. Maybe he's deaf."

Harry gave Casey the ball. Casey said, "Listen, mister, unless you leave the field right now, I'll have to call the police..."

But it wasn't Casey. It was the teen-age umpire. They were gathered around him: the children; the innocents. Watching. Waiting.

He could have thrown his life around any one of them. "I'm sorry. You're right...I...I just wanted to get the feel of the mound." He smiled at the pitcher. "You ought to wind up, son. Like I did. I wanted you to see it." He turned to the umpire. "And that pitch...that pitch was a strike."

The umpire said, "You'll have to leave now."

Harry stared at the children.

Then the pitcher said, "We have our rules."

Harry nodded imperceptibly, then turned and started out toward center field.

The teen-age umpire shouted, "Play ball!"

But the children did not move. They watched Harry... waiting for him to pass through the center field gates.

ABOUT THE AUTHOR

STEVE SHAGAN was born and raised in Brooklyn, New York and has subsequently lived in Madrid, Rio de Janeiro, Mexico City and Tel Aviv. When World War II broke out, he left high school, lied about his age, and joined the Coast Guard. Confronted with a great deal of spare time, he began writing "word portraits" of the sea. After the war, he held a variety of jobs, including factory worker, stagehand, film printer and, finally, freelance publicity writer for a film studio. This led to a job as producer of the *Tarzan* television series. "Then one day, I just began to write *Save the Tiger*." The novel was a success and became an Academy Award-winning film. In addition, Mr. Shagan received an Academy Award nomination for Best Screenplay and won the Writers Guild of America Award for Best Original Drama. His next novel, *City of Angels*, was a bestseller and became the hit movie "Hustle," starring Burt Reynolds. Mr. Shagan received his second Academy Award nomination for his screenwriting work on "Voyage of the Damned." While he was in Berlin writing that screenplay, he stumbled onto the fact that Nazi Germany had been totally self-sufficient in energy due to its success with synthetic fuel. Discovering that there had been fifteen Hitler-sponsored plants using a process called "hydrogenation," Mr. Shagan decided to look up the word for the process. The result was *The Formula*. Once he began work on the book, he never relented, even turning down a $300,000 screenplay re-writing job. With the novel already a success and a movie on the way, Mr. Shagan is certain to remain one of the top original screenwriters in the film industry. In the offing are a television movie about the Kent State/National Guard incident, a novel about the movie industry and, possibly, a Broadway play. Steve Shagan is presently living in Los Angeles with his wife, Betty, his teen-age son, Robert, and his cat, appropriately named Tiger.